IMMORTAL SORCERESS

BOOK 5

DEATH OF THE SORCERESS

KRISTA WALSH

RAVEN'S QUILL PRESS

OTTAWA, ON

Raven's Quill Press

www.kristawalshauthor.com

Publisher's Note: This is a work of fiction. Names, characters, places, and incidents are a product of the author's imagination. Locales and public names are sometimes used for atmospheric purposes. Any resemblance to actual people, living or dead, or to businesses, companies, events, institutions, or locales is completely coincidental.

Cover Design: Deranged Doctor Design/2023

Death of the Sorceress / WALSH -- 1st ed.

Paperback ISBN: 978-1-998398-08-9

For everyone who fights for what they love

1

Katerina

Everything I'd believed was a lie.

I'd believed the blood witch, Mikhail, was a typical power-hungry magic user, digging up rare spells and gaining obedient followers with the traditional tricks of lies and charisma.

I'd believed the fear demon, Shogaur, was a nasty coincidence—maybe a vengeance ploy.

I'd believed Alodie, the sorceress who had cursed me to my immortality when she'd slaughtered our entire community eight hundred and fifty years ago, was the root of all my problems.

I'd believed the witch hunters who had dosed me with a tea that stripped me of my magic and immortality had been out to get rid of *me*.

None of those things was correct.

Every step of the way, I'd acted based on faulty assumptions. As a result, I was now racing to find out what the witch hunters were truly after and why they'd thought targeting me would help them achieve it.

Magic surged through my blood, and I formed a fireball between my palms. It started small, no larger than a chestnut, but as I channelled more magic, the flames spread, remaining compact, dancing and spiralling as it grew into the size of a watermelon.

A watermelon of death.

Or so I hoped.

I allowed it to hover above my open hands, then widened my arms and watched the fire follow the path of my fingers, creating a band of searing hot flame. My strength wobbled, and I nearly lost my grip on my magic, but before it extinguished, I caught it and raised my hands. The fire broke into two separate strings that extended from my fingertips, nothing less than fire-touched whips.

With another breath, my magic steadied, and I reversed my heat. The fire cooled, chilled, hardened, leaving me with two sharpened blades of ice. I wove them through the manoeuvres Adrian had taught me centuries ago, my skills rusty with disuse but gradually coming back to me as I worked my daily practice.

After a few minutes, the ice grew slick in the summer heat.

I dropped the blades into the forest debris, closed my eyes, and reached for my deeper magic, the power that didn't come as naturally to me and required more intense concentration.

I tapped into the dryness in the air that lurked beneath the thick, clinging humidity. It tingled over my fingertips, crept up my arms, and scurried around the edges of my gloves until it was trapped by the runes etched into the leather from my knuckles to my elbows. Bracing myself with another breath, I summoned sparks that jumped from fingertip to fingertip and made my hands dance.

The static charge of my power built, burned, until it reached a breaking point. I aimed my hands outwards and let loose a dozen lightning bolts that arced across the water.

As soon as I released my magic, I staggered backwards on the shoreline and dropped into the sand. My heart raced, my lungs heaved, and sweat pooled in the small of my back.

For over a week, I'd spent hours a day working to return to where I'd been at the height of my monster-hunting days— those dreamlike days when my lover, my best friend, and I had travelled the world looking for magic users and creatures that threatened the balance between magical and mundane.

There had been a time when I couldn't walk into a magical-dominant city without people bowing and stepping aside for me, knowing I was there to save them or stop them.

In recent decades, I'd allowed that reputation to grow stale.

I'd hidden in my little corner of northern Ontario, made a home for myself in the small community of Manitoulin Island, and allowed the world to pass me by. I'd only stepped out of my comfort zone when the threats drew close enough to be inconvenient, or when they came for me directly.

Now I was paying for my choices.

Rogue members of the witch hunters, the vampire hunters, and the Hunter's Guild had taken advantage of my weakness. They'd summoned Fegor, the demon bound to Alodie, to bring the sorceress out of her imprisonment in the infernal realms, and from that moment sixty years ago, my life had been forced towards an end point I couldn't see.

I refused to walk their path anymore.

My eyes were opened to their plan. I might not know what they were after, but I knew I couldn't let them win. They were messing with a balance they didn't understand, and I wouldn't let them undo a thousand years of work because of their short-sighted fears.

But after so many days of practice, I appreciated how far I still had to go to become what I once was.

Murisa's potion, the one that had broken through the poison blocking my magic and my immortality, had done wonders clearing away the cobwebs, but it wasn't enough.

It was also possible I was projecting Emrick's fears onto my own insecurities.

Frustration bubbled within me at the thought of him—the servant of Death who had become my heart, my soul, and my home since he'd escorted me away from the bloody remains of my massacred family almost nine hundred years ago. In the week since my magic had returned, the stubborn man had refused to accept that our bond had been restored and his touch would no longer be fatal to me. Worse, he refused to sit down and talk about it because he didn't want to concede that I might be right—or that I might not care if I was wrong.

My hands curled into fists of their own accord, and fire flickered between my fingers.

I drew in a deep breath and let it out slowly, allowing my magic to seep back into my blood with the influx of oxygen.

Anger was useful, but not if it expended my energy when I needed to conserve it. Practice was good. Overuse would exhaust me.

I repeated the words over and again until my tempestuous emotions calmed, and then I flopped backwards onto the sand and stared up at the sky through the thick trees that surrounded my home.

"You're getting stronger, but your footing needs work with your ice swords."

I squeezed my eyes shut. "If I can't see you, it means you're not actually here, right?"

The chuckle that followed was so unexpected, I opened my

eyes to make sure I hadn't lost my mind and gained aural hallucinations along with my returned magic.

But nope, there was James Barrett, ex-vampire thrall, ex-frenemy, recent… friend? Permanent pain in my ass.

As usual, he wore dark clothes that made his muscles pop—dark green T-shirt, black jeans, black boots. All the better for running around in the shadows in the middle of a sunny summer's day. I would have said it was old combat training habits dying hard, but I suspected he enjoyed how people hurried out of his way wherever he went. Made grocery shopping much less of a headache.

He dropped onto the ground beside me, pulled his knees to his chest, and stared out over Lake Huron where it ebbed and flowed against my private beach. "You don't have to push yourself so hard."

"I'm not. I'm pushing myself a perfectly normal amount."

He snorted, and again I looked him over. The Barrett I knew didn't snort, and he didn't chuckle. He also didn't talk much. Or emote.

For years, I'd seen him as a large brick who was useful for throwing into fights.

But ever since Adrian's final death, when my old friend had run into a fire spell to save his thrall from facing the same fate, Barrett had changed.

His position on magic had certainly changed. A few months

ago, he might have congratulated the witch hunters for what they'd done to me, his hatred of magic had run that deep.

After the rogue hunters' actions had led to Adrian's death, his priorities had shifted. I'd watched him put a bullet in his hunter friend's skull without a glimmer of remorse, and Tony had been as mundane as the junk food he'd favoured.

Doling out that fragment of our vengeance hadn't been enough, not nearly, but it had been a bonding moment.

"We see what you're doing," he said. "We know what you're trying to become. But you're not where you were six hundred years ago when it was just you and Adrian against the world. You have a team now, all of us ready and willing to march beside you into whatever battle is coming."

I gritted my teeth and pushed myself up. "I know. And believe me, I'm grateful. I know you guys are capable of kicking all kinds of ass without my help, but I'm the immortal among you. I'm the one who should break down doors and walk in first, regardless of how much power stands behind me. To do that—to make sure you guys stay safe—I have to be the best I can be. I can't slow down."

"Hm."

There he was. This was the Barrett I knew.

I waited for him to say something else, and when he didn't, I summoned a fireball into my palm and released it to hover in front of us. A simple display. One of the first tricks I'd learned after Emrick had broken down the mental barriers that had held me back for the first fifty years of my life.

I snuck a glance at Barrett, but he didn't react to the flames. He watched the fireball's slow spin, the tiny sun letting off little flares.

Then I waved my hand beneath it, and the ball split into six tinier spheres that I sent over the lake. They shot into the water and disappeared with a sizzle, little plumes of steam rising where they'd landed.

I wiped my hands together. "I have come too far and gained too much to let anyone take it from me again. I know you guys want to be involved, and I won't say no, but protecting you is as important to me as obliterating them."

Barrett turned his head to look at me, his dark eyes intense. "After what happened last week, there is not a single person in this family who wouldn't say the same. That's what a unit is, Kat. We defend each other. We protect each other. We each offer everything we can. No matter what these hunters are planning, they'll have to face all of us."

My stomach tightened with fear. "That's what terrifies me, Barrett. The hunters know that. They know who we are, what we're capable of. You know their resources. They'll have dossiers on every one of us, and they'll be just as ready—if not more so—than we are."

"Then we need to out-resource them, and no matter how

much you train or how powerful you are, it can't rest entirely on you."

I sank my chin onto my knees. I hated when he was right. "All right, then. What do you have in mind?"

"I think we should start by talking to Poppy. It could be time for her and her mother to enjoy a family reunion."

2

Katerina

N°."

Proserpine Lister didn't hesitate to turn down Barrett's suggestion the second the words left his mouth.

She crossed one pink-clad leg over the other, waggled her fluffy purple slipper, and sat with all the determination of a woman who had broken away from her family and had no intention of crawling back to them.

Cuddles, her long-haired resurrected cat sat beside her in solidarity. His yellow eyes were fixed on me, and the tip of his kinked grey tail flicked back and forth in warning. Despite the hundreds of washes with expensive pet shampoo, his stench of decay tickled my nose, adding an unexpected weight to his glower. Gods help anyone who messed with his necromancer.

"The Hydrangea Circle is the most powerful coven in Ontario," Barrett said, not the least bit cowed by her scowl or Cuddles's posturing. "If they fight with us, our position against the hunters will be that much stronger."

Poppy turned to me, her arms crossed tightly, her long, bright blue fingernails tapping an irritated rhythm. "You would sell me out to my own mother, kitty Kat? Really? You know how hard I worked to put that bitch behind me."

I did, and I didn't blame her. Having met Hera Lister, I wouldn't have been in a rush to claim her as my mother, either. Cold, stern, ambitious—she was the head of a current beauty-focused coven and the ex-high-ranking member of the notorious Death Raisers, a coven of necromancers I'd dealt with frequently during the sixties and seventies.

I'd crushed them in the eighties, but that hadn't stopped Hera and her husband, Arnold, from passing their skills and knowledge on to Poppy. She'd been heading down a dark road until she'd run into me and I'd set her on a kinder path. Sure, I'd done it by threatening to kill her if she ever again used her magic for evil, but the lesson had sunk in.

To say our relationship had gotten off on a difficult foot would be an understatement, but hey, look at us now. BFFs and working together to prevent the mean old witch hunters from doing… something.

A something we would have a much easier time determining

with the help of Poppy's mother.

And so we'd come full circle.

I grimaced. "Sorry, Pop. I wish we could leave her off the list of potential allies, but as it stands, we need all the help we can get. You know the resources the hunters have on their side. You've faced them yourself a few times."

Both in her old role and in her new one.

Although I'd always had issues with the way the hunters ran things, I'd appreciated the support they'd given my mission to protect the balance between magical and mundane. To the point that, months ago, standing directly opposed to them would have made me question whether I was defending the right side of this particular battle. Today, I had no doubts. Magic was a necessary part of this world. The foundations of existence ran on it, whether the mundanes realized it or not.

Yes, it was dangerous.

Yes, there were magic users who used their power to harm instead of help.

But point me at a single person on this planet, magical or otherwise, where the same might not hold true. People were more complicated than their magical inclinations. I didn't understand how these rogue hunters could be so clueless as to not see that.

Poppy muttered under her breath and closed in on herself as Cuddles hunkered down beside her, eyes still pinned on me.

Murisa Bhatt, technomancer, biomedical engineer, and injection of cheer into our dour group, took Poppy's hand and drew it into her lap.

"This could be the opportunity you've been waiting for."

I raised an eyebrow. "Opportunity?"

"Poppy's been trying to figure out how to introduce me to her parents."

A flush spread across Poppy's cheeks, highlighting the rich undertones of her skin and making her brown eyes shine. I couldn't help but smile at her embarrassment.

"More like trying to find excuses not to, eh, Poppy?" I asked.

She darted out her slippered foot and kicked me in the shin, making me cackle.

Murisa grinned. "She thinks I didn't notice what she was doing, but there's only so many times you can say your dad's busy getting his car waxed before you realize your girlfriend's trying to keep you away from them."

Poppy and I exchanged a look. Having met her father—and found him in his garage waxing one of many cars—I suspected that particular excuse was one of the more honest ones.

"Well," I said, "there you have it. We can make it a family trip. We'll pile into Barrett's SUV, drive to Burlington, and ask your mother to pretty please leave her coven at our disposal—hey look, the potential for grandbabies."

Now it was Murisa's turn to cackle as Poppy's jaw dropped and her eyes rounded into saucers.

I held up my hands to defend myself. "I'm not saying you need to provide them. I'm just saying the woman might be mollified if she knows you're considering it."

"She'd dig my grave herself," Poppy said with absolute seriousness, which only made Murisa laugh harder. Cuddles finally shifted his attention from me to his people, a low growl rumbling in his chest as his notched ear flicked at the noise.

I leaned forward so my elbows rested on my knees and took Poppy's other hand. "Come on, Poppy. I know this is your worst nightmare but think of how much worse it might get if we don't try. We don't know what the hunters are doing. We know they have the recipe for a compound that can block our magic. They put it in a tea, but how else will they use it? They could weaponize it. Strip us of who we are for the sake of 'saving the world.' For starters."

Poppy gritted her teeth and sat back in her chair, her hands caught by two people egging her on while Barrett sat across from her, his expression blank but his opinions as loud as if he were shouting them. Cuddles climbed into her lap and set to work grooming his testicles.

Poppy hunched her shoulders. "I'll give her a call. But you owe me, kitty Kat."

"Anything," I promised. "Except babysitting."

Poppy, Murisa, and Cuddles headed to the privacy of their bedroom off the basement rec room to make their call, and I retreated to the haven of my own room to collect my thoughts.

Getting the Hydrangea Circle in our back pocket was a good first step, but we would need more than witches to force the hunters off their path.

I really wished I knew their plan.

I paced the length of my room, trying to put together all the hints the hunters had dropped during our last encounter.

Your ego has blocked your view. You think everything is about you, Tony had said. Then he'd talked about magicals and how the future wasn't safe until every last one of us was dead or leashed.

Everything pointed at the hunters using me as a step forward, but who was their end-goal? If I was the bait, as Tony's words suggested, they had to want someone close to me. As much as I valued every person in this house, I couldn't see how any of them would be important enough to gain the hunters' attention.

Barrett had been a vampire's thrall up until a few months ago, and before that he'd been a soldier in the Canadian Armed Forces. For the hunters' purposes, he had a solid background, with good knowledge and experience of strategy and how the magical world worked—everything perfectly in line with their official mission statement. But they had oodles of his type in their ranks. Maybe none as advanced in statuedom, but some came close.

Poppy and Murisa were incredibly skilled witches, but Murisa had only just come into her power as a technomancer, and Poppy had been doing her best to stay under the radar for the past five years. Mostly to avoid me.

Rhys's second sight might be useful for the hunters, but Maera and I had done our best to keep his ability hidden, and his mastery of it remained hit-or-miss.

That left Gavin.

A likely target, I had to admit. He'd only recently discovered he had magic, and although he was powerful, he was a novice at controlling the fire he summoned. His lack of control made him useless to anyone looking to wield him as a weapon, but his newness also made him mouldable. In the wrong hands, he could become a dangerous force.

I was in the middle of wondering if I should talk to Barrett about keeping a guard around our reluctant sorcerer when the temperature in my room dropped.

I stopped pacing and watched the mist that appeared in the doorway leading to the balcony. Emrick stepped out of the afterlife, and as always happened at the sight of my other half, my heart skipped a beat, my stomach tightened, and my skin warmed.

Centuries of habit urged me to step into his arms and wrap myself in his delicious scent of campfire and loam, but I forced myself to stay still. I knew him well enough to accept that at my first step forward, he would retreat. With my emotions already in turmoil, I couldn't handle the rejection.

I took in the stylish cut of his white-blond hair—just long enough on top that a few strands swept across his pale brow. Silver eyes, as bright as moonlight dancing across the ocean, watched me. His perfect lips and the hint of stubble along his jawline made my legs quiver.

Why did he have to be so damn handsome?

My gaze travelled down the smoothness of his neck to the breadth of his shoulders and tapered waist hidden beneath his dark blue T-shirt. His faded jeans showed off the rest of his assets to the greatest advantage, and I deserved a medal for respecting his wishes and keeping my distance.

All because he feared he would kill me with a kiss.

To be fair, if I were anyone else, his touch *would* kill me. He was a servant of Death, after all. The purpose of his existence was to escort magical souls to the afterlife… or usher them there ahead of schedule with a brush of his bare skin.

I forced my eyes back up to meet his, and my breath caught at the intensity I found staring at me. He stood with his back to the wall, his gloved hands tucked behind him.

The pose triggered the frustration I'd successfully tamped down during my magic practice. He only took that pose when he was around mortals—a way of reducing the risk of accidental contact. He'd stood that way when our bond had frayed. But our connection was as strong as ever, and I wanted to shake him.

"Do you need something?" My question came out sharper than I'd meant it to.

He raised an eyebrow, and a smile teased the corner of his mouth in a way that awoke my desire alongside my anger. "I wanted to check in and see how you're doing. If you've learned anything about the hunters' plan."

As tempted as I was to offer some snarky reply about him lying to get in my room, I didn't have the heart for it. He shouldn't need an excuse to visit me, and the fact he thought he did left me tired and sad.

I slumped onto the side of the bed. "Nothing. I'm guessing no rumours have floated your way via the afterlife?"

Emrick had filled me in on the spirit gossip. Turned out I was a hot topic among the dead. Something about me bringing waves of destruction in my wake. I didn't see how it could happen—while I might talk a big game, burning things to the ground out of spite wasn't really my jam—but if they worried my response would be that catastrophic, whatever was coming had to be big.

"I wish I did. The magical souls either don't know anything or they're staying quiet."

In the silence that followed, awkwardness lurked, toeing the carpet and poking its nose in my underwear drawer. How it could exist between us after almost a millennium boggled my mind, but it just went to show that immortality was no barrier to complicated issues. If anything, that was a perk of being mortal. You could die and take your complications with you.

It wasn't fair. Emrick and I weren't supposed to have awkwardness after so many centuries together. Worse, neither of us would be in this situation if he hadn't broken his promise to me.

Seventy-five years ago, I'd ordered him to stay away from me. It had been a last-ditch effort to save him from losing so many fragments of his soul that he faded into nothing. Mikhail's plotting and Shogaur's return had brought him back into my life, and although I'd done my best to keep my distance, I'd failed.

Miserably.

I couldn't do it.

The bond that tied me to him and this world was strong, but nothing compared to the emotional bond that had formed after eight hundred and fifty-three years of having him by my side.

So I'd caved, I'd let him back in—and now he was the one pushing me away.

For so many reasons, it was the wiser move. By staying with me, he risked losing the rest of himself. The fight with Shogaur had stripped him of more than one memory, and I didn't know what might disappear next.

But I also didn't know if I had the strength to survive what was coming without him.

"You haven't changed your mind?" The question came out before I could stop it, and I hated how pathetic I sounded— desperate and needy. Anger would have been better, but it had abandoned me.

Emrick's expression softened, but despite the yearning that reached out to touch my own, there was no crack in his determination. "Has Murisa discovered anything new with your blood?"

Murisa had worked so many miracles in the past few weeks, but putting Emrick's fears to rest had not yet been one of them.

"No." I hated admitting it. "The immortality is holding, though. No fluctuations, no issues."

Emrick tilted his head without breaking eye contact. "But you're still taking the potion?" His stare bored into me as though he could peer into my soul to ensure I wasn't lying to him.

I blinked, then gritted my teeth. Of course he'd been paying enough attention to know Murisa had been supplying me with the counterpotion to clear my blood of the hunters' poison. "She thinks I'm done with them, but she has one more dose on standby."

Disappointment shifted across his eyes like clouds over the moon. I knew he would have preferred if I'd said I was finished with them. That my magic was holding without any kind of magical intervention. I wished I could have lied to him. "That's something. Hopefully we'll know more soon."

I nodded, struggling to keep my spine straight under the weight of my pained longing. "Hopefully."

The awkwardness left my underwear drawer to dance naked in front of the large picture windows, and I picked at a loose thread on my comforter.

Time passed, and the silence grew thicker, filled with all the words we both wanted to say.

Emrick broke it first as he pushed away from the wall and shoved his hands in his pockets. "I'd better go."

I swore he sounded as though he wanted some reason to stay, and I wished I had more to offer besides my desire that he would.

"I'll see you later, Kat. I love you."

I didn't have time to return the sentiment before he disappeared.

3

Emrick

I PACED THE barren fields of the afterlife.

All around me, souls drifted like pinpricks of light, some lost, some wandering, some waiting.

Never had I empathized with them as much as I did now.

On the other side of the barrier between worlds was the one person whose soul called to me with intense love and power. I wanted to go to her, take the chance that we could be together without my world ending.

But the price was too high.

She worried I would trade too much of my soul for her and become a wraith; I worried a single touch might turn her to dust and send her soul to the afterlife.

Adrian had always believed she and I would find a solution

to our problem and move forward, but what would he think now, after everything that had happened to keep us apart? How could he believe we were anything but doomed?

The thought of being without her sliced me up. I couldn't imagine an eternity of craving her touch and being denied it. But I wasn't willing to rush my desires in case I guaranteed my own destruction.

So I would hold firm. We would wait. Fifty years. A hundred. Until we had some kind of proof that she was here to stay. That our bond hadn't weakened to the point where it could no longer protect her from me.

On that day, I would kiss her until the tether between us grew taut with her breathlessness. Her desire for me now would be nothing compared to mine for her once I knew she was safe.

I let out a breath and allowed hope to wrap around me.

What I needed was to get my mind off her. In calmer, more peaceful times, I would have distracted myself with work. Death knew I was busy enough with my responsibilities. I could have disappeared for a few months before checking in on Murisa's progress. What were a few years to an immortal?

But with the hunters coming for Kat, there was no way I would stray too far from her, no matter how painful it was to stay close.

As had become a common refrain over the past couple months, I wished there was more I could do to help her find the answers she needed. I meant what I'd told her earlier—I had scoured the afterlife for anyone who knew what the hunters might be up to, but no one was talking. I'd even managed to find some of the magical hunters who'd died recently, but they claimed to know nothing.

Unfortunately, I hadn't been able to speak with any of the hunters Kat and her team had dispatched in front of their unofficial headquarters last week. All of them had been mundane, safeguarding them from my wrath. I'd cleared away their mortal bodies to prevent any nosy neighbours from being witness to a magical battle outside their homes, but my role had stopped there.

Since then, I'd tried to dig deeper into the rumours floating through the afterlife over the past few months. Those rumours had taunted me—warning me of danger to come, of destruction so vast the spirit-herders would be overworked. A few spirits had suggested that if events continued as they were, the balance of the world would tip towards Death.

And at the heart of all their worries was the immortal sorceress.

For months, I'd believed the warnings had to do with Kat, though the logic behind it hadn't made sense. Then the witch Abigail had revealed herself to be the sorceress Alodie, another Palonian survivor, and I'd believed *she* was this bringer of darkness. The explanation had fit so much better given her desire to obliterate Kat and reclaim the youth that had been stolen from her during the failed immortality ritual.

After Alodie's death, the rumours had subsided for a while, but now they were back, more urgent than ever. From everything I'd heard, whatever was in the works would push Kat beyond the boundaries she'd set for herself and strike her down a path darker than any she'd walked in nine centuries.

I couldn't imagine what would cause such a precipitous change, and no one had anything other than vague murmurings to offer me. To say I was apprehensive would be the understatement of the millennium. The clock was ticking. If we didn't figure out the hunters' plan soon, I feared the world's foundations would tremble.

I forced out another breath and slowed my pacing, taking in the empty fields that stretched in front of me, beautiful in their emptiness. If only I could take on the sense of peace the muted colours and still waters provided. Maybe then I could see my way forward.

Specifically, a way forward that wouldn't sacrifice everything I had left. I held my hands out in front of me. Here in the afterlife, the increased paleness of my skin didn't stand out as much, but I knew how I appeared in the mortal world. Adrian had said he could almost see through me. I was becoming more shadow than man. All it would take was a few more bad decisions before I no longer felt the pull to visit Kat, all memory of her gone.

A shiver ran down my spine, and I dropped my hands to my sides. I would play this smart. Kat needed me to remain whole, so I would limit my actions to the afterlife and trust her and her team to handle the rest.

Resolved, I left the empty fields and made my way to the river. Somewhere along these shores, someone knew something. If I had to go person to person to ask my questions, I would find a connection to the witch hunters and drag what I needed out of them.

Yet before I reached the river, a pull on my middle tugged me backwards.

I paused and examined the sensation.

Was it the bond? My anxiety spiked as I braced for the burn in my chest warning me that the connection between Kat and I had grown frayed and unstable—as it had when she'd drunk that poisoned tea.

Fears ripped through me that the hunters had discovered another way to attack Kat's tether to this world. What if the next time they got to her, they didn't block the bond but severed it?

The tug in my middle grew stronger, and I rushed out of the afterlife towards Kat's room.

My movements grew sluggish, as though I were running through water. I pushed harder, desperate to break out of whatever haze I'd fallen into, but it was like the world was sliding away from me. I couldn't get a grip on the mists I'd mastered centuries ago. My limbs felt heavy, my blood thick and slow. Even my thoughts were fuzzy.

With a last burst of effort, I parted the mists, and Kat's room came into view. She was still sitting on the bed, shoulders slumped, face buried in her hands.

"Kat?" Her name came out muted to my own ears, as though I were standing in a room designed to dampen sound. I called out again, and my voice sounded even farther away. My heart raced against my ribs, so rapid I tasted blood at the back of my throat.

She looked up and saw me. Confusion furrowed her brow, and she rose to her feet to step towards me.

Her lips formed my name, but I couldn't hear it. Was it panic, or the ever-increasing tug on my middle that filled my ears with an unshakeable buzz? I reached for her, desperate to grab hold of anything that might pull me from this syrupy trap, but even as I extended my hand into her room, the scene faded and another overlaid it. I stood in two places at once. One was familiar—the only place I wanted to be, beside the only person I wanted to be with—and the other was a large room filled with strangers staring in my direction.

Black spots danced in my vision as I struggled to catch my breath. I didn't understand what was happening. Who were these people? Where was I?

A small corner of my frantic brain assessed the strangers with their weapons and urban fatigues, and the obvious answer hit me like a punch to the gut.

Hunters.

How was this possible? What had they done to me?

Even as fear for myself galloped in my chest, a deeper terror overwhelmed me. If they had me, what did that mean for Kat?

With what little grip I retained on Kat's room, I forced my attention to her. I had no idea if she could hear me, but I refused to abandon her without warning. Channelling all my strength into my lungs, I shouted, "Whatever happens, don't come after me! I love you."

Her eyes widened as she threw herself at me, but the way between us closed before she made contact.

She faded, and this other room, filled with nothing but concrete and wide eyes, was all that existed.

4

Katerina

I STUMBLED INTO my bedroom wall as the last of the mist faded from my room.

"Emrick?" I shouted, desperate for him to come back.

What had just happened? One second, he'd been standing on the edge of the afterlife, ready to step into my room. The next, his attention had been focused elsewhere, his expression one of confusion followed by fear.

And then he'd vanished.

Whatever happens, don't come after me. I love you.

His voice had barely come through. As though he'd called from kilometres away instead of standing less than two metres from me.

And why did his words sound like goodbye?

My heart raced, and I spun in a circle as I called for him again. Nine hundred years, and we'd never found a way for me to contact him in the afterlife. He'd always come to me, always knowing when I needed him. More than once in my long life, I'd resented that one-sided nature of our relationship, but never more so than in this moment.

Because that hadn't been a proper goodbye. That hadn't been him saying he'd thought it over and realized it would be better if he didn't return to my side. He'd been warning me about something.

Don't come after me.

If he were in the afterlife, he wouldn't have said that, because the only way I could reach him on that plane would be if Death took me again. If he wasn't there, he had to be somewhere in the mortal world. But then why…

My bedroom door flew open as Gavin barged in. Fire danced over his extended palm as he looked around my room. When his gaze landed on me, he frowned. "I heard you yelling. Is everything okay?"

My pulse raced, my heart beating so quickly my tongue felt prickly. Panic had rooted my feet to the floor, and my thoughts were static. But beyond the panic was a certainty that no, everything was most definitely not okay. And with that certainty came the knowledge that if I didn't act soon—if I didn't ignore Emrick's order—I would lose him for good.

Answers tumbled over each other in their hurry for me to understand, and I braced myself against the wall as they fell into place. Emrick was somewhere in the mortal world—somewhere that would be dangerous for me. Not many people in the world had the power to keep a servant of Death trapped on this plane.

But I could think of one group that might have found a way.

I squeezed my eyes shut to register the truth staring at me and sucked in a breath to gather my courage.

Once I was certain I wouldn't lose myself in a deluge of overblown magic, I met Gavin's eye. "Gather everyone downstairs. I know who the hunters are after."

5

Emrick

I TURNED TO the people gathered around me, searching for whoever led them. There were at least a dozen in the room, ranging from their early twenties to their mid-fifties. Although they didn't wear an official uniform, every one of them sported cargo pants and a fitted T-shirt. The attire screamed military, which had been my first clue about who I was dealing with.

The other clue had been the cold look in the eyes of some of the older people and the haughty arrogance in the younger. Half of them had seen more of the world than they should have with their mundane blood, and the other half believed they could handle whatever was coming.

Neither group had any idea what they'd done by bringing me here. They might think they claimed some kind of authority, but no one—not even a bunch of upstart hunters—could control Death.

Finally, my eye fell on the woman at the centre of their group. Unlike the others in their ready-for-battle gear, she wore a pressed cream blouse with a high collar, a buttoned dark grey jacket, and slacks that flared over her heeled boots. With her coiffed hair and painted nails, she looked more like she should be at the top of a boardroom than surrounded by people ready to throw themselves into a magical fight.

A few of the hunters looked her way, as though deferring to her for hints on how to proceed. This had to be the witch hunter general the hunters had told Kat about. The leader of the Ontario witch hunters who had obviously gone rogue.

I processed all these thoughts as I worked to stay calm. They couldn't touch me without killing themselves. I was the most powerful being in this room, and they would do well to remember it.

Beneath my self-assurances, I couldn't help but wonder how the hell they'd dragged me here. What magic had they used to make it possible? And if they knew what I was, why did they look so certain they were in no danger?

The only exception was a young soldier standing behind the others. Her eyes were wide, and her shoulders were hunched. She watched me warily, and when I moved, she jerked away.

At least one of them understood that the fire they played

with would burn them. I was done being jerked around. These bastards had come after Kat and almost succeeded in stealing her from me. They were the reason Adrian was no longer with us and why Gavin's life had been upended. The damage they'd caused could never be repaired, and from everything we'd learned, they had more planned.

This was my chance to protect Kat from those plans. Sacrificing one more fragment of my soul would be worth it to prevent these hunters from causing more pain and suffering. Even Kat would agree with me.

In time.

Saying a prayer to Kat's gods that this piece of myself wouldn't be the last, I strode towards the woman.

Only to jerk back as intense pain, like hot iron tickling my nerve endings, sent my muscles into spasm.

I landed on my back, spine arched, and a cry spilled through my lips. The agony stretched on, shocking every cell in my body and cascading along every vein. Being mostly spirit, I hadn't thought it possible for me to suffer like this anymore. Yet somehow these people had targeted the part of me that remained human.

Was that how they'd summoned me here?

Nothing about this made sense, and while the pain continued, my thoughts were too fragmented for me to try to understand.

Eventually the torture subsided. Gasping for breath, sweat dripping down my face, I pushed myself up on shaking arms and looked at the woman. She stared back at me without sympathy. If anything, I would have said she looked bored.

"Now that we've got that out of the way," she said, "perhaps you'll play nice."

I scowled and rose to my feet. Whatever they wanted me for, they wouldn't get it. I reached for the mists to take me back to the afterlife. Nothing happened. I tried again, and all I sensed was a sturdy wall preventing me from reaching my home. For the first time since I'd made my deal with Death, the doorway to the afterlife was blocked.

Whatever the hunters wanted, whatever they'd planned, they'd ensured I had no way out.

6

Katerina

It took less than three minutes for Gavin to round everyone up in the living room.

For all my urgency, I was the last one to join them, having needed to take thirty seconds to catch my breath and jump-start my cognitive functions. When I walked into the living room, everyone fell silent and turned my way.

"The hunters have Emrick."

Why draw it out?

It had taken me all of three and a half minutes to process what I'd witnessed, and although I didn't understand how they could have snared him, I knew in my gut I was right.

A furrow formed on Barrett's brow. He was the only one not sitting, looming behind Maera's chair, as close as he could get to the front door. Guarding the entrance? I wouldn't put it past him to be so cautious. "How is that possible? How are they not piles of dirt?"

I rubbed my arms to fight the chill that chased me despite the hot, muggy day. "I don't think they got hold of him physically. He was about to step into my room when something stopped him and pulled him back." I swallowed hard and closed my eyes against the pain of him being there and then *not*. The desperation in his eyes when he'd warned me away was a knife-strike to my heart. "However they did it, they have him."

"How do you know it's the hunters?" Gavin asked.

Impatience clawed at me. Why were we sitting here discussing details when the obvious stared right at us? "He told me not to go after him, which means he knew I'd figure out who'd taken him. Who else could it be?"

"If he warned you away, shouldn't you listen? They could be using him to get to you." Poppy kicked her feet up on the coffee table, but I wasn't fooled by the casual posture. Her shoulders were stiff, the lines around her mouth hard.

I read between the lines of her suggestion and crossed my arms. "What have you heard?"

Her nostrils flared, a dead giveaway that she swas hiding something from me. "What do you mean?"

"If you know how or why or where they have Emrick and you don't spit it out, Proserpine Lister, I swear to the gods…"

She held up her hands. "I don't know anything specific, I promise. You know if I did, I would never hold it back. Not with Emrick involved." She cleared her throat. "But I did reach out to my mother like you asked me." Her lips flattened into a straight line. "The conversation went about as well as you might have expected, but whatever. That's a later problem. The important thing is she's heard all kinds of rumours about the hunters lately. Most of them she discounted as being ridiculous, but now she's looking into them again."

"What kind of rumours?" Maera asked, and I was glad someone had the presence of mind to inquire because I was too busy holding myself back. Not from Poppy, who had only just gotten off the phone, but from hunting down Hera and tearing her head from her shoulders. I'd looked that bitch in the eye and told her someone was out to get me, and she'd mentioned nothing about these *rumours*.

If she'd thought to let the hunters deal with me before she dealt with them, I would have a few eye-opening responses for her when this was over.

But first things first. Maera's question hung in the room, and Poppy shifted uncomfortably in her seat, dropping her bright yellow Converse shoes to the floor and leaning forward on her knees.

Cuddles padded into the room, headed straight for Poppy's shoes, and lay down to bat at her laces.

Murisa gently nudged the necromancer with her elbow. "Tell them. We can't do anything about it until we're all on the same page."

Poppy sighed and bowed her head into her hands, tugging on the thick mass of curls. Then she sat up and looked me in the eye. "Look, I don't know what in this tangle is true and what's not, okay, kitty Kat? So don't lose your head right away. Not until we know for sure."

I clenched my hands into fists and did my best to keep breathing. Throwing myself at Poppy wouldn't speed up getting answers.

Neither would throwing my chair. Or the coffee table. Or the whole room. That was my panic talking, and I couldn't let emotion control me.

"All right," I promised.

Poppy hesitated a moment longer, assessing me, making up her mind as to whether she believed me. "Hera says the hunters have been digging into a lot of history lately. Books, myths, legends. They're digging for something."

"Any idea what?" Barrett asked.

In my experience, it was never a good thing when magically-minded people—whether magical themselves or not—showed an obsessive interest in any subject. It usually meant they were seeking power hidden in secrets long since buried.

Also in my experience, those secrets were buried for a

reason.

Poppy frowned, and the flicker of confusion that passed across her features did nothing to put me at ease. "She has no idea. Her contacts at the libraries and research facilities have passed along some of the titles the hunters are looking for, but there doesn't seem to be any connection between them. Articles about death and immortality, evolution, chaos theory. She read a bunch of them off to me, and it sounds like some kid's thesis material."

"If they were taking three different master's degrees," Murisa added, looking equally perplexed.

"Can you get Hera to send us the list?" I asked. "I don't care if we need to break it up and spend the next seventy-two hours reading the most boring dissertations until our eyeballs bleed, I want to know what these people are looking for." I looked to Rhys. "Unless you've Seen anything?"

His cheeks flushed to match his hair, and he shook his head. "Nothing helpful. More of what I Saw last week."

The last big vision Rhys had shared had been disturbing enough. *Fire extinguished. Ice melted. Words silenced. Death is coming for Death.*

Part of it sounded as though the hunters intended to come for my magic again, but they'd done that and failed. If they had a plan to come after it from a different direction, they'd be disappointed. Thanks to Murisa's counterpotion, I was ready for them this time, and I'd made it clear I was willing to kill to protect what mattered to me.

I turned back to Poppy. "What else has Hera heard? If her contacts are delivering titles, that's a little more specific than rumour."

Murisa and Poppy exchanged a glance, and Poppy shrugged. "Supposedly, the magicals within the hunter organizations are on edge. Some of their coworkers are making them uncomfortable, there's a rise in office bullying, that kind of thing. The execs haven't addressed it, but more than one hunter witch has given their notice and returned to their coven. Some might have even left the country."

On paper, the witch hunters, the vampire hunters, and the Hunter's Guild were not evil organizations. If they were, they wouldn't have survived their nascent years without Adrian and I wiping them out. Their official mandate was the same as mine—to protect the balance between magical and mundane.

Over the years, more magicals had joined their ranks, giving the impression of fairness in their dealings.

In reality, I knew all three groups tended to look at magicals outside their organizations as beneath them. The magical world was something to corral and punish instead of nurture and protect.

But if Hera's sources were right that the hunters were turning on each other, there was more going on behind the scenes than I'd realized.

"It fits with what we know," Gavin said as he leaned back into the couch. "What did Tony say? Their group split off from the main hunters about a decade or so ago. And by all accounts, they're gaining power."

"They have a least one witch hunter general in their ranks." The words tasted bitter.

The general had given the order to create the magic-blocking tea from the recipe Alodie had given the hunters. They'd had the money and resources to prepare the compound, make the tea, and distribute it under the guise of a legitimate business—if only for a few hours. This faction was no small deal.

I cleared my throat. "If there's tension within the hunters, maybe we can use that to our advantage. Turn them on each other."

Murisa looked up at me from beneath her long lashes. "So you're going to go after them despite what Emrick said?"

"Of course I am." How could any of them believe otherwise?

Rhys shifted in his seat. "What if he knows something we don't and didn't get a chance to tell you?"

"Then we figure it out for ourselves." Red crept around the edges of my vision, and I looked around the room at each of my team. "What the hell have we been doing for the past week if not preparing for this fight? Them taking Emrick is not going to make me back off. In fact, they've guaranteed the opposite. They have no idea what they've done."

I rolled my neck and tried not to think of Emrick in trouble. A thousand years, and I'd never faced this particular problem. He had always been the safe one, able to step into the afterlife whenever he needed to escape. Able to lay hands on any threat if they got too close. He was untouchable. Yet somehow our enemy had touched him.

Rhys nodded, though he didn't appear thrilled with my decision. Gavin glared at the coffee table, Maera stood up to prepare a tray of snacks, and Poppy and Murisa looked at each other. Barrett was the only one who met my eye, and I found the same fire burning behind his stare as the one that raged in my soul. These people were behind Adrian's death. It didn't matter what danger awaited us—these bastards were going to pay.

I shifted my attention back to the witches. "Poppy, you get that list of titles from Hera, then I want you and Murisa researching any possible way these non-magic users might have captured Emrick. Barrett, Gavin, Rhys, I want you digging up and reading those texts the moment we get them. I need to get to—" I stumbled and pressed my lips together, closing my eyes and breathing in through my nose as I worked to keep my rising fear at bay.

I was about to say I needed to get to Toronto so I could

poke around hunter territory myself, but Emrick wasn't here to take me. Maybe he'd never again be here to take me. Maybe he was gone, and I'd never know what had happened to him.

I forced my thoughts away from that dangerous, sucking pit and cursed every hour of delay the drive would take me.

A bump against my leg made me open my eyes, and I found Cuddles brushing against me. My emotional aura had to be dark if the undead cat who'd never warmed up to me was showing empathy.

"I'll help with the articles," Maera said softly. "Barrett can go with you to Toronto."

I looked at my housekeeper, who stared back at me with an expression of such deep compassion and understanding she nearly triggered the tears I'd just swallowed.

Stiffly, I turned to Barrett, who nodded. "I can be ready in twenty minutes. You figure out who we need to talk to, and we'll head straight there."

I considered the time. It was a little after five o'clock in the evening, so we'd be reaching Toronto close to ten depending on traffic. But that was fine. The people I needed to find tended to work late.

"If you learn anything, you call me," I said to the rest of my team. "If you *think* you learn anything, you call me. We don't have time to waste on this. Never mind whatever danger Emrick might be in, the witch hunters have trapped a powerful being whose existence is tied to the balance of the world. Whatever they want him for, it can't be anything good."

The faces around the room were grim as the truth of my words settled over us.

If the witch hunters succeeded in their plan, the foundations of the world as we knew it could be in jeopardy.

7

Katerina

BARRETT AND I reached Toronto a little after nine-thirty. He'd driven faster than I'd ever seen him go, and out of appreciation for his rule breaking, I'd been on my best behaviour as a passenger.

Normally, I enjoyed torturing the man with my taste in music cranked to the loudest volume, but tonight I craved silence. I wanted to drown in my fears of what would happen if I failed. In a twisted way, I hoped the intensity of my terror would push me through any fatigue that crept in as the hours passed.

Barrett's ears were also saved by the fact that any noise unrelated to our plans to save Emrick and make the hunters suffer irritated my last nerve. I'd nearly crawled out of my skin at the squeak of the windshield wipers when we'd passed through a rainstorm halfway through Sudbury.

Barrett himself stayed blissfully quiet throughout most of the drive. His attention was on the road, taking us into the heart of downtown without once questioning where we were going or what I intended to do once we got there.

Which was good because my plans remained vague.

We needed to talk to someone who had an in with the hunter circles. Unfortunately, our only connection to the hunters themselves had decomposed into a pile of earth on a quiet residential street. For months, Tony had been our go-to guy for everything hunter related. Not to mention he'd been a long-time acquaintance, if not friend, of Barrett's.

To learn he'd been feeding us lies every step of the way, luring us deeper into this net the faction had spread to catch us, had been a huge hit to my ego and my confidence. That weaselly, cheese-powder-covered asshat had outsmarted me, and if I were to live another thousand years, I didn't think I would ever forgive myself for being fooled. I was so used to Barrett's hatred of me I'd discounted Tony's. Accepted it as the default position of any hunter.

If I'd seen through him sooner, maybe we could have stopped his rogue group before so much destruction had been wrought. Before Adrian had sacrificed himself.

For centuries, I'd prided myself on being the greatest hunter the magical world had ever seen, but that pride had obscured the truth. Tony had said as much. I'd been too arrogant, too certain that I was the target for the hunters' plans.

The revelation that I wasn't gnawed at me as Barrett navigated his way through the city streets.

All these years—all these deaths—all to bring me down so they could get past me to someone else.

How many signs had I missed along the way?

Tony had said his group had been around for about a decade, but someone had summoned Alodie's demon at least sixty years ago. How long before that had they put their plan into motion? I doubted they'd summoned Fegor on a whim and—oops!—happy coincidence, along came another Palonian sorceress with a grudge against a certain self-proclaimed guardian.

No, someone had put time and research into digging up my past to discover what would hit me hardest. I'd never kept what happened to me a secret, but I also hadn't been vocal about the details, much preferring they stayed buried. So whoever had begun this movement would have had to dig through centuries of information, tracing my route across the world to discover the little region tucked into the Lake District of England where my community had been massacred. They would have had to figure out what Mae, Alodie, and Blythe had done to carry out their ritual—how, by binding themselves to Fegor without first summoning it onto this plane, they'd sentenced themselves to joining their demon in the infernal realms.

Only Alodie had opted to take the plunge—Mae and Blythe having chosen death over imprisonment—but she had been enough to wreak havoc on this modern world.

All that research would have taken decades. Centuries.

The witch hunters were far from a new group. Some version of them had existed as early as the sixteenth century, even if the organizations as we knew them today had only become official about three hundred years later.

At what point had they begun to use me?

At what point could I have sat up and noticed we weren't living in harmony as I'd believed we were?

Hells, I'd trusted them enough to ask for their help and support going after Mikhail and Shogaur. I'd believed they were reliable enough to stand with me against some of the greatest magical threats the world had seen in recent years.

Now I wanted to beat my head against the window for being so naive. I'd been around for almost a millennium, and I could still be surprised by how twisted human nature could be.

"Stop it," Barrett said as he pulled into the driveway of Adrian's house in Kensington Market.

Or not Adrian's house anymore.

Technically, it was mine, as stated in Adrian's will. While Barrett had inherited the house in Muskoka and a villa in Italy, my friend had bequeathed most of his extra residences to me as options for when I said goodbye to Manitoulin and began a new life for myself. A new identity under which to continue my immortality. A new base of operations for this fight I'd sworn myself to.

I couldn't accept the change without mentally keeping the house in Adrian's name. To be here without him was strange enough; to consider it mine was a step I wasn't yet ready to take.

Another life lost because of my shortsightedness.

Barrett wrapped his fingers around my upper arm and squeezed until I met his eye. "This is not your fault."

When I tried to pull away, he tightened his grip, and his jaw bulged. "You've been beating yourself up since we left Spring Bay, and I haven't said anything because I know you're not in a place to listen. But I'm not about to go around asking questions with you spinning every answer into how you might have done things differently."

My blood pressure rose, heating my cheeks and making my ears pop. What did he know about what was passing through my head? What right did he have to direct my thoughts?

His dark eyes burned as he released my arm and squeezed the steering wheel instead. By the way his knuckles bled white, I was grateful he'd chosen to vent his feelings elsewhere. "Do you think I didn't torture myself over what happened to Adrian for months after we lost him? Do you think I still don't wake up in the middle of the night asking if I could have moved faster? Noticed the spell circle sooner? We all make mistakes, Kat. We all have regrets, and we all miss things. You may be immortal, but you're still human."

It wasn't the first time he'd said something similar, but tonight it sounded less like an accusation. Another shift in our relationship. I was used to Barrett blaming me for everything, not empathizing with me.

I cleared my throat, but my words still came out thick. "You'd think I'd have learned to stop trusting people by now, Barrett. The number of times I've been betrayed. The number of times someone acted the opposite of how I expected them to. All these years, and I haven't figured out how people work."

He let go of the steering wheel and flicked his thumb over the windshield wiper handle. I'd never seen the man fidget before. "Be grateful you haven't. You might get hurt and you might get pissed off, but imagine how bored you'd be if you could anticipate everyone's next move. I think if that were the case, you wouldn't have panicked at finding yourself mortal. You would have been relieved for the out."

A rough laugh escaped me as I realized how right he was.

In fact, it had shocked me how desperate I'd been to stay alive when my immortality had been blocked.

Seventy-five years ago, after I'd forced Emrick away, I'd wondered often about what my end would look like, and I would have sworn I'd grown comfortable, if not eager, with the idea of reaching it.

People weren't meant to live forever.

The world changed too quickly, and keeping up with it was an exercise in exhaustion. I adapted as best I could, lagged behind on other things, and embraced the reputation of eccentric youth wherever I wound up. Yet no matter how hard I fought to float with the current, the fight often didn't feel worth it.

I'd come to believe that if the opportunity presented itself to call it quits, I would jump at it.

I hadn't anticipated that the opportunity would arise right when I'd found a new family. One that supported me and fought at my side, challenged me, irritated me. Loved me.

In the end, I hadn't been willing to let it go so easily.

"I guess you're right. The world is only bearable because of the different types of people who live here." I slumped in my seat and rubbed my brow. "But that doesn't excuse my lack of awareness. If anything happens to Emrick…"

Another laugh threatened to bubble out of me, this one closer to hysterical. What would happen if it did? Our bond would break, and I would again become mortal and happily go down in a blaze of fire, taking every last hunter with me.

If Emrick met his final death, I wouldn't survive him for long.

There was a strange sort of comfort in the idea, even as it set off another wave of barely suppressed panic.

What if his final death meant he wasn't there to greet me when I met mine?

What if I never had a chance to see him again, even beyond this world?

My breathing quickened and dark spots drifted in front of my eyes. I grabbed the door handle and forced myself to focus on the remains of a cobweb dancing in front of the vent as cold air blew into my face. Barrett had clearly been distracted if he hadn't noticed it.

We would get to Emrick in time.

There was no other option.

And the only way to ensure we did was to tackle the tasks ahead of me. "We'll start with the shops. Ten minutes to drop off our stuff, and then we're back in the car, and we don't stop until we learn something."

Barrett turned off the engine and opened his door. "Let's make it five."

8

Emrick

I THREW MYSELF at the invisible walls of my cage and swallowed my screams as agony wracked my body. My nerve endings crackled, and I clenched my teeth until my jaw popped. But no matter how hard I shoved my shoulder against the barrier, I made no progress into the empty grey room beyond.

Exhausted, I stumbled backwards to the middle of the circle and fell to my knees. Sweat dripped down my face, and I wiped it off with the back of my arm as I blinked away the black spots dancing through my vision. My muscles felt as though they'd been shredded, my lungs ached, and my head throbbed. With every breath, my heart lurched in my chest as though it were bouncing around untethered against my ribs.

It wasn't the first time I'd endured this torture in my attempt to push my way to freedom, but so far whatever they'd used to cage me had held firm.

The circle was roughly six feet across, giving me enough room to pace if not to lie down, and offered a view of concrete walls uninterrupted by any windows and a stretch of concrete floor. There were no markers to reveal where I was or where in the building I might be if I did manage to escape.

Not that I would stop trying. Not that I would *ever* stop trying.

After my warm welcome, the hunters had left me on my own. I sensed living people standing sentry outside the door, but no one poked their head in to make sure I was still here. I didn't know if I was more relieved or unnerved by their absence. It meant I could try whatever I wanted to get out of here and not have anyone step in to stop me, but it also meant they were confident I wouldn't succeed.

Somewhere in this building, the witch hunter general was no doubt enjoying my attempts. I couldn't wait to get my hands on her and watch the terror spill into her eyes the millisecond before she decomposed at my feet.

The vision fueled me, pushed me through the fading agony, and motivated me to stay focused on my goal. Whatever it took to return to Kat. Any pain was worth that.

Still on my knees, I closed my eyes and turned my efforts from the cage walls to the barrier between this world and the next. I reached for the mists, the familiar sensation of the empty void all souls passed through when they died.

When nothing happened, I concentrated instead on Katerina and our bond. My heart bled at the thought that she was out there waiting for me. Worrying about me.

After seventy-five years, we'd finally reconnected, and now here I was, unable to get to her.

While I doubted she'd listen to me, I prayed she'd stay away. I'd been concerned enough about her going after the hunters when we'd believed she was the target. Knowing they were after me, I didn't want to imagine how they might use us against each other to get what they wanted.

But even as my prayers drifted into the void, I knew they were futile. My beautiful Katerina. My heart and soul. My reason for maintaining any connection to a world where people willingly and eagerly destroyed the beauty around them for the sake of greed and power.

Despite my warning, I knew she would find her way here—wherever here was. She'd never been the type to sit quietly once she identified a threat that needed to be put down. Especially when that threat targeted the people she loved.

I was honoured to be on that very short list, even as I feared what it would cost her.

To protect her, and probably the rest of the world depending on why the hunters wanted me, I had to find a way out.

If the afterlife was beyond my reach, I would return my efforts to this cage. These arrogant, pitiful humans believed they could ensnare Death. I refused to give up until I'd proved to them how wrong they were.

On wobbly legs, I rose to my feet and once again threw myself at the invisible wall, pouring my haggard screams into the room.

9

Katerina

Barrett pulled up outside Rune the Day and parked the car.

I stared through the windshield at the brightly lit display in the window. The night was quiet, the store was quiet, the car was quiet… but my mind was in shrieking, raging, wrestling turmoil. The vague sense of dread that had come over me when Barrett had turned onto the street was dragging me towards full-blown panic. I drew in three slow, deep breaths before attempting to speak.

"I guess I should have anticipated a visceral reaction to returning to this place," I commented around the heartbeat thrashing inside my chest.

Barrett pressed his lips together and gave me time to

compose myself. Last time I'd been here, a figure in the shadows had tried to take advantage of my temporary mortality by throwing a knife into my chest. It didn't matter that I was now immune to similar attacks, trauma was trauma was trauma. You could be twenty-four or eight hundred-and-seventy-seven years old—when you got stabbed and nearly bled out, it stayed with you.

"At least the store owner was quick to help you," Barrett said.

His answer earned him a very lady-like snort. "He was not. You threatened to tear out his spleen if he didn't get his ass in gear and pump me full of healing potions."

His jaw ticked. "You heard that?"

"Emrick filled me in."

Everything about those few moments was hazy in my memory. I clung to vague impressions of standing outside my body and watching the scene from afar, but the details were lost. Emrick had described some of it. He'd told me how he'd stood next to me on the edge of the afterlife as we'd watched Barrett and the witch pull me away from Death. Emrick had seen it all because he'd been there with me, encouraging me to hang on, urging me to go back.

My throat burned, and I squeezed my eyes shut against the impending tears. He'd been there for me at all my lowest points, and now it was my turn to be there for him. Which meant getting out of this car, going into that shop, and doing whatever it took to find out where these hunters were working from since we'd burned down their house. If I was lucky, this guy could elaborate on the rumours Hera had mentioned.

Rune the Day was the first stop of many, but I chose to be optimistic that we would learn everything we needed tonight.

A bell chimed over the door when we pushed our way in. It was just past ten o'clock, long after every other shop in the area had closed—the empty fast-food place next door excepted— but occult shops in this city, the ones that dealt in genuine articles, tended to stay open late.

I'd never asked why. Maybe it was for all those last-minute "crap, I need this rare ingredient for this super urgent spell" emergencies. Or maybe because the bulk of their customers preferred to do their shopping in relative anonymity.

Even though the lights were on and the owner stood behind the cash, his readiness for his next customer didn't stop him from widening his eyes and doing a wonderful impression of a fish trying to jump out of the frying pan at the sight of me.

"Y-You."

He was in his mid- to late thirties, with wire-rimmed glasses and a mop of brown hair over a pair of soft brown eyes. His black T-shirt and black jeans matched Barrett's, with the addition of a black apron tied around his neck and waist.

Not that anyone would ever confuse the two men, of course.

Barrett gave the impression that he could snap your neck with a look. Mr. Apron looked like he could snap his own neck by tripping over his inventory.

But I'd learned not to underestimate the witches of this city. The meekest of them had the potential to hold an absurd amount of power.

This guy, for instance. He looked like the most useful thing he could do was properly label his herbs, yet according to Emrick and Barrett, he'd saved me from a fatal stab wound with those properly labelled herbs and a few mumbled words.

"I understand I have you to thank for my continued existence." I leaned on the counter with both arms, gracing him with my warmest, friendliest smile.

He paled.

Oops. I pulled back the wolfishness for a more moderate grin.

"C-can I help you? I swear, I had nothing to do with whatever happened to you. I didn't know anyone was hiding in the parking lot. If you think I—"

I frowned. "Why are you so afraid"—I squinted at his nametag—"Ben? If you haven't done anything wrong, you have nothing to worry about."

"You're her, aren't you? The sorceress. The immortal."

"My friends call me Kat. But sure, that's me."

"You hunt witches."

I shrugged. "Only the ones who cause trouble." I narrowed my eyes. "You cause any trouble lately, Ben?"

"N-no, ma'am. I swear. Ever since you—I mean, Mikhail—wiped out three quarters of my coven, I run this shop and keep my head down."

I bristled. The deaths of his covenmates most certainly hadn't been my fault. Mikhail had eliminated at least four of them himself, and I'd taken down the rest in self-defence. Except for that one, but that had been a ricocheting spell circle—also not on me.

Ben must have read the disapproval on my face because his eyes widened further and he took a step back. "I'm not involved in anything you'd have issue with. What's left of my coven only practices healing spells. We don't have anything to do with the groups the hunters have been targeting."

My curiosity piqued, I allowed my smile to fall into place again and rested my chin on the back of my hand. "What groups, Ben?"

His gaze drifted to the door, then to the bookshelf on the opposite side of the store, then back to mine. "I don't know. Groups. You hear stuff when you work in places like this. People come in looking for all kinds of things."

"Dangerous things?" I purred.

"Not in and of themselves." Ben drew his shoulders back and raised his chin. Apparently I'd triggered his defensive bone.

"Of course not." I pushed myself up so I leaned on my hands instead of my elbows. I glanced at Barrett, and he headed off to browse the shop's wares, leaving me with Ben. "Listen, Benny, I owe you a few times over for what you did for me last week, so I won't ask to look in your stock room or poke around in your sales books. All I want to know is what you've heard about the witch hunters, the vampire hunters, the Hunter's Guild, and whatever groups they've been paying extra attention to lately."

Again Ben's gaze slid towards the front door, and this time I followed it with my own.

"Are you expecting someone, Benny?"

"N-No."

He was nervous again. Interesting.

"Are you worried I'll learn something I shouldn't and turn on you despite my promise of gratitude, or are you worried someone will walk in and discover you've been talking?"

He blinked his large eyes at me, licked his dry lips, and nodded his head towards the storeroom.

I looked to Barrett, who nodded and continued poking around the smudge sticks as I rounded the counter and followed Ben into the cramped storage space.

"You didn't hear this from me," he said.

I leaned back against the wooden shelving unit and crossed my arms. "As far as I'm concerned, I was never here."

He let out a breath and appeared marginally reassured, though his shoulders still brushed the bottoms of his earlobes.

"I don't know much, but rumours are bouncing across the city about how the hunters are crashing coven meetings left, right, and centre. They've always been strict about how often we meet and what we get up to, but lately, they've been coming down hard."

I gritted my teeth. That didn't sound very friendly.

"Has anyone been hurt?"

Ben's eyes flashed with the first glimmer of anger I'd seen since I'd arrived. "No, but at least a dozen witches have disappeared. Never during the raids, always a few days later. No one knows what's happened to them. We've filed missing person reports, but there are hunters everywhere you look. I suspect the ones in the police department are hushing it up."

I knew well enough how true that might be. It was the only reason Rhys was still walking around instead of in jail for inciting a mob during the Shogaur incident.

"Do you know where the hunters are based out of these days?"

Ben's anger faded into mild confusion. "I don't know where they've ever been based. As far as we know, they move around, not wanting us to pin them down and carry out some kind of revenge plot or something. Who do they think we are? Something out of American Horror Story? We're witches, for the goddess's sake. Do no harm."

I sniffed. "That's all well and good for you, but remind me why most of your old covenmates are dead? All the better for you if you keep your nose out of it, though."

Even if his clean nose meant I wasn't likely to get the information I needed from him.

I cleared my throat and nudged my toe into a dip in the floor. "Let's say I wanted to talk to a witch who dabbled in the… less savoury elements of your craft. Where would you suggest I begin?"

He flushed and stared over my left shoulder. "I don't know anyone like that."

I laughed. "Stick to inventory, Ben. You're a horrible liar." I erased my smile and dropped my arms. "I promise not to do anything to them. They'll get off with a warning this time— which, by the sounds of it, is more than the hunters are offering. I need to get to the hunters before they do something worse than interrupt a few coven meetings. If you don't know where they like to hang out, point me to someone who might."

He shifted his weight on his feet, then met my eye. We stared at each other for a good, long minute before his shoulders drooped. "Kelly Boldare out of the Fool & Chariot, a shop out in East York. She dabbles in all kinds of things, but her coven got hit last week. One of her witches, a guy named Freddy, disappeared without a trace a few days later."

Either Freddy had been up to no good and the actual hunt- ers had been a little excessive in dealing with their problems, or Tony's gang had crossed some serious lines.

As soon as I sniffed out the truth, one side or the other would have me to deal with.

"Thanks, Ben. That's two I owe you now."

He scowled. "Don't think just because you're immortal and terrifying, I won't collect."

"I'd be disappointed if you didn't." I hesitated at the door. "Would you and the rest of your coven be willing to stand with us if it comes to a fight? Purely in a healing capacity."

Ben narrowed his eyes. "What's going on? I know who you are, and I know what you do. Why are you asking me for help?"

Emrick's silver eyes flashed behind my eyelids, and my heart twinged. "Because I think I'll need it. I think, if we want to see the seasons change again, we'll all need to work together."

He stared at me for a few seconds, and I braced for him to refuse. To my surprise, the lines around his eyes hardened, and he nodded. "My healing knowledge is yours when you need it. My old coven wanted power, and look where it got them. I want to practice magic. I want to learn and improve. But at the heart of it all, I want to help."

He reminded me so much of Poppy that, even after our rough beginning, I found myself liking him.

"I'll be in touch."

I collected Barrett, and we drove straight to the Fool &
Chariot. The clock was inching closer towards eleven, and
my jaw cracked with a yawn. Soon enough, our luck on these
easily accessible witches would run out, but while a single one
remained awake, I didn't intend to call it a night.

Despite the hour, Barrett didn't look the least bit tired. Oh,
the perks of an occasional drop of vampire blood. Adrian may
have left me a few dozen beautiful properties across the globe,
but the real gift he'd left me was ensuring Barrett remained in
peak condition to fight at my side.

"Do you think this woman will talk to you?" he asked as he
rounded the corner.

"Not readily, maybe, but hopefully that'll change when
she realizes she'd be smarter to talk with me than wait for the
hunters to arrive. I never thought I'd see the day where it would
be *us* against *them*. Maybe it's too bad we blocked Shogaur from
coming back. He could have let us know the hells had frozen
over."

A furrow formed between his eyebrows. "Are you really
going to give these witches a pass on whatever dark magic
they've been practicing?"

"If it gets us the hunters? Sure. I can look the other way
one—well, shit."

Barrett pulled the SUV to a stop, and I stared out the
window at the scene unfolding before us.

Hunters stood with their guns aimed at a woman standing outside the shop. She had one arm wrapped around a man's chest while her free hand held a knife to his throat.

"Put your weapons down." Kelly's voice was laced with so much magic my bones quivered. "This is your last warning. Obey, or your colleague dies."

I scrambled out of the car, but whatever I planned to do, I didn't have a chance to put it into action.

One of the hunters moved, another turned to stop him, and Kelly jerked the blade across the man's neck. As the blood poured from his body, a blast of power burst from the witch and knocked me off my feet.

10

Katerina

KAT?" BARRETT SHOUTED.

"Get back in the car!" I didn't wait to see if he followed orders before I combat-crawled across the parking lot towards the woman who now stood in a sphere of floating blood.

Her eyes were black, her hair was drenched red, and her teeth were bared with the effort of maintaining her defensive spell.

When Ben had told me this coven dabbled, I hadn't realized just how loosely he'd interpreted the definition of *dabble*. While I didn't have an inherent issue with blood magic as a rule, I did draw the line at using blood from the unwilling, and slaughtering was right out.

The dead hunter slumped to the ground, and the blood

around Kelly shifted from a protective sphere into an offensive blade that flew towards the hunters. Most of them ducked beneath it, but the woman on the end wasn't so lucky. The liquid scythe sliced through her neck, and the next thing I knew, her head was rolling towards me.

With a grimace, I shifted into a crouch and darted towards the witch. Her power coiled around me, but I reversed my fire magic and cooled myself down until goosebumps rose over my skin. Once my power was firmly in hand, I threw up a frozen shield that received the brunt of her spell. Shattered ice rained over me, and I grabbed the shards and hurled them in Kelly's direction.

A shriek rang through the night as one of the shards tore into her arm, and she hugged the injured limb to her chest to staunch the bleeding.

Another wave of power hit me, this one not nearly as strong or as focused, and I swallowed my scream as pain hugged my bones. She was throwing around some seriously dark magic, and when I finished here, I would have another word with Ben to find out just how *uninvolved* he was. It was possible our truce would be short-lived.

"Stop making it impossible to keep my promise," I shouted through clenched teeth as I tackled Kelly to the ground.

Bullets flew overhead and smashed into the shop windows. Glass sprayed everywhere, and I threw up my arms to cover our heads.

More shots rang out, but when none of them hit my body, I peered up to find the hunters focused on Barrett, who'd brought out the full artillery from his trunk. His enchanted semi-automatic made no noise when he squeezed the trigger, and the bullets did little damage, but a few seconds later, a series of soundwave explosions rattled my eardrums. The hunters clapped their hands over their ears, and more than one fell to their knees. Murisa had levelled up her toys.

I grabbed hold of Kelly's wrists, hauled her to her feet, and dragged her into the store. The shattered window was a less-than-effective barrier between us and the hunters, but I wrestled her towards a blank space of wall and pressed her against it.

"Let go of me!" Kelly screeched in my ear.

I adjusted my hold to keep her in place and glared at her. "Before I do, I need your word that your blood magic ends tonight. Right now."

The last thing we needed was for me to release her only to have more dark magic sweeping through the parking lot, and her blazing black eyes didn't do much to reassure me. Although the power was already seeping out of them, revealing their natural blue shade.

"Are you crazy? Why would I promise that? You see what I'm dealing with here? I was just in my shop, running my business, when these assholes drove up and threatened to firebomb my store." She twisted her head to yell out the broken window. "That's my livelihood, fuckwads!"

"You're peddling death, witch," one of the hunters called back, and I squeezed my eyes shut.

I hated dealing with children.

If this woman didn't give me her promise soon, the hunters would rally, and we'd be at a wild disadvantage. Already, more gunshots were sounding off, and I prayed Barrett was keeping his head down.

Deep breath in, slow breath out, and once my patience stabilized, I opened my eyes and stared down at the woman glaring daggers at me. "Listen. On any other night, if I had come here and found you practicing unethical blood magic, you'd be dead. I wouldn't have hesitated. I've seen enough witches go down that path to know it's only a short trip from killing one hunter to slaughtering an entire warehouse of witches to gain a twisted immortality."

Her lip curled in a sneer, and I knew she'd heard of Mikhail's failed efforts—if she hadn't been in that warehouse herself and experienced the close call firsthand.

"However," I continued, "it's your lucky day. I promised someone I wouldn't kill you if you told me where to find the hunters. Since I found the hunters trying to kill you, I can deal with them and consider your current display of horrible judgement an act of self-defence. But if I catch you with a toenail over the line again, you'll meet the same fate as that woman you decapitated. Sound good?"

I didn't loosen my hold as she glowered at me, nor did I break eye contact with her. When Kelly finally broke down and nodded, I chanced looking away from her to peer through the window at my actual persons of interest.

The moment I eased the pressure on her arms, Kelly shoved me away and ran for the back of the shop. Seconds later, the lights went out, dousing the parking lot in shadow, and the back door slammed shut.

Grumbling to myself about the witch's lack of assistance, I summoned a fireball into my palm and let it rise in front of me until it hovered above my head, lighting the pavement a few metres around. Armed with my power and relieved that we could take blood magic out of tonight's encounter, I returned outside.

Barrett walked towards me, his semi-automatic firm in his grip. I drew more fire into my hands, letting it spread up my arms to the tops of my elbow-length gloves. When I was ready, I took in the five hunters standing together. The headless corpse and Kelly's sacrifice lay on the ground between us, and my heart clenched that the person who should have swooped in to clean up the mess before panic hit the news centres was nowhere to be found.

My sorrow and fear burst into fury, and I allowed my fire to blaze a little brighter.

I strode forward. "All right, who's going to be the smart one who tells me where my lover is? That person might be allowed to walk away."

I scanned the five. Three men and two women, four of them in their twenties and thirties, and one of them pushing fifty. They shared the same arrogant set of their chin, as though they believed there was nothing I could do that would make them speak.

Once upon a time, that might have been true.

Centuries ago, I'd sworn never to take a human life if I could avoid it. Recent months had pushed me to disregard that personal vow for one reason or another, even though doing so filled me with a deep sense of guilt and shame.

These bastards?

They had Emrick.

I would set fire to every last one of them if that's what it took to get him back.

One of the two women must have read as much in my expression, because she stepped forward and drew in a breath. Before she could utter a syllable, the older guy raised his weapon and shot her twice in the chest.

My eyes grew as wide as hers as she slumped to the ground, blood pooling around her body.

"What the fuck, my dude," I said to the guy.

He sneered at me. "What we've set in motion won't be stopped. If some of us are too cowardly to see it through, they don't deserve to be in our ranks."

By the twist of Barrett's mouth and the twitch of his eye, he was one bad excuse away from blowing this person's head off, and I wasn't about to stop him.

"If the plan is already in motion, there can't be any harm in telling me what it is, can there?" I asked.

It was a long shot, but whatever. All I had going for me right now were long shots.

The younger hunters looked to their leader, and I swore the second woman stepped away from him. Wise. At the moment, standing next to this son of a bitch was the worst place to be for anyone who wanted to see morning.

"Jared…" one of the others said.

"Shut the fuck up, Victor." Jared's sneer deepened as he looked me over. "You'll find out soon enough, sorceress. I'm not about to ruin the surprise."

"Come on." I took another step. "You want to see the look on my face when I find out, don't you? And if you don't tell me, you won't be around to experience it for yourself."

He took his own step forward, and I flicked my fingers in Barrett's direction, ordering him to hold his fire.

Jared closed in on my personal space. "This moment is

already sweet enough. Watching you scramble. Seeing your desperation. You believe you can prevent what's coming. You believe you can save your disgusting reaper. But you have no idea. You're already too late. The only thing left for me to enjoy will be the moment you realize it."

His confidence—his utter certainty—that Emrick was gone for good was enough to shake my hope that I would figure this out in time. Even as fear quaked my bones, rage swept in even hotter than before that this sadist should make me doubt myself.

I closed the rest of the distance between us until our faces were almost touching. He reeked of onion and garlic, and I wrinkled my nose. "You think you're the cleverest, bravest prick to ever stand against me, don't you? From where I'm standing? You're nothing but dog shit smeared on the bottom of my shoe. You are nothing. Your plans are nothing. Your little group? Nothing. The only reward you're earning by keeping Emrick from me is my wrath. Consider yourself grateful you won't be here when I unleash it."

The glimmer of fear in his eyes was more satisfying than anything else he might have said, but I didn't give myself time to savour it. Without another word, I summoned an ice spike into my hand and drove it through his throat. His eyes widened as he gurgled around it, and blood trickled out the corner of his mouth. He collapsed next to the body of the young woman he'd murdered.

With him dead, I turned my attention to the remaining three. "Would anyone else like to offer their two cents?"

The other woman looked ready to run, and one of the men had a glower to match their leader's, but the second man—Victor—trembled as he pointed to the phone lying on the ground. "We've never been to the base, so we don't know where it is, but he did. There's probably information on his phone."

I bent down to pick it up and passed it to Barrett, who slid it into his pants pocket. "I'm going to suggest the three of you walk away. Take a trip. Get as far from the hunters as you can. Whatever your group is involved in, it's not going to end well. Either your leaders get what they want and the world will suffer, or I get what I want and the hunters will be wiped out. Anyone standing in my way won't be there for long."

Two of the three nodded and ran. The third one held my gaze, his blue eyes glittering under the streetlights, and I knew in my heart he and I would be seeing each other again real soon.

11

Katerina

ONCE I WAS sure the hunters weren't about to return with a second assault, I went back into the shop.

Barrett lingered by the dead bodies, and by the time he joined me inside, I'd already confirmed Kelly had bolted out the back.

He found me behind the sales counter poking around in all the drawers and cubbies. "What are we hoping to find?"

"Something. Anything that makes me feel like we made progress tonight."

Barrett arched an eyebrow, and I huffed. "Yes, all right, I know. The night wasn't a complete bust. We came here to find information about the hunters, and we got information about the hunters. *And* prevented a witch from being abducted. All in a day's work."

Sure, she'd used overt criminal blood magic to keep the hunters away, giving them credibility for being here, but despite all I'd witnessed, I believed she hadn't been the instigator. Not to mention, the few words their leader had shared before I'd killed him had confirmed we were on the right path.

Every step I'd taken was leading me the right away. I couldn't let myself be disappointed by the setbacks.

I drew in a series of deep breaths to find my composure, then rummaged through the books tucked under the counter, hoping to find some contact information we could use to find Kelly. I had a sneaking suspicion the Fool & Chariot was in for some downtime while they put their shop to rights, but that didn't mean I was about to let her slip away.

It took a few minutes and one broken drawer lock before I found what I was looking for. I snapped a photo of Kelly's address with my phone.

"Just in case," I answered Barrett's silent question.

"In case you decide the only way to deal with the hunters is to dabble in magic you hate?"

A shudder ran through me at the thought of the damage witches like Kelly could cause if set loose, but until we had a better idea of what we were dealing with, I couldn't say never.

"With luck, we'll scrounge up some allies who don't rely on illegal blood magic to get them out of a pinch, but based on everything the hunters told us and that leader guy's bad atti-tude, we might not have a choice."

"And you think this woman would be willing to help? I hate to break it to you, Kat, but she didn't seem the type to stand and fight if the option to run presents itself."

He wasn't wrong. "She owes me for saving her life tonight. At the very least she can throw me a few names of people who might be more inclined to stand for their freedom."

I looked around the empty, glass-covered shop, and my shoulders slumped. "There's nothing else for us here. Let's head out."

As we passed the bodies—still on the ground, still not yet piles of dirt—I jerked my head towards them. "Were they able to tell you anything?"

Barrett grunted and held up the dead man's phone. "Nothing useful. Guy's print and face didn't register, which tells me it's not his primary phone, but we might get something off it if Murisa can crack the lock."

I reached for the door handle of Barrett's SUV and noticed how badly my hand was shaking. Not wanting to give myself away, I refrained from wrapping my arms around my middle as I slid into the seat, but of course the ex-soldier, ex-thrall, ex-frenemy noticed anyway. Despite the hot and humid night, Barrett turned the heat on low until my shivers stopped. By then, we were halfway back to Manitoulin.

The dead hunter's phone sat in the console between us, taunting us with whatever information it contained. We agreed the best option would be to return home and get Poppy and Murisa to give it a shot. Once in the technomancers' capable hands, I was certain the phone would spill its secrets.

When my adrenaline finally levelled out, I turned off the heat, cranked the AC, and sank into my seat to stare out the window at the passing scenery. All too quickly, the view of the looming rock faces along the highway gave way to trees and lakes, which changed again as we entered Espanola. Home was close, and from there, armed with new information, we could figure out what came next.

Like how many more blood witches I'd have to help if I wanted to put the hunters in their place. The irony of that sentence staggered me.

"Don't you hate when you have to fight for the wrong side to save the right one?" I asked.

Barrett grunted, and I chuckled. Perhaps he wasn't the best person to draw into deeper subjects. I'd rarely known the man to speak ten words together unless he was lecturing me.

But I had to talk out my train of thought before I worked myself into a spin, and, lucky him, he was the only one here to listen.

"Take that witch tonight. I might not have an issue with blood spells, depending on where they get the blood from and what they do with it, but that display tonight? It puts her right on my list of Problems I Need to Deal With. Yet for now, I don't have time to spare for her, because the people who should be dealing with her for me are the ones who pushed her to go to those lengths."

I tapped my fingers against my thigh. "Or did they? For all we know, she was already working her dark magic, and our dramatic entrance interrupted the hunters' attempt to take her down, which, in that case, oops. But if Ben is right about what the hunters have been up to, then those guys provoked her by going after her coven, and she was trying not to go the same way as her friend."

Barrett nodded but remained infuriatingly silent.

"For all we know, the hunters' intentions are benevolent and their plan would save the world an eternity of magical problems. Unlikely, since they refuse to tell me what that plan is, but I guess it's possible. Unfortunately for them, I no longer care if their goal is to wipe out world hunger. They took Emrick. Unless they're feeding him tea and cake and only abducted him to pick his brain about the needs of the afterlife before letting him go, I will reduce every last one of them to charred meat sacs."

Again, Barrett nodded. This nod surprised me. After all we'd been through, I'd expected a look of disdain or contempt. At least an eyeroll. This was the guy who'd once given me shit for storming a coven meeting without a solid plan and failing in my efforts to corner Mikhail. He'd called me anticlimactic. A disappointment to my reputation. Despicable for having magic and not doing enough to help.

He *hated* magic.

And now he was agreeing with my desire to immolate a not-insignificant group of people because they'd kidnapped the love of my eternity?

"Who even are you?"

He replied with a crooked smile as he changed lanes around a truck that had pulled to the side of the road. "You always did think the worst of me."

"Because you only ever showed me the worst."

This time Barrett straight-up laughed, nearly stopping my heart with the shock, but he didn't argue. "I may not like magic, or the way magic users like to lord over everyone else, but I do understand passion. I understand love. I understand the desire to keep the people we care about safe, no matter the cost to anyone else. I also know, after years of working with you, that you're usually a lot of talk. If we have the chance to free Emrick and stop the hunters without killing them all, you'll take it. So forgive me for not clutching my pearls at your melodramatic proclamation."

While I appreciated his perspective and couldn't say he was wrong, his assumptions did pave the way for one important question. "And if the only way to get him out is to go to war?"

His jaw flexed, and he pressed his lips into a hard line. "I'll help you pour the gasoline."

We got home around three o'clock in the morning to find everyone except Maera awake and waiting for us.

"Mum baked a pie before she went to bed," Rhys said, pulling off the cake cover to reveal the remains of strawberry-rhubarb perfection. "We saved you a piece."

I squinted at it. "That's not a piece, Rhys. It's a crumb. You left Barrett and I a crumb that we will need to surgically divide in order to ensure we both get a fair share."

Barrett peered over my shoulder. "I'll fight you for it."

While Rhys set to work cutting the minuscule slice in half and wasting dishes by setting those barely bites on two plates, the rest of us grabbed our seats.

Barrett threw the phone onto the middle of the table, and Murisa snatched it up.

We'd given everyone a rundown of our night on our way here, so it was the work of a moment to catch them up on any details we'd left out. Muroppy—as the Poppy-Murisa duo had come to be known—were already murmuring and whispering to each other by the time we'd finished.

"It shouldn't take too much effort to get past the lock screen," Murisa said. "The hard part will be once we're in. Breaking through all his passwords and what have you."

Poppy took the phone from her. "Unless he was kind and left everything we need in a notes file."

Gavin snorted. "Who would be that stupid?"

Barrett raised his hand, and when everyone directed their wide-eyed stares his way, he shrugged. "I can't be bothered to remember sixteen thousand passwords."

Poppy grinned. "Good to know where to start when I'm looking for birthday ideas for you."

"Or bank statements," Murisa added.

"Shopping history," said Poppy.

"Preferred games."

"Favourite porn sites."

Rhys snorted a laugh, and for a blessed moment, the tension around the table evaporated, leaving me able to take my first real breath in over twelve hours.

After I finished my three bites of pie—Barrett finished his in one and a half—I left them to chat and escaped to my room to shower.

Exhausted as I was, I washed the day away with single-minded focus. Once all trace of blood was gone, I threw on my softest, comfiest pyjamas, then left the warm steaminess of the bathroom for the cold darkness of my bedroom.

I didn't bother turning on the light. The waxing moon was three-quarters full and shining through the glass door. The silvery glow danced through the trees, tracing mottled patterns on the walls, and I stepped onto the balcony to drink it in.

At this hour of the morning, so close to dawn, the world was quiet. The breeze rustled the leaves, the gentle waves of Lake Huron kissed the shore, and I sank into their natural magic.

With my eyes closed, I was almost able to imagine that the cool breeze on the back of my neck was the mist that surrounded Emrick whenever he passed from the afterlife into our world. I could almost pretend my hand on my waist was his. That the brush of my shirt against my shoulder was the caress of his lips.

Salt water slipped into the corner of my mouth, and I wiped the pads of my fingers across my face to dry my tears.

Exhaustion tugged at me, luring me to bed, but I knew if I lay down, I would wind up staring at the ceiling wondering if Emrick was all right, or if I had regained my immortality only to lose it and the man I loved a week later. If that were the case, I would break. The hunters would win regardless of whether they succeeded with their plan.

My chest tightened, a hand of dread and fear gripping my heart and squeezing, and I dropped to my knees, unable to breathe.

"Shh, it's all right, Kat," Maera murmured in my ear as she wrapped her arms around me. In her embrace, I lost my ability to hold myself together.

Deep sobs wracked my body, and she hugged me tighter, squeezing my pieces in place while I couldn't do it for myself.

"Come on, let's tuck you in. You need to sleep or you'll be useless in the morning. Emrick needs you at your best, right?"

Maera helped me up and kept her arms around me as she guided me to bed.

I curled onto my side, and she settled beside me so we lay face to face.

Her soft hands brushed the hair out of my eyes, then she curled her fingers through mine and rested them on the pillow between us.

Once my sobs eased, she chuckled gently. "This brings back memories, doesn't it? How many nights did you and I spend just like this? Only back then, it was me crying on your shoulder. Bad breakups and fights with mum. Jack's loss—oh, that was a bad one."

I tightened my grip on her hand. Even after seventeen years, any mention of her late husband brought a deep sorrow to her eyes.

"What did you always tell me?" she asked. My throat was too tight to get the words out, so she rubbed the back of my hand and answered for me. "No matter how dark the night, the dawn always comes. Even if we need to set something on fire to make it happen."

Through my tears, I smiled, and Maera wiped my face with her thumb.

"Emrick will hold on. He's old, he's powerful, and he loves you more than I've ever seen anyone love anyone else. If there is any chance he can return to your side, he'll take it. And the same goes for you."

I sniffled. "Even if he ordered me not to."

Maera scoffed. "That man knows you too well to believe you'd listen."

I laughed, but the pain that shot through me at his urgent command nearly pushed me to sobs again. "He seemed so scared. Like he knew he wouldn't be able to find his way back to me. Not this time."

"Well, he's been known to be wrong. Whatever comes, it won't happen without a fight. You'll show these bastards you won't be cowed because of a few threats and some murder attempts. You'll show them who the real power is in this world. Spoilers, as Rhys would say, it's not a bunch of upstart, pretentious cowboys who think that because their organization has a bunch of money, they get the last word."

For a second, I blinked at her.

How long had it been since I'd heard Maera go on a tirade that wasn't over me dragging Rhys into trouble?

Despite the weight hanging on my shoulders, I barked out a laugh and kissed the back of Maera's hand. "I am so grateful you've stayed with me all these years."

She smiled, and at the sparkle in her green eyes, I was taken back to when she was sixteen. As though no time had passed at all. "You may drive me up the wall, Katerina Palon, but you know I love you. And you know I believe that if anyone can save that spirit-herder, it's the woman who'd burn down the afterlife itself to get to him."

12

Emrick

A SLAMMING DOOR jerked me out of my wandering thoughts. The slam was followed by the clack of heels on concrete that echoed across the empty room. I looked up to find the witch hunter general coming towards me, dispelling the shadows as the motion-sensor lights flicked on.

Although my power was dulled in this cage, almost muted, I sensed enough from the woman to read a glimmer of her life energy now that she was on her own. Mid-fifties, healthy enough aside from her failing eyesight, which she mitigated with thick wire-rimmed glasses. No internal plights or ticking timebomb in her brain. As far as Death was concerned, she was far from ready for its offered hand, never mind my own opinion on the subject.

Today—tonight?—she wore her brown hair in a chin-length bob held back by a black headband. A string of small pearls lay around her neck over a pink turtleneck, which she wore under a grey jacket. Her black slacks were a size too tight around her waist and flared too loosely around her ankles, and her footwear was impractical chunky-heeled shoes.

This was a woman who sat behind a desk and let her lackeys do the work. She only showed up when the messy part was over. I'd seen the type often enough to know she would be hell to work with—and that she had buttons to press.

I sneered at her and pulled my knees up, resting my elbows on top of them. "Let me guess. This is either where you come to torture me or regale me with your reasons for locking me up."

She cocked her head and stared at me, her brown eyes dragging across my body, lingering at certain points. There was nothing sexual about her stare. It was coldly, disturbingly clinical. The kind of look a funeral director might give someone who came in asking about their services, sizing them up for their coffin.

Discomfort hugged my spine, but I kept my face impassive. If she thought to scare me, she wouldn't succeed. I couldn't care less about her opinion of me or my wellbeing as long as Kat was safe.

"My name is Witch Hunter General Margaret Cartwright. My people tell me the sorceress calls you Emrick."

Surprised laughter burst from my chest. How was that for a greeting?

I neither confirmed nor denied her non-question, nor did I give a shit what her name was. I didn't want to talk to these people. I didn't care about their plans, because there was nothing I could do to stop them from in here. I didn't care about their intentions for me for the same reason. To a point, I didn't care what their intentions were for Kat, either, because I believed she could handle herself and because knowing how they wanted to hurt her would make me worry.

So I shifted my gaze past the woman's shoulder, pointedly ignoring her, and hoped she'd get the hint and leave without another word.

Of course I wasn't that lucky.

"You've been a tricky one to pin down, reaper."

I bit my tongue to hide my reaction to the title and gave her a closer look. Just as I was searching for her buttons, she was trying to press mine. But why? She already had me caged—what more did she want? I took in the pulled-back shoulders and raised chin, the hint of excitement in her eyes. Her tone was all business, but my capture had boosted her confidence. My being here brought her one step closer to something.

The silence stretched between us as she waited for me to comment on her statement. In the end, she was the one to break it. "Do you know we've been trying to catch you since the mid-nineteenth century?" She shook her head as though the inane fact astounded her. "We've got every attempt on record. They tried demonic traps, baited lures. In the sixties, they even went so far as to hire a coven to work a summoning circle on you. They all failed, of course."

She walked the perimeter of my cage, peering at me down her nose. "It turns out that, for all they understood about the important role you play, they didn't fully grasp what you are. Because you're not a demon, are you? You're not a spirit. You're something… quite different."

I didn't do her the favour of following her path around me. I didn't move a single muscle. Inside, however, my skin crawled. To her, I was the trapped tiger waiting for the opportunity to leap free and tear her throat out. To me, I was just a tiger in a zoo, on display for all and sundry to ooh and ahh over, knowing all too well how powerless I was.

Never had I craved the emptiness of the afterlife more.

"We came so close a few weeks ago." An edge of frustration lined her words. "With Ms. Palon on the edge of death and your bond severed, you were finally distracted enough that we almost grabbed you. But still you evaded us."

Goosebumps rose on my arms. At first, I had no idea what she was talking about, but before I could throw it in her face that they hadn't come as close as they believed, I remembered a dark parking lot. I remembered Kat's bloodied body on the ground and her spirit beside me debating whether she would return to the waking world or not. In that moment, I'd felt a *pull*. Something beyond the afterlife calling for me. My determination to remain by Kat's side had helped me ignore it, but the general was right—they'd been close.

"Even with all our research, I'm still not sure I understand you," Cartwright continued. "Everything we have on file is from the sorceress who called herself Alodie and what our people were able to learn over the years by eavesdropping on Katerina and her friends. What do they call you? Gast ludman?"

I couldn't hold back the cringe at her horrible pronunciation of Kat's term for me. *Gàst-ladman*. Spirit-herder. Thanks to pop culture references, the concept of a grim reaper with cloak and scythe was more familiar to most people, but that title had always offended Kat's sensibilities. Her revulsion for it made me smile. In her mind, a reaper would be what I became if I lost myself, if I sacrificed so much of my soul that I faded into little more than a shadow. Still tied to Death, still collecting souls, but without any memory of her or our time together or the man I'd been before I'd made my ill-fated deal.

I wasn't about to share any of that with this woman, however. If anything about my nature remained a mystery to the hunters, that would help in preventing them from using me.

The woman shrugged. "Not that it matters, Emrick. We

know enough. We know of your connection to the afterlife, which is fascinating, but it's only part of why you're here. You're here because of your connection to the foundations of life itself. To the foundations of *magic*. You have no idea the important role you're about to play in safeguarding our future."

I couldn't hold back the snort of derision that bubbled up at her fervent arrogance. Zealots being zealous. Centuries might pass, but some things never changed.

Her dark eyebrows, too thick for her bony face, climbed towards her hairline. "You might not believe me now, but give it time. Soon enough, you'll see exactly how crucial you are in humanity's path to greatness. You're the lynch pin. The keystone. Whatever you want to call it, you are at the heart of a global shift."

Despite myself, knowing I should keep my mouth shut but itching with curiosity, I said, "Fine, I'll bite. How exactly do you expect me to help you with anything from in here?" I rolled my eyes to indicate the cage I sat in.

The smile that spread across her face chilled me to the marrow of my bones. "It's very simple. We're going to use you to remove all trace of magic from the world."

13

Katerina

I WOKE UP with a jolt, a cold sweat once again running down my spine.

My pillow was soaked, my sheets were clingy, and I rolled out of bed before they suffocated me.

At some point after I'd fallen asleep, Maera had left me. While I'd been more than a little grateful for her company last night, I was even more grateful I didn't need to explain myself this morning.

The dream that had chased me through sleep haunted me even with my eyes open. Visions of Emrick slamming against a wall trying to escape, calling for me but ordering me to stay away. Him fading, becoming nothing, disappearing. All while I stood by screaming his name but unable to close the distance between us.

The sense that I was running out of time strengthened with the rising sun, and I was glad I'd only slept for four hours. Any more than that, and I would have felt as though I'd wasted the day.

I stripped off my pyjamas, pulled on a fresh uniform of black T-shirt and leather pants from my dresser, and marched into the bathroom.

Despite the early hour, mugginess battled the air conditioning, and I splashed water into my face to wake myself up. It dripped down my cheeks, replacing the tears I'd cried last night. In the light of the morning, I had no more tears to shed. In their place was a sizzling fury that curdled my bone marrow and filled my muscles with energy I looked forward to expending. Violently. For my family's sake, I hoped Muroppy had gotten something off Jared's phone so they could point me towards a good outlet.

Awake, refreshed, and cranky, I headed downstairs to the bedroom Poppy and Murisa had claimed as their own.

Only when I reached the rec room and caught sight of the low sunrise through the patio did I stop to wonder if they might still be asleep. I paced the room twice before deciding I didn't care and banged my fist on their door.

Muffled voices reached me from inside, and I returned to my pacing while one of them rushed to get up.

I'd expected Poppy to open the door, but Murisa's bright eyes greeted me. Despite the hour, she looked more awake than I was and moved with pep as she gave me space to come in.

"We figured you'd be awake soon," she said as she took careful steps towards the table where she and Poppy did most of their work and sank into a chair. The curtains were drawn, and Poppy was huddled under the blankets with a pillow over her head. Murisa had turned on a table lamp, which cast a soft glow across the items strewn over the table's surface. "We didn't find much off the phone, but there are a few things you might be interested in."

I settled into the chair opposite Murisa and pulled the phone towards me. A cable connected the device to Murisa's tablet, and she scrolled through a bunch of apps until she found what she wanted to show me. "He didn't have a lot of texts, which suggests this wasn't his main phone, he deleted them as they came in, or he didn't have a lot of people texting him."

I glowered at the phone as though it were the man who'd owned it. "Considering the manners he showed last night, he didn't strike me as the sort to have a great turnout at his birthday party."

An expression of sympathy crossed Murisa's face. "That's sad. Everyone deserves guests for their birthday." The sympathy lapsed into anger. "Then again, by the sounds of it, his parties would have ended up with a lot of people dead, so it's probably for the best he was a loner."

I didn't bother rushing her. She'd given up most of a night's sleep to get whatever information she could, so I'd allow her a few minutes' stream of consciousness.

Even without my prodding, she stopped and shook her focus into place before continuing. "The texts we did find, however, are interesting. Most of them come from this one number we weren't able to track. Before you ask, we're working on it. But you can see, they seem to talk about you. *Sorceress sighted at The Sage Toad. Sorceress en route. Maintain visuals in case incentive is needed.* You get the idea."

A red haze filled my vision, and I clenched my fists to prevent fire from licking off my palms and setting everything in this room ablaze. If they were keeping an eye on me to grab me as possible *incentive*, it meant they needed Emrick in a more active capacity to achieve their aims and weren't above torture to get him to comply.

These bastards would suffer badly when I got my hands on them.

"Then there are these other texts," Murisa said, moving on as though she hadn't noticed my rising anger—or maybe because she had. "They refer to their headquarters, I think. See this one? *Drive around back. Construction blocking parking lot.*"

Her face split into a wide, excited grin. I waited for her to explain the revelation, but when the silence stretched out, I realized that *was* the revelation. I blinked at her. "You're kidding me, right? How does that narrow anything down? It's August. Most of Canada is under construction right now."

From across the room, under her blankets, Poppy snorted.

Murisa smirked at her, but her smile quickly faded as she looked back at me. "It is, but the detail does help us a bit. Even if we don't have a name attached to the other phone number yet, I can tell you it was sent from somewhere in or near Toronto. If it's outside the city, it's not by much. Our next step is to get a better idea of location with a few tracking spells. Now that I've had some sleep, I'm ready to get moving."

She didn't say it in a way to make me feel guilty, but I felt a pang nonetheless. Once Emrick was safe, I would pay for these two to go off and enjoy a few weeks' vacation.

"Even without that," Murisa continued, "we know we're looking for a place that has a second parking lot, a rear entrance, and is under construction. Considering the hunters' numbers, it's not likely to be a house, and considering they'll be prepared for you to attack, it's probably not in a busy residential or commercial area."

I raised my eyebrows. "Warehouse?"

"Likely."

A bitter laugh escaped me. "That would be fitting, wouldn't it? We started this whole mess with Mikhail in his warehouse. Makes sense we stand to end it in another one."

Murisa rested her hand on mine. "Nothing is ending, Kat."

"Everything ends. That's the beauty of life. But to hell if I'm going to let someone else dictate the terms."

Murisa's gaze turned as steely as my tone, and she nodded her agreement.

"Fuck, you two are depressing," Poppy groaned from across the room as she threw her pillow at my head.

By noon, I was crawling out of my skin. I needed to move, to learn something, to set someone on fire—I really didn't care who it was as long as they weren't in this house.

Muroppy were locked in their room casting their spells, Rhys was holed up in his room—studying, supposedly, and no one wanted to pry—Maera was baking, and Barrett and Gavin were nowhere to be found.

Deciding their activities were at least something I could look into, I headed outside and walked the path down to the beach, which was usually where I found them.

Sure enough, they stood on the rocks that lined the shore, their presence shielded from the house by the leaf-laden spruces and maples. Gavin summoned a series of fireballs and shot them over the lake, while Barrett warmed up his muscles with a few stretches and defensive moves. He held a knife in his hand,

and I recognized it as one of the daggers Murisa had enchanted for him.

The witch had used my tainted blood sample—filled with the compound that had blocked my magic—and reverse engineered it to learn the recipe the hunters had used. The same recipe my people had used nine hundred years ago to etch the runes on my gloves.

The recipe had been lost when the last of the sorcerers had died out sometime in the sixteenth century. It was strange to see the once-familiar silver glimmer on something that wasn't the leather encasing my arms.

By working the enchantment on the dagger, Murisa had effectively created a magic blocker that would defend against spells, magic users, and mundanes. Dangerous in the wrong hands—such as the hunters who also had access to the recipe—but a good edge of protection for anyone on my team.

Except, of course, for one small detail.

"You don't think the magic-hating witch hunters will be throwing spells, do you?" I asked as I approached.

Barrett's balance didn't wobble at my interruption, and I wished I could reverse time and claim a do-over, come up with something so shocking he toppled into the water. Next time.

"Who knows what they'll have." He didn't look up from his focused stare at the lake. "The regular hunters have been known to use bottled spells against their enemies. Whatever it takes.

This group might take the same approach."

"You don't think that would be a little hypocritical? To bash magic and still use it?"

"Tell me there aren't companies you hate but use all the time."

It took me shockingly few seconds to come up with five. "Touché."

"Besides, I'm thinking long term. The hunters won't be the last enemy we face. It's better to be prepared."

The words were barely out of his mouth when Gavin turned on him and launched a fireball at his head. I cried out a warning, but Barrett was already sliding his feet and swirling out of the flame's path. He raised his dagger and freed a second one, crossing them in front of his face seconds before the fire hit. The enchantments caught the magic, and the fireball extinguished on contact.

Not a single follicle of Barrett's short curls was singed. His dark brown eyes gleamed with satisfaction, and he pulled his lips back in a contented snarl.

From the edge of the rock, Gavin grinned like a fool. He shook the fire off his hands, tamping his magic, then brushed his fingers through his black hair to sweep it out of his face.

"You have to admit, I almost got you there."

"Not even close," Barrett said.

"What do you say, Kat? Could I have won?"

I smiled and summoned my fire, channelling it so it lashed out like a flaming whip. The tip of it slapped Barrett's fingers. He hissed and dropped his knife as he jumped back, and my smile widened.

"I think you made a pretty solid effort, but there's always room for improvement."

I strode forward with every intention of picking up the knife and returning it to Barrett. Unfortunately for him, I happened to catch his under-the-breath grumble about cheating and found myself hip-checking him before I could second guess it. The next sound to greet my ears was a rough curse and a splash as he ended up in the lake. The sound after that was Gavin's gut-deep laughter getting cut off as Barrett launched himself out of the water and pulled the other man in.

I sat on the rocks, dipped my feet in the lake, and watched them wrestle as both tried to dunk the other one under the surface.

Nostalgia hit me so hard and fast I couldn't breathe.

My sister and I used to play the same way, both of us trying to get the upper hand, seeing how far we could push our powers without hurting the other. Kyla always won, of course. She'd had more control over her fire than I'd ever had when I was mortal, even if she was six years younger than me.

What would the world have looked like if she'd been the one to survive the immortality ritual? If she'd been the one tethered to Emrick?

Would she have fought as hard as I had to maintain the balance in this world? Would she have sacrificed so much to repay a debt no one else seemed to think mattered?

I rubbed my chest to remove the sudden tightness, and it was a relief when Poppy's voice reached me from the house.

"Kat? We've got something."

14

Katerina

"GUELPH?" I STARED at the map Murisa had draped across the table, peering around the fur Cuddles had left behind.

"On the outskirts," Poppy confirmed, brushing a few stray tufts away and dodging the undead cat's clawed swipe at her hand.

Guelph was about an hour and a half west of Toronto, which fit with the area we'd expected. A thrill of excitement ran through me as I scanned the streets. Somewhere in that labyrinth was Emrick. We were one step closer to finding him.

I ran my finger along the highway. "What's our next step?"

"I suggest we bring in our resident Seer," Murisa said. "We can use the satellite view online and maybe get lucky, but if Rhys can trigger a vision to guide us in the right direction, we'll probably get there faster."

"Failing that, our best bet might be to get in the car and look for the place ourselves," Poppy added.

Barrett frowned. "If you do that, we'll need to suit up and be ready for anything. They'll be expecting us, so we'll have to stay on guard."

Gavin nodded. "We'll go with you."

I looked at them both, but my attention settled on Gavin. "Are you sure? Once we find them, things will get messy pretty quickly." I tapped my fingers on the table, not wanting to pry but also needing to make sure my team was on the same page. "None of you are under any obligation to help with this."

Barrett grunted, making his opinion known. I was touched but not surprised. The man had more than a little revenge to serve.

Poppy crossed her arms. "Even me? What about my debt?"

Cuddles glared at me, and I took it as a threat of what would happen if I answered incorrectly.

"Paid in full, Pop." As if there could be any doubt after all she and Murisa had done over the past few weeks. "If you two wanted to pack up and leave, you could walk with my gratitude."

I hoped they didn't—I *really* hoped they didn't—but I wasn't too worried. I'd given Muroppy a challenge, and neither of them was the type to walk away from a possible world-changing breakthrough. But given the problem we faced, I also wouldn't blame them for hightailing it out of here.

Poppy grinned. "No way, kitty Kat. I'm not running away when the fun's about to start."

My chest loosened with relief, and I returned her smile, then looked at Gavin. "What about you? You have no reason to stay. You owe us nothing, and you haven't even been home after… everything."

With Muroppy's help, the memories Gavin had lost during his time with Shogaur had returned to him. Enough that he'd remembered his parents, his career, where he'd left his phone. As far as I knew, he'd been in regular contact with his parents in Hamilton, but he'd quit his job and had yet to take the trip to see them, even while we'd been in Toronto.

His face flushed, and he dropped his gaze. "Yeah, I'm not ready for all that. If I went home and my parents started fussing and my magic came out? I've gotten better at controlling it, but"—he held up his hand to let fire dance over his fingers and up his arm—"it's still unpredictable when my emotions come into play."

I nodded. "I wish I could say that part gets easier, but it doesn't."

He rolled his shoulders. "I will go see them, but not until I'm sure I won't hurt them." He raised his chin. "Besides, if you're going up against these hunters, it only makes sense to have some extra fire power behind you, right?"

My heart squeezed at his willingness to stick around. That this man, who hadn't had more than a glower to offer me for so many months, wanted to stand beside me meant more than I could express.

I swallowed the thickness in my throat and focused on the practical matters at hand. "In theory. But remember these bastards are armed with the same compound Barrett's dagger is enchanted with. They used it to make tea, but we have no idea what other surprises they have in store. It's possible they've found a way to neutralize our power, in which case we'll need to rely on good old-fashioned weaponry."

"I may have only recently started training, but that doesn't mean I'm useless." His words were hard and bitter.

Barrett clapped him on the shoulder. "He's pretty good with all kinds of weapons these days. I wouldn't worry about him."

Gavin nodded. "No one is ever getting one up on me again."

The pain in his eyes, the memories that haunted him from his days with Shogaur, screamed at me with familiar intensity.

"All right, consider yourself one of the team."

Poppy picked up Cuddles and set him on her lap to scratch behind his ears. He closed his eyes in bliss. "I've already said I'm sticking around. That includes going with you to check out this warehouse."

Murisa pressed her lips into a thin line. She said nothing,

but I owed her a million favours, so I shook my head. "You should stay here, Poppy. Someone needs to go through those titles Hera sent us, and we don't know what we're going to find when we get there. It might—"

Poppy stiffened, and Cuddles's eyes flew open. "If you say it might be dangerous, Katerina Palon, then you don't know who you're talking to. Did you forget my history? I'm not some fragile bird who's going to get her wings clipped. I'm a badass necromancer who nearly took over her coven while destroying our rivals, and the only reason I didn't is because your inconvenient ass got in my way. I'm going, and that's the end of it."

I looked at Murisa expecting to find disappointment, but her brown eyes were rock hard, glowing with the same fire that had lit within Poppy.

"We heard what the hunters said, Kat. We were there for that fight. Whatever they're after, it will affect all of us. We won't stand for it. The texts might be important, but seeing things for ourselves will help more. Wherever you go, we're right behind you."

My throat tightened, preventing me from saying any of the things that popped into my head. I settled for a nod and curled my hand into a fist.

Guelph was six hours away. If we left within the hour, we could be there by nine o'clock this evening. Not a bad time to do a little reconnaissance. I doubted we'd be lucky enough to achieve anything more than finding the warehouse tonight—even that was questionable unless Rhys got lucky. But before we made a move, we'd need to pool our resources.

Maybe round up a few of those allies I'd considered.

I swallowed a groan.

We were in no way prepared to go up against the hunters as we were. While we'd won against them in Toronto, we'd faced a fraction of their numbers. And if they could neutralize our magic, that would leave us with half of what we brought to the table.

As much as I hated to admit it, my formidable team was screwed on its own.

"I don't suppose you had another chat with your mother when you asked her for those titles?" I asked Poppy.

The lines around her eyes hardened, and she rolled her jaw. Her long, bright yellow nails disappeared into Cuddles's fur. After a moment to compose herself, she tossed her curls over her shoulder and said, "I may have. Words were exchanged."

I waited, and she cast a look at both Barrett and Gavin.

They made as if to leave, but I held up my hand to stop them. "I understand you're embarrassed and pissed off, Poppy, but we can't afford to keep secrets right now. The five of us aren't enough to storm the castle. We need backup. Will she help us?"

Murisa laid her hand on Poppy's knee, and Cuddles leapt to the floor with an irritated meow. "Tell her. You know you need to at some point."

Poppy crossed one leg over the other and slumped deeper in her seat. "She said she'll help." I drew in a breath, ready to express my relief, until she cut me off. "If."

The breath caught in my throat. "If?"

She nodded. "She wants to see you, kitty Kat. I guess you made an impression during your last visit."

My mouth went dry. Even though I had my power back, the influence and authority Hera Lister exuded was enough to leave me feeling like a six-year-old girl who'd been caught stealing cookies from the pantry.

"What does she want to see me about?"

Poppy grimaced. "I don't know, but knowing my mother? She probably wants to make a deal. Hera does not agree to anything unless it benefits her."

Red danced in my vision. I hated this woman for trying to control the board, but what other option did I have? Emrick was missing, the hunters were preparing, and if I wanted to stand any chance of destroying them, I had to be willing to give as much as I got.

"Fine," I gritted out. "Call her back and let her know I'm ready to meet with her."

"Are you sure? You know she won't settle for anything less than your soul."

I bared my teeth. "She's welcome to demand it, but unfortunately for her, someone else claimed it centuries ago."

15

Katerina

IT HAD ONLY been a week or so since I'd visited Hera and Arnold Lister in their Burlington mini-mansion, but it was as if I'd never been here at all.

The thousand-dollar floral arrangements in the front yard had been swapped out for a brand-new array, these ones vivid purple-blue instead of the softer purple-pink of last time. The once-black shutters were now a rich green, and there was a different absurdly expensive car in the driveway.

Everything else, though, was exactly the same. Ostentatious and designed to intimidate.

Unlike Hera, the house stood no chance with me. I'd spent too many years living in places like this not to feel comfortable walking across the pristine lawn.

Poppy stayed close to Murisa, who was polite enough to follow the driveway to the front door. Or maybe she was trying to make a good first impression—that would explain why she'd insisted on leaving Cuddles at home when Poppy had been determined to bring him. I didn't have the heart to tell Murisa that nothing she did would win Hera over. The woman had as much warmth as the concrete flower urns that littered her front yard.

I paused on the front step, letting Poppy take the lead. She didn't wait on ceremony. Without bothering to knock, she threw open the front doors and waltzed into the foyer with its slate-grey granite tiles and crown moulding. Unlike the exterior, which had undergone a complete makeover since last week, the same ferns maintained sentry duty inside. They still made me want to avoid them lest they jump out at me and sink unseen teeth into my flesh.

This time I'd be able to set them on fire, but I'd prefer to avoid such a step unless absolutely necessary.

"Mom, Dad, I'm home!" Poppy shouted as loudly as she could, projecting her voice into every nook and cranny of the foyer, up the stairs, and straight through to the parlour.

I bit down on a smile and peered around the corner into the garage, which was where I'd bumped into Arnold last time. He'd been curious enough about why I'd come to invite Barrett and me for a chat with Hera, but I doubted I'd receive such a charming greeting on this visit.

Not that I needed charming. What I needed was help, and I hated the position that put me in. The last time I'd barged in on Hera, I was worried about myself, so I'd still held a few cards in my hand. This time, I was here to save Emrick, giving her all the power. The moment she realized it, she would be merciless.

"Proserpine, do keep your voice down, dear. Not all the neighbours need to know our business."

Hera swept into the foyer from a room beyond the stairs looking every bit as powerful and authoritative as she had before. Her dark skin glowed with its golden undertones, her makeup was flawless, and her grey hair was cut almost to the scalp. Her eyes were harsh as they took in her daughter, lacking an ounce of warmth or affection, and my rancour rose.

Did this woman not realize what she had? Did she have any idea what I would have given to watch my son grow up? Even if he'd fought me every step of the way. Even if he'd made me bang my head against the wall as I asked myself why he insisted on making every possible bad decision, I still would have spent every single day of my life grateful to have known him.

To Hera, Poppy was a tool, and one that hadn't worked the way she'd hoped. If she could have exchanged her daughter for an improved model, I had no doubt she would have done so.

Instead, I was the lucky one who'd earned Poppy's loyalty. And I was smart enough to appreciate her worth.

"This must be Murisa Bhatt?" Hera's gaze flicked down her nose in what would easily win every Most Offensive Award on the planet, but Murisa, to her endless credit, received Hera's condescension with a sunny smile.

"It's so lovely to meet you, Mrs. Lister. Poppy's told me so much about you. As thanks for inviting me to join you today, I made this for you."

As she reached into the bag slung over the back of her wheelchair, Hera took the opportunity to say, "I didn't invite you, Ms. Bhatt. My daughter simply informed me you were coming."

I was watching closely enough to catch the faint tightening around Murisa's eyes, but her smile never faltered. If anything, it grew brighter. "All the same, this is for you."

She held out a purple velvet bag tied with silver ribbon.

Hera accepted it ungraciously, untied it, and pulled out a tiny silver tin, about two inches by one. When she opened it, specks of dust floated to the floor to mar the spotless tile. Hera's lip curled ever so slightly. "Should I thank you? What is this dirt, exactly?"

"Vampire ash, spelled to keep it from breaking down. I understand you're working on a few recipes for a skin rejuvenation creme. The smallest pinch of that should increase the efficacy significantly."

I wanted to give the woman the highest of fives. There was

no better way to win Hera's approval than by offering her the path to victory. By the gleam in Hera's eyes, I suspected Murisa had earned an invitation to Thanksgiving dinner.

"That's very thoughtful." Hera stepped aside. "Please, come in. I understand we have much to discuss."

Her weighty stare fell on me, and I returned it, not giving her an inch. Last week, I'd had to force myself to meet her eye, doing my best to cover up the fact I'd lost my magic. Today, power crackled under my skin, and I wanted her to feel it. Anything to hide that I felt even more vulnerable than on my previous visit.

Poppy and Murisa led the way into the parlour. Hera followed them, and I brought up the rear. I wasn't in a place where I was comfortable with anyone at my back.

Arnold waited for us inside. He handed Murisa a cup of tea, though Poppy declined. Hera's tea sat on an end table, her card table nowhere in sight.

I accepted an absurdly tiny cup but set it untouched on the table beside the couch as I sat down. I still hadn't gotten over my aversion to hot beverages post-magic loss.

"Proserpine tells me the witch hunters have declared war," Hera said. As always, I appreciated her readiness to jump right to the point.

Arnold dropped into the armchair beside his wife's, and Poppy took the seat beside me. Murisa angled her chair close to Poppy, and I didn't blame her for not wanting to shift to the couch. Although not quite as firm as they appeared to be, the cushions were far from cozy. The Listers were not a couple who encouraged guests to extend their stay.

"They have," I said. "They've abducted a servant of Death for reasons unknown. Having met Death, I imagine the afterlife is not a fun place to be right now."

Hera frowned, the shift in expression subtle but intense. I hadn't thought the woman's disapproval could be more potent. Under its severity, I was surprised the hunters didn't show up at her door to apologize and offer to weed her garden.

"I've had issues enough with them in the past," she said, "but such an overt move seems out of character, even for them."

I crossed one ankle over the other. "We believe the act is part of a greater manoeuvre. As you know, hunters across all three organizations have opened their doors to magical allies, bolstering their strength, knowledge, and power. From what we learned from an inside party before his… unfortunate demise, the group we're currently looking at is made up of mundanes only. No magicals allowed. Everything points to a bigoted faction trying to stir up trouble. Their actions so far have proved they know what they're up against, and I have no doubt their intentions for this servant of Death are far from neighbourly."

"And you expect my coven to help?" Interest flickered in Hera's eyes, overshadowed by her pending refusal. I could hear it on her lips already, and I hadn't asked the question yet.

I breathed through my rising anger and met her eye. "I do. Not for my sake or for what Death might do over Emrick's containment, but because of what it will mean for your coven if the hunters get what they want."

"Which is?"

"I don't know." I hated having to reveal my ignorance to this woman.

"No."

Her definitive answer set my teeth on edge, even though I'd expected it.

Hera set her palms on the armrests as though preparing to show us out.

"Sit down, Mother," Poppy ordered.

Hera's eyebrow arched. No grand shift in her face, just an infinitesimal quirk of the fine hairs, but she stayed put.

Poppy remained stiff, exuding the same aura of authority as her mother did. "We're here eating our pride to ask this of you, and I suggest you keep your ass in that chair and listen."

"Pom, don't speak to your mother that way." Arnold didn't raise his voice, but the reprimand hit like a slap anyway. Poppy didn't flinch.

"Sorry, Dad, but I'm done sitting around letting you two ignore how massive this is. The hunters are closing in on *something*, and it should scare you that we don't know what. From the little they let slip when we were at their previous base, their aim isn't to help magicals live in this world. They unleashed Mikhail on Toronto's covens. They allowed a sorceress to summon a fear demon. They stripped Kat of her magic. Of her immortality. If they can do that to a nine-hundred-year-old powerhouse, imagine what they could do to you."

Hera's eyes flashed at the threat, but Poppy didn't back down. I wanted to throw my arms around my necromancer's neck and hug her, but I remained where I was and spun my tiny cup around on its saucer.

Tamping down on my smugness and my amusement, I said, "Poppy makes a good point. It's possible they have no interest in you or your coven, but considering Tony is the one who pointed me in your direction when I lost my magic, you're on this group's radar. How long will it be before they knock on your door looking for something? Possibly to destroy you."

Hera and Arnold exchanged a glance, and then Hera's eyes sought out mine. "What sort of help are you requesting? I don't imagine you need a financial boost, and I don't know how much my witches can assist in any tactical approach. We pride ourselves on living a non-violent life these days, Ms. Palon. Peace doesn't lend well to fighting."

I smiled, infusing it with as much charm as I could muster. "I believe you, Hera, but I also believe your witches are capable, strong, and unwilling to allow a bunch of hunters to threaten their magic. I need people at my back when I make my stand against them. Based on our information, they number at least a hundred. Whether they'll all be at their headquarters when we arrive, I can't say, but I need to ensure we have at least enough people to match theirs, armed with whatever it takes to force them into submission."

Hera sniffed. "If you believe I have a hundred witches at my disposal, then you haven't done your research."

I widened my smile. "And if you believe I don't know the influence you have in this community, then you've underestimated how closely I've been watching."

The coven leader and I stared at each other across the room until the tension between us grew as taut as a guitar string. One pluck and the resulting note would shatter every window in the room.

Finally, Hera dipped her chin. "Very well, Ms. Palon. You'll have your witches. I'll ensure they're on standby when you need them. In the meantime, we'll set to work preparing potions and spells that may be of use. In return..." Her mouth twitched, and I stiffened, braced for the worst. "I demand that you leave the Hydrangea Circle alone from here on out. No more snooping into our goings on, no more checking in on our purchases and coven meetings. We will be free of your... management."

Magic prickled in my fingertips, and I smoothed an imaginary crease out of my leather pants. "A request like that, Hera, makes it sound like you have something to hide. But I'm sure that's not the case, is it? I'd hate to think I'd be better off leaving you to the hunters."

The woman didn't react, as though she'd also mastered the art of encasing herself in frost.

"The only plans I have in mind are to work without over-sight, *Katerina*. We're not children who need to be monitored."

"If only history allowed me to believe that." Even as I pushed back, I knew I would comply with her request. Emrick was worth a rogue coven or two. In the short term. "You have fifty years without me looking over your shoulder."

"A hundred and fifty," Hera said.

"Seventy-five. What will it matter after that? Unless you plan on following in Mikhail's footsteps and working a spell to gain immortality?"

A slight flush rose on the woman's cheeks, but I marked it as a sign of her anger and not embarrassment at having her lofty ambitions called out.

"Very well. Seventy-five years where I never have to hear from you."

"Deal." I rose to my feet, and Poppy joined me. "I thank you for your time. I look forward to fighting at your side."

Her eyes widened, and I guessed my suspicions were correct that she'd had no intention of joining the battle herself. Now her pride wouldn't allow her to sit it out.

She inclined her head towards me, and I took my leave.

"It was lovely to meet you, Mrs. Lister, Mr. Lister," Murisa said behind me, and I heard Arnold murmur something in a pleasant tone as I walked out the front door.

If Murisa could burrow her way into their lives, more power to her. I, on the other hand, never wanted to cross this threshold again.

"That went better than I expected," Poppy said as she helped Murisa into the back seat. "I do see one glaring issue with your plan, though, kitty Kat."

"Oh?"

I slid into the driver's seat and started the car as Poppy slammed the passenger door shut. "We gained a few witches. Great. Where are we getting the rest of our fighters?"

I grinned and adjusted the rear-view mirror. "We're going to take a little trip to see a vampire queen who owes me a debt."

16

Emrick

I LOST TRACK of how long I was left alone to dwell on what the hell Cartwright meant when she said the removal of *all* magic.

Was she considering the destruction of every magical element across the globe? The deaths of every magical being? Eliminating all trace of supernatural power that ran through the earth?

The woman had no idea what she was talking about.

But it didn't matter. That kind of worldwide destruction wasn't possible. Especially not with me as their only weapon.

Was it?

For hours, I tried to force my thoughts in any other direction. It wouldn't serve me to obsess over the aims of a fanatic and her followers. What I needed was to find my way out of this cage.

Yet as time stretched on, after every failure to escape, I found myself mulling over not only how Cartwright might pull off her wild idea but the ramifications if they succeeded.

The planet as we knew it wouldn't survive.

I gave it fifty years before systems everywhere began to break down. Faster in some areas, slower in others. Did these people have no concept of how deeply their seemingly mundane lives were rooted in the otherworldly? So much of what they called science was based on magical foundations. The tides, photosynthesis, electricity. Just because humans understood how it worked didn't mean there wasn't magic involved. Magic was the undercurrent of life itself.

Even if the hunters tried to wipe it out, other groups would step in before they took their plan too far. They couldn't achieve their goal in one fell swoop.

Why did they think possessing me would help them succeed?

I wanted to tear at my hair and pace until I worked it out, but I refused to show the hunters how deeply they'd crawled under my skin. In the light that had spilled into the room on Cartwright's entrance, I'd spotted the cameras in the corners. Six of them watching me from various angles, taking in my every move, my every reaction. They'd turned my captivity into their entertainment—something else I'd make them pay for at the first opportunity.

If I wanted to bore them until they dropped their guard, I had to remain stock still. I'd drawn one leg to my chest so I could rest my elbow on it and stretched my other leg out in front of me. It was a show of casual disregard for anything they threw at me. A display of confidence in the face of their threats. I wanted them to know I spent every second they left me alone imagining the different ways I would pick their souls apart and leave them as wasted nothings in the afterlife.

Then again, if I found a way to make contact with the afterlife, their plans would end before they began. I would leave the bulk of the hunters for Kat and her team to clean up, but Cartwright was mine. I would wrap my gloved hand around her throat and squeeze, bit by bit, until she accepted what a mistake she'd made in caging me. Only once she admitted it would I send her Death's way.

I still couldn't figure out how they thought to use me, and that ignorance nagged at me. It made me worry I was missing some key element—something that gave the witch hunter general her easy arrogance—her solid belief that she would achieve her goals without any obstacles or snags.

Yes, I had power. I was tied to Death, which meant my essence was part of the natural order of the world. I wasn't magical anymore—at least, not with the same power that drove

Kat's magic. Or Poppy's, or Rhys's.

So it wasn't like the hunters could use me as some kind of battery. I had no idea why they'd want to, anyway. They wanted to remove magic, not steal it for themselves.

I tapped my fingers against my outstretched thigh, allowing myself that one small fidget while I followed my line of thought.

Cartwright knew what I was. She knew my connection to Death, but somehow I doubted her aim was to use me to destroy Death. The idea was laughable. You want to destroy the world within a week? Wipe out Death.

Using my access to the afterlife, however…

My fingers stilled, and a shiver ran down my spine.

My corner of the afterlife was a waiting space more than a final resting place. The dead passed over the stretches of open field, the dead grass, the barren trees with their empty branches, and waited by the still river for the ferry to take them to whatever came next. Some spirits got stuck before they crossed, unsure where they wanted to go, or not yet ready to leave, but those lost souls were rare compared to the hundreds of thousands that passed every day.

For me, it was the end of the line. I wasn't allowed to know what came next—not until Death released me from my servitude—so I'd come to see the afterlife as home.

I knew all its ins and outs, all the ways it connected to the mortal world. I'd always perceived it as an unseen layer of existence. That was why I could step through the mists and come out wherever I wanted. I was able to bring Kat with me along the outskirts, giving her access to the entire world within heartbeats.

If Cartwright used me to access that waiting space, she would have the power to extend her magic-destroying plans planet-wide.

My stomach twisted, and I squeezed my hand into a fist before forcing my fingers to relax and lie still on my thigh.

I wouldn't open that doorway for them.

However they planned to get me to cooperate, they were doomed to failure. I had been around long enough that nothing they said would turn me. Had they found a way to kill me? Fine, I would accept my fate with pleasure. My only regret would be not having a chance to say goodbye to—

Kat.

I'd warned her when they'd taken me not to follow, but I had no doubt my sorceress would ignore my order. She knew who had me, and she would make these stone walls crumble before she let them harm me. Just as I'd longed to turn them all to dust when they'd stripped her magic away.

But these rogue hunters had power. Resources. If Kat got within a kilometre of this place, they would know. And once they knew, they wouldn't threaten to hurt me—they would target her.

I bowed my head and squeezed my eyes shut. Somewhere in the building, I swore I sensed someone's smugness rising.

They had me, and unless I found a way out or Kat anticipated their every move, there was nothing I could do to stop them.

17

Katerina

"TELL ME AGAIN who these people are?" Poppy asked as I pulled up in front of another mini-mansion, this one on the outskirts of the small city of Orillia.

Apparently, we were on a roll with ostentatiousness today.

Unlike Hera's private palace, however, this pretentious movie-set of a house belonged to the Orillia vampire nest.

A wide driveway led to tiled front steps framed by two white, cylindrical columns. Inside were another two columns wrapped in sculpted vines and nightshade blossoms, the white marble standing in stark contrast to the black marble floor.

Vampires loved their statements.

"Orillia is the queen of this nest. She owes me a favour."

"I thought Orillia was the city."

I pressed my lips together to wait out my wave of heart-shattering grief. When I'd come here with Adrian a few months ago, he and I had carried out almost the exact same conversation. The lack of his presence at my side made me ache. "It's both. But don't worry, no one refers to her by name. It's all 'Her Majesty' or 'the queen.' I prefer not to refer to her at all. Makes life easy."

Poppy nodded her understanding, but her lips were bloodless except for where she'd chewed through them. "And it's safe?"

"As safe as vampires can be. They won't hurt you if you don't give them reason to."

"What would they consider reason to?"

I shrugged. "Being rude, threatening them, smelling too good."

She paled further, and I looked away so she wouldn't see the smile creeping up on me. I couldn't help teasing her. She made it too easy, and I was in desperate need of a moment of levity.

"You ready?" I asked.

"Maybe I should stay in the car."

"Come on, Poppy," Murisa said from the back seat, laughter lining her words. "It's another fun adventure. We're racking them up now while we're young so we can retire early and not have to deal with these problems once we're old."

Those were the wisest words I'd heard in a long time.

I climbed out of the car, and Poppy helped Murisa into

her wheelchair. The front steps were in no way accessible, but that didn't stop Murisa, who'd enchanted her chair to hover on command. She couldn't maintain the spell for long stretches of time, but she'd ensured she could navigate the world regardless of how difficult the world tried to make it for her.

Tenacity, thy name was Murisa Bhatt.

I knocked on the door, and a man I vaguely recognized answered it. After a moment, I realized it was the same low-ranking vampire who'd let us in on my last visit.

I clapped him on the shoulder as I stepped into the house. "Hey, good job. You made the cut."

He stared at me blandly, not reacting at all, then stepped back and said, "Her Majesty will see you shortly. If you'd be so kind as to wait here."

I gave him a grin that I hoped told him exactly how happy I was to wait, and he disappeared to do his vampire butler thing while Poppy and Murisa gawked at the decor.

I couldn't blame them. The space was designed to make visitors feel small and insignificant. The ceilings were tall, and the colours were extreme—from the black-and-white foyer to the rich crimson carpet that covered the curved staircase.

The sideboard no longer stood against the wall next to the queen's favourite parlour, and I wondered if her experience getting drugged and abducted made her less inclined to leave her refreshments so easily available.

We didn't have to wait long before a woman appeared at the top of the stairs. Not the queen, but no less familiar. Tonight, Trillium, the queen's second, wore a crisp white gown that clung to her curves and brushed the floor. The slit along her thigh was high enough for me to confirm that, despite her smooth stride, she was not, in fact, floating above the steps.

Somewhat disappointing.

"Ms. Palon." Her smooth, honeyed voice caressed my ears. "I confess, I didn't expect to see you again so soon. I thought we might have to wait another few centuries for the pleasure."

I forced a smile. "Believe me, Trillium, if I didn't have to be here, I wouldn't be." I realized how that sounded, cleared my throat, and added, "I'm sure you're busy enough without me showing up on your doorstep looking for a return favour."

Her dark eyes glittered, but no crimson ring surrounded the iris. The nest had obviously resolved their feeding issues. "We always have time for the woman who saved our queen."

Poppy's eyes widened and Murisa's jaw dropped, but I ignored them. This wasn't the right time to get into the story. It wasn't all that interesting anyway. Twenty-four hours of my life, a few dicey battles, and time spent arguing with my favourite men.

A fond memory, all the blood and vampires aside.

"If you'll follow me, Her Majesty will see you."

Trillium led us into the parlour. Orillia sat in her usual

armchair, the stem of a blood-filled wineglass pinched between her fingers where it rested on the armrest. Her cold blue eyes rose to meet mine as she crossed one leg over the other. Her blue slacks hugged her toned thighs, and the cream-coloured blouse fell open just enough to give a peep at the assets hiding underneath.

Despite her youthful features—she must have been turned no older than eighteen—she exuded power. Probably more now that her position on the throne had been solidified.

"Katerina," she greeted without standing up. "A pleasure. I'm sorry Adrian and Barrett couldn't join you this time. Please. Sit."

My throat tightened as I settled on the sofa, but I graced her with a smile. "It's a real shame. But their absence is a big part of why I'm here."

Her white-blonde eyebrow rose with interest. "Oh?"

"I'm preparing to go after the people behind Adrian's final death."

"I thought you'd already done that when you killed the sorceress. She was the reason for your immortality, wasn't she?"

Trust there to be no secrets from vampires. They had eyes and ears everywhere, which had always royally pissed off the vampire hunters.

"We thought so." I leaned back, the image of casual comfort. "It turns out we only excised the tumour. We didn't get rid of the cancer."

"Consider me intrigued."

"What do you know about a mundane faction of hunters sprouting up across Toronto?"

She bared her teeth, her impressive fangs on full display. Murisa let out the tiniest squeak, and Poppy shifted uncomfortably on the couch beside me. I found it easy to remain non-reactive. It wasn't like Orillia was angry with *me*.

"They've popped up around here, too, the bastards. More than one of my people have been taken down due to 'breach of treaty.'" She emphasized the final words, giving them the weight of air quotes, and goosebumps rose on my arms. Clearly, I wasn't as immune to her rage as I'd thought. "I argued with their local leader and was warned, not so subtly, that if I imposed or obstructed their patrol, my nest would suffer for it. The sons of bitches have us chained."

I understood her fury. Orillia was one of the rare vampire queens who understood the importance of keeping up with the times, staying under the radar, being reasonable with feeding. She kept a firm hand on her people, treated her thralls as loyal employees, complete with perks and benefits, and had even gone so far as to create a peace treaty with the local shifters to ensure no conflicts arose over territory. If every nest were like hers, I wouldn't have developed such a loathing for dealing with vampires.

"We have reason to believe the issue with the hunters goes deeper than them wielding a stricter-than-usual hand." I filled her in on our recent experiences with the witch hunters, right down to my losing my magic and immortality for those terrifying days.

By the time I finished, there was murder in the queen's eyes. Her fingernails had lengthened into talons, and I worried the stem of her wineglass would snap under the pressure and ruin her beautiful blouse.

She took a slow, calming sip, then handed the glass to Trillium, who set it on the sideboard.

"They'll bleed for this," Orillia said.

I shrugged. "You and I are on the same page as far as that's concerned. Does this mean you'll stand with us?"

The queen eyed me, then shifted her gaze to Trillium, and the two carried out a silent conversation. I wasn't sure if they could actually share thoughts or if they simply knew each other well enough to communicate without sound, but it left the rest of us sitting and twiddling our thumbs until they finished.

After a long, drawn-out minute, Orillia returned her attention to me. "Unfortunately, Ms. Palon, I don't believe we're in a position to help."

I clenched my teeth and waited for her to explain. The silence stretched, as awkward now as it had been before, but with far more anger on my side. If she thought she could refuse my request without the barest of explanations, she was sadly mistaken. A debt stood between us, and I wasn't beyond demanding it be paid.

I sensed Poppy's and Murisa's gazes on me, but I kept my focus firmly on the queen, until, finally, her shoulders sagged. Only a fraction, but enough for me to notice.

"Perhaps if you had come to us a few months from now, I might have better news for you, but the events of March have shifted the dynamics of my nest." Her hard blue stare flicked to Trillium, who met my gaze squarely.

"There are some in the nest who believe the ease with which Her Majesty was removed from her throne is evidence that she is weakening and no longer fit to rule. There have been… murmurs of an impending challenge. If Her Majesty were to offer you her people to fight, there would be no guarantee they would obey."

I exhaled slowly and closed my eyes, centring myself so my frustration didn't leak all over the queen's expensive furniture.

Five months ago, I had risked my life—well, mostly Barrett's and Rhys's—to rescue Orillia and plunk her ass back in her fancy chair, and now she couldn't summon a hundred vampires from her vast nest to help me save Emrick?

Fucking vampires.

On a deep inhale, I opened my eyes, and by the way Trillium shifted on her heels, I guessed my expression showed the depth of my displeasure. "I see."

"I am sorry, Katerina." The queen sounded sincere enough in her regret that I might have been mollified if my other half's existence didn't hang in the balance. "I hope in time the Orillia nest will be stable enough to come to your aid when you need us."

I rose to my feet and stared down at her. "If this goes poorly, there won't be time. For either of us. I hope you enjoy your seat while it lasts, Your Majesty."

18

Katerina

I WAS STILL shaking by the time we made it back to the car.

Neither Poppy nor Murisa said anything, and I suspected they were afraid if they uttered a syllable, I would burst like a fireball and blow up the vehicle.

It was possible they weren't wrong.

For the past six months, tense had been my constant state. Every time I'd solved one problem, another had arisen, with this tangled web becoming more complex with every knot I unravelled. I'd done my best to keep a level head, to remain calm and confident, but over all this time, my nerves had grown increasingly taut. I didn't know what would happen if I finally let go.

I suspected we would find out soon. Day by day, hour by hour, I felt my control slipping. Everywhere I turned, more people were out to mess with me. To trip me up. To take everything I cared about.

It didn't matter that I'd walked this earth for almost nine hundred years, these attacks stung. I didn't want to be the target of anyone's wrath. All I wanted was for the world to be a quiet, peaceful place where everyone stuck to their lanes—magical beings existing and enjoying their existence without making life difficult for mundanes, and mundanes existing and enjoying their existence without slaughtering magicals.

Was it too much to ask?

Apparently so, because the hunters, the people who had sworn to help maintain that balance, were the ones tipping it.

But not all of them.

The realization came to me like a thunderclap, and I pulled the car onto the road.

"What are you thinking, kitty Kat?" Poppy asked, giving me a narrow side-eye. "I know that look. It's the one that says someone somewhere is about to have a bad day."

I grinned. "You might be right, Poppy. But not as bad as someone else's day is going to be if I get my way."

Murisa cleared her throat. "I don't suppose you care to share?"

For a few minutes, I didn't. I was still running my idea through my head and steaming from Orillia's refusal. Even if my magnificent plan worked, the vampires would have been an asset. But, despite my resentment, I couldn't deny the queen had made the right decision for her nest. She had to look after her people. That was her role—as much as Emrick's was to escort souls to the afterlife and mine was to set fire to anyone who upset the world's delicate balance.

As my earlier revelation settled over me, some of my anger fizzled out, and I was ready for a brain other than mine to critique my genius idea.

"We've been so focused on the hunters standing against us, we've overlooked the rest of them." I merged onto the empty highway. "How much do you know about the hunter organizations?"

Poppy shrugged. "That they've been around for a while, think their shit don't stink, and love nothing more than to show off their massive codpieces."

She was not incorrect.

"I know a little more than that," Murisa said. "As a group, they're about three hundred years old, but aspects of their governance stretch back further. Why?"

"Because I think I've figured out how to turn this PR night-mare to our advantage."

When neither woman looked at me with abject awe, I grumbled under my breath and settled into Lecture Mode. "When the witch hunters first formed centuries ago, they were all mundane. They were petty men who resented that other people had more power than they did. To make themselves feel better, they accused their neighbours of all kinds of things to get a leg up in their communities. Enough of them bought into what they were saying—or perhaps realized their accusations were more than simple power plays—that they formed a group under the witch hunter general. I'm sure you two know all about that fun time in history."

Poppy scowled, and Murisa nodded sedately in my rearview mirror.

"Sometime in the nineteenth century," I continued, "there was a shift in the hunters' hierarchy. A group of witches decided they were tired of light and dark witches being lumped together, so they petitioned to join the organization. They offered their skills and knowledge and promised to help track down and deal with magic users who had shaken their moral compass so far they were stuck pointing south. A similar shakeup happened around the same time within the vampire hunters and the Hunter's Guild."

Witches, vampires, and magical creatures—the triple threat, each with their own group to clean up after them. If they got there before I did.

"Since then, each group has prided itself on its diverse membership. It's been their prime selling point in policing magicals. 'See? One of your own believes you're in the wrong, so you must be.' A lot of the time, it's still bullshit, but optics counts for a lot. They have the *appearance* of fair dealing, and as a result, the magical community doesn't rebel. This new group, however, is mundanes only. They've embraced their bigoted roots, and if word of their existence, let alone their rising power, gets out, control will be more difficult for the main group to maintain."

Poppy bobbed her head as she finally tapped into my brilliant train of thought. "You think if we reach out to the main group, the ones still working with the magic users, they might back you up?"

"This does not look good for them. For all the issues I have with their organizations, I can't deny they serve their purpose. I can't be everywhere at once, and magic users rely on them. They trust the hunters to protect their place in this world. Dark witches pose as much of a threat to light witches as they do to mundanes, and no one else has the courage to challenge them. If it comes out a rogue group of hunters has turned on the magical community, there will be a lot of light witches who side with their dark neighbours out of self-preservation."

Murisa sucked in a breath. "That could mean war."

In the haze of my epiphany, I'd failed to recognize that tiny side effect, but Murisa was right. How could there not be? Among magicals, there would be a scramble to choose the best magic to ensure their survival—and a rush to wipe out the hunters before they turned on them. The rogue hunters had to know this, which meant they also had to be hurrying. There would be no time to consider the consequences, no chance to interrupt the missile trajectory before it struck the epicentre of the magical world.

From there, the balance between both sides would degrade faster. With everyone fighting to gain the upper hand, there was no way they'd be able to keep their battles secret. Word would spread, the media—social if not traditional—would catch on, and the veil would be lifted. From there, the violence would only expand until the entire world was pitted against each other.

My guts churned as the scene played out in my imagination. So much blood and death and destruction, and all because a small group of people had decided I was the correct person to target.

They were about to learn a very important lesson about fighting in their own weight class.

Poppy frowned and squinted through the windshield. "What the hell is that?"

It was closing in on two o'clock in the morning, and up until now, the highway had been clear except for us and a couple of trucks parked on the shoulder. Now a few more of those trucks had stopped up ahead, along with a half-dozen cars blocking the stretch of road.

My pulse leapt, and my fingers tightened around the steering wheel. Whatever it was, I didn't think we wanted to get any closer. I checked the rear-view mirror, and jerked hard on the wheel, turning us around while leaning on the gas.

Except the trucks from the shoulder had followed us and were now stopped in both lanes, blocking our retreat.

"Fuck," Poppy breathed.

My only options were to drive straight through—and pray I didn't kill us in the collision—or stop. Neither option appealed to me, but at least with the latter, we stood an increased chance of survival. I hit the brake hard enough the wheels screeched, then threw the car in park.

No movement came from the trucks ahead or the barricade behind. The interior of the car was silent except for three terrified women struggling to control their breathing.

"Do you two have spells ready?" I asked through the lump in my throat.

Blood rushed in my ears, and magic wound through my heart and spilled down my arms. I held it back to avoid melting my steering wheel, and sweat broke out on my brow at the effort of keeping it in check.

Poppy reached into her satchel and pulled out a few colourful vials full of, I was sure, nasty surprises. From the back seat, the buzz and whir of tiny enchanted mechanicals joined the pulse of my racing heart.

"Whatever you need us to do, we're with you, kitty Kat."

"What I need you to do is take the wheel. You and Murisa

are my backup, but as soon as I give you an opportunity, I want you to get the hell out of here."

Poppy frowned. "Kat, we're not leaving you with—"

"Get back to the house," I ordered. "Get Barrett and Gavin, and open communication with the hunters. We need them on our side."

My phone rang from the console, but I didn't take my attention off the vehicles blocking us in. Up ahead, the truck drivers sat in their cabs, watching me watch them. Behind me, the drivers of the cars were getting out and taking position behind their open doors. They were armed with guns, and one of them held what looked like a crossbow.

I swallowed through the trepidation throbbing in my veins and latched on to the thrill of the fight that buzzed deeper, far beneath the surface. These guys wanted a fight? I would be happy to give it to them.

On the third ring, Poppy grabbed my phone. "It's Rhys."

I didn't acknowledge her, so she went ahead and put the call on speaker.

"Kat? Are you there?"

"I'm here," I replied through clenched teeth.

"Stay off the highway, okay? I just had a vision, and it was bad. Like, really bad. I think Poppy's going to get hurt if you don't avoid it. I saw cars and fire and blood." His voice trembled, and although I wished I could give him a tight squeeze, I was more than a little grateful he was far from here.

"Thanks, Rhys. I'll do what I can to get them out of here. I love you, buddy. You know that, right?"

"Kat, what—shit, you're already on the highway, aren't you? Can't you turn around? You have to try, you won't—"

I nodded at Poppy, who hung up the phone with a shaking hand.

"I'm not leaving you." Her voice was steely, though I picked up the faint tremor beneath her stubbornness. "I don't care what might happen, you're not going to fight them alone."

I shot her a look, and she shook her head. "No, Kat, I'm fucking serious. I spent most of my life trying to live up to my mother's impossible standards, and when that failed, I threw myself into a coven that ended up using me to try to take out our rivals. You gave me a chance to prove I can earn what I want—and that what I needed was different from what I ever imagined. I told you when you lost your power—I'm not going to abandon you when you need me."

Murisa leaned forward between the seats. "Neither will I. Whatever they want, they'll have to face the three of us. How many are there? Twelve? Fifteen?" Her laugh was more bitter than I'd ever heard from her before. "We'll make them wish they'd brought triple that number."

Their determination, their drive to fight, wrapped around me like a warm hug but did nothing to quell my fear that if they fought beside me, they'd be the ones to fall.

Because I doubted these people wanted me dead.

Not when Emrick still existed.

"I love you guys," I said, meaning every syllable, "but someone needs to return to the house to work with the rest of the team. Whatever happens tonight, we can't let these bastards get what they want."

Murisa pulled out a mechanical, and it spread its bird-like wings. "Gather the magical hunters," she said to it. "Whatever it takes."

The bird opened its mouth, and Murisa's voice came out of it. *"Gather the magical hunters. Whatever it takes."*

She waved her hand over it, and the bird launched from her palm and out the window as Poppy rolled it down. "That message will reach your house within a few hours. No matter what they do to us here."

Tears pricked my eyes as I let go of the steering wheel and rested my fingers on the door handle. I wasn't ready for this fight. I doubted the witches were, either. But the hunters had pushed the issue, and we would rise to meet them.

"Keep your distance from me," I warned. "I'm not about to go easy."

Poppy bared her teeth. "If you think I am, you're fooling yourself."

I opened the car door, stepped out facing the trucks in front of us, and immediately formed a fireball the size of a beach ball. It hovered over my palms and spun in circles as it grew.

"Katerina Palon," a voice called from behind me. "I suggest you come with us quietly, or we will use force to ensure your compliance."

"If you think that's how to sweet talk me, you haven't done your homework," I shouted over my shoulder, but I held off on attacking. If I was going to take their lives, I wanted to make damned sure I was fighting the right people. "Where is Emrick?"

"Safe. For now. I make no guarantees if you don't agree to come with us."

That was all I needed to know. Any hunters with magical know-how would know better than to mess with Death. That was a mundane's short-sightedness talking.

Without further delay, I launched my fireball at the two trucks blocking our exit and grinned as they exploded in the night.

19

Katerina

THE SURPRISE OF my attack didn't hold the hunters back for long. The drivers of the two trucks were out of the fight, but that left fifteen pissed-off magic haters behind me.

Within seconds, they'd taken formation and bullets were flying. Poppy ducked behind the car. From this distance, her potions would never reach their targets—not without a little help.

She pulled vials from her satchel and handed them to Murisa, who tucked them into the backs of her enchanted beetles and released the mechanicals through the window.

I distracted the hunters by summoning more magic into my hands and flicking fireballs at the trucks on either end of the barricade.

More mechanicals skittered past my feet, nearly invisible in the darkness. Once they entered the glow of the headlights, cries went up and the stomping began.

I winced at the crunch of metal and plastic, knowing how much work Murisa had put into those little critters, but Murisa shrugged off her losses and released another squadron.

The ones that made it past the hunters' heavy boots chirped and sang before their casings opened to release the potion vials hidden within. Screams drowned out the chirps, and more shots echoed along the quiet highway. A fire broke out next to one of the cars, and the driver rushed to back up the vehicle before it was consumed.

In the chaos, I stalked closer to the barricade, pumping more fire into my hands. Poppy crept behind me, and as soon as she was within range, she threw two vials over my shoulder. One hit its target, and the woman collapsed to the ground wrapped in a green haze that left her vomiting on the asphalt. The other shattered against the hood of the car, and the spell fizzled out before any damage was done.

The hunter standing closest to the dud sneered and raised his weapon. I grabbed Poppy's arm and dragged her with me to the ground as he fired.

"What the fuck happened to my potion?" Poppy demanded.

Rage burned in her eyes as she rolled out of my grip and back to her feet, three more vials ready in her hands. She launched them at Mr. Cocky, but her only reward was his widening grin.

He spread his arms in invitation for us to keep trying, and dread pooled in my gut. Needing to prove my suspicions, I guided my magic into a giant fireball and hurled it at a woman standing a few metres away from him.

The fire turned to smoke before it reached her.

A creepy smile spread across her lips, and she turned to stare at me, giving me a finger wave so obnoxious I was almost impressed. The balls on that bitch.

But the fact she wasn't on fire confirmed my fears.

The bastards had done it. They'd found a way to nullify our magic, and we were at their mercy unless we got close enough to go toe to toe with them.

Not for the first time tonight, I wished Barrett were with us.

"Poppy, get back," I ordered. "Murisa, roll up your window."

The witches had nothing more to offer here. Murisa's mechanicals seemed to be able to get under the line of the hunters' defences, but how long before she ran out?

"Kat—" Poppy argued.

"The hunters," I reminded her.

She met my eye, and her desperation bored into me. I ignored it. The only guarantee of survival was retreat. If I got into the car with them, the hunters would pursue and none of us would stand a chance. I was the one they wanted. If I kept them busy, Muroppy could lead the charge without me.

Poppy must have read my every thought because her desperation wilted into resignation. Then she flexed her jaw and sprinted towards the car.

Three shots rang out as the hunters tried to stop her. A yelp sounded behind me. I didn't turn around to check on Poppy but kept my attention on the hunters. Mr. Cocky had once again aimed his gun at my chest, and Ms. Finger-Wave looked ready to blow me away at my first bad move.

The engine revved behind me; the tires squealed. A last shot fired in the direction of the car, and all eyes fell on me.

My heart raced, its rhythm echoing in my ears. I tasted blood with every new breath—adrenaline and fury rushing through me, setting fire to my veins. Flames flickered over my arms, and my fingertips prickled with the buzz of electricity.

The hunters watched me. Some looked amused, some curious. They believed they were safe behind their barrier. That misjudged bravery left space for arrogance, and oh, how I looked forward to snatching their confidence in my fist and crushing it into pulp.

They had Emrick. If they thought a little nullifying barrier would be enough to stop them, they had critically underestimated my love for that man.

"Your only hope of escape is gone, sorceress," Mr. Cocky said, projecting his voice above the small fire still burning from the mechanical's explosion and the raging inferno of trucks behind me. "What do you say? Will you surrender?"

I stared at him, then took in the rest of the scene. There were four vehicles and two trucks parked across the width of the road. Three hunters lay on the ground, leaving twelve standing and ready to take me.

I memorized their positions, did my best to assess the limits of the invisible barrier, then closed my eyes. Emrick's face flickered across the backs of my eyelids. Not from the last time I'd seen him—confused and horrified—but as he'd been the last time he'd touched me. Our interrupted kiss. His promise that we would pick up where we'd left off as soon as he returned to me. He'd broken so many promises over the years, but this one made me royally angry.

That anger bubbled inside me, coiling around my internals and spilling to the tips of my fingers. I stoked it, manipulating every rising ember of fury into a deeper stillness that made my fingertips prickle. My hair crackled, sparks danced over my skin, popping across my leather gloves.

I opened my eyes and met Mr. Cocky's stare. "I don't think so."

Aiming for as much destruction as possible, I released a dozen lightning bolts from my palms, directing them at every car and truck along the line.

The vehicles not protected by the nullifying power jumped

at the impact, and sparks skittered across the dry road. More than one of the hunters had been standing too close to the strike and either collapsed to the ground or had their clothing catch fire, throwing them into a panic.

Only a few of the bolts petered into nothing, and I avoided that area to focus my efforts on the spaces vulnerable to my magic. I drew on my fire, letting it engulf my hands until the dark highway was alight with my rage. As soon as I released my fireball, I reversed my heat, summoned ice spikes into my hands, and hurled them at the remaining cars. Windshields shattered, and tires exploded.

The hunters rushed to stop me. Bullets sprayed through the flickering light, and more than one found its target. The impact of a shot to my gut pushed me backwards, but I screamed through the pain and summoned more lightning as I edged closer to the cars, aiming for an angle that would get me access behind the barrier.

My power was draining quickly, but I didn't slow down. The witches were gone. They would handle the rest of the hunters while I dealt with these sons of bitches who'd made an otherwise shitty evening worse.

I peeled my lips back in a smile and pumped more magic into my palms, letting it fill my veins and soak into my flesh. My vision swam golden as power surged through my blood, and I watched fire pour out of my hands and shoot up behind me to form wings of flame. Mr. Cocky and Ms. Finger-Wave stared at me in horror as they fired off more shots. I barely felt the pain as their bullets ripped through my chest. I was their nightmare. I was what these bastards bragged of hunting in theory but never had the guts to go after in reality.

I was happy to give them their chance.

With a cry, I snapped my wings and released them like blazing swords that sliced through the roof of one of the trucks and consumed three of the hunters standing nearby.

More shots rang out, and another bullet slammed into my shoulder.

I screamed and reversed my heat, summoning more ice spikes. My magic stuttered, growing sluggish, but I pushed through the delay in accessing it, gritted my teeth against the grinding agony in my rotator cuff, and hurled the spikes. One of them lodged in a hunter's chest; the other melted in midair and landed as a puddle on the ground.

That was the cutoff point for their protection.

I scanned the area, trying to figure out what they'd used to produce their shield. My eye landed on a tiny box sitting on the roof of the middle car. I needed to get my hands on that box. If Murisa and Poppy had ten minutes with it, I was sure they could figure out how it worked. We could strip the hunters of their ultimate defence and reduce them to ash.

Until then, I'd have to work around it.

But my head was spinning and my vision had blurred around the edges.

I was running out of time.

With most of the hunters in the left lane out of commission, I took advantage of the opening and jumped onto the hood of one of the defunct vehicles, then onto the roof. I stumbled on my way back down, blinking through the black spots that had begun to spread through my periphery.

Another bullet tore into my leg. I bit back a cry and retaliated with more ice spikes.

Finally, I made it past the barrier. Two spikes plunged into my targets, including one through Finger-Wave's throat. Her eyes widened, and she gurgled around the stake before slumping to the ground.

I staggered again. If I was lucky, I had another minute to take down the remaining hunters before my strength gave out.

But even as I summoned more fire into my palms and prepared to blast the remaining two vehicles, I spotted more people coming out of the shadows. More vehicles driving up from farther down the highway.

I wobbled on my feet and let my power fly. More fire, more lightning. More hunters fell, and I drew on the dregs of my magic, sucking it through the straw of fatigue.

Whatever these people threw at me, I would not go down without a fight. More power, more ice spikes. More screams and death and the reek of charred flesh.

More shots echoed through the silent night and drove into my body.

My power slipped away from me. I'd overspent my reserves, and exhaustion, pain, and blood loss had weakened me.

"Come now, sorceress," a woman's voice called from the darkness. "We told you it didn't have to be this way. It's a shame. I would have liked your lover to see you hale and hearty. Now he'll be lucky to see you at all."

I fell to my knees and summoned one weak fireball between my palms. With everything I had left, I threw it at the woman speaking. As unconsciousness took me, I wrapped myself in the satisfaction of her high-pitched screams.

20

Emrick

IMEASURED MY breaths, counting each inhale, each exhale, and the spaces in between. I'd been doing so for the past few hours as a way to keep my heart from beating a hole through my ribs in its mad dash for freedom—from the moment I'd sensed the tether between Kat and I grow taut.

Our bond had settled and now pulsed normally in my chest, but something had happened—or almost happened—and my need to know what it was had driven me to the brink of insanity. Even now, I teetered on the edge. One more pull on our bond and I was likely to go careening headfirst into madness.

The doors at the back of the room opened, and light spilled through the darkness.

I looked up from where I was sitting with my head bowed

on my crossed arms and scowled at Cartwright as she made her way up the aisle towards my cage. Her heels clicked across the floor in the steady rhythm of someone who had things to do and no time to waste. But as she approached, I noticed the witch hunter general wasn't her usual put-together self.

Instead of her jacket and blouse from earlier, she wore blue surgical scrubs, and the side of her face was covered in carefully taped gauze. Our dear general had seen some action since the last time she'd visited.

But even as my hopes rose that she'd lost the battle, her brown eyes met mine, and the satisfaction pouring from her gaze made my skin prickle with unease.

She said nothing as she ran something through her fingers, and despite my efforts to hold her gaze and show no curiosity about what she carried, my eyes betrayed me and dropped to her hands.

To a pair of gloves. Familiar, runed, leather gloves.

The ground fell out from under me, and anger flared through my veins, undoing all my attempts to keep my breathing level. I dropped one knee to the ground, shifted my weight to my other foot, and slowly rose to my full height. My skin vibrated with the force of my fury, my spirit feeling too restrained by my physical frame.

Despite the protection my cage afforded, Cartwright must have registered my otherworldly desire to rend her limbs from her torso, because her expression flickered with uncertainty. Then she steeled herself, her confidence renewed that the wards would hold me. A small smile twisted her ugly mouth.

How I wanted to punch that smile off her face, then watch as her flesh and bone fell to dirt at my feet.

It would happen. I didn't know how yet, but whatever this woman had done to Kat, she would suffer the same damage tenfold.

"Where is she?" I demanded through clenched teeth.

I hated how impotent I felt. I wanted to consume this entire room with the mists of the afterlife. I wanted every stone to crumble, and every soul in this building to wither away like desiccated fruit in a drought. Death's power wrapped around me, pulsing with the energy of the void. I soaked in it, letting it fuel me. They would not contain me forever—they couldn't— and when I broke free, I would destroy anyone who stood between me and my sorceress.

Because I had to assume that if Cartwright had taken those gloves off Kat, she was in no condition to fight her way free. The only other time someone had forcibly removed them from her person, she'd come within seconds of passing too far for me to reach her. I'd banished the demon responsible to the infernal realms, and I had no problem serving the same fate to Cartwright.

"She's safe," Cartwright said blandly. "For now."

I squeezed my fists at my sides and forced myself to relinquish my hold on my power. The more I drew on the after-life, the less connected to this world I felt. That detachment wouldn't help Kat.

The general tightened her grip on the gloves, a silent threat. "What do you think, reaper? Are you ready to hear me out?"

She sounded so sure of herself, as if she knew she'd backed me into a corner.

And in this moment, I wasn't sure she hadn't.

From the second I'd felt the pull on our bond, I'd run through every possible scenario of how I would respond to them using Kat against me. I'd imagined finally smashing through the cage and doling out the destruction these bastards deserved. I'd imagined grieving, accepting the loss of my beautiful sorceress for the sake of the rest of the world. In every scenario, however, I'd been clear to myself about one thing: as much as I loved Katerina, I couldn't let our love be the cause of the world's demise.

Now that I was faced with the reality of the situation, I didn't know if I could hold to that vow.

The thought of her in their grasp, them free to do whatever they wanted with her—including stealing her gloves, the only piece of her old self she'd managed to hang on to for almost a millennium—I struggled to cling to reason.

"Let me see her."

It was an easy demand to make, and their compliance would

give me a few precious minutes to decide what I wanted my future to look like. Either I burned the world to the ground or the hunters did, but it seemed likely the end was pretty fucking nigh.

"No."

I was hardly surprised by the refusal. So far, they'd given me no ground to stand on. As if they knew showing weakness in one thing would encourage me to test their boundaries else-where. Unfortunately for the general, I'd had fifteen hundred years of practice in out-stubborning souls who didn't want to cross into the afterlife. Cartwright might be determined, but she had nothing on the dead.

I crossed my arms and held her gaze. "Bring her here and let me see for myself that she's all right, or I'm not doing anything for you."

She quirked an eyebrow. "Do you know what we have in our labs, Emrick? We possess the compound that can block her magic. You remember what it did to her the last time she consumed a dose, don't you? I don't believe it went well for either of you."

Red flashed in my vision. "If you go near her with that compound—"

I struggled to rein in my emotions, but it was too late. Cart-wright smirked. "You'll what? You have no hand in this game. You are here to serve us. The only question is a matter of how easy you make it for yourself. You help us, and we're willing to negotiate. If you don't…"

Her shrug told me more than enough of what they would do to Kat if I didn't give in. But even as I trembled at the thought of how far they could push her—even as I felt the world quake around me as my terror grew—the words of surrender lodged in my throat.

I knew what Kat would say if she were here. I knew the exact look she would give me. This woman and her minions wanted to wipe *magic* from the world.

Part of me was tempted to let the hunters do it. It wouldn't take them long to realize their mistake, and they would suffer as greatly as everyone else. But we were talking billions of people facing slow, agonizing death. The trees and grass shrivelling like their counterparts in the afterlife. The ocean drying up, and the muddy beds becoming nothing more than the same dust that made up every person in this building.

Could I consign the world to that fate?

It was either that or trust Kat to find a way to end this mess.

She'd come a long way from the young woman who'd been trapped in Shogaur's snare. The hunters might have herded her to this point and boxed her in, but they were far from the greatest foe she'd faced. These people might have strapped her to a table and stripped away her magic, but all that would do was enrage her. And a Katerina enraged was a Katerina to be feared.

She also wasn't fighting alone. Cartwright hadn't mentioned having anyone else, which meant somewhere out there Barrett would be forming a plan, with Gavin offering whatever support he could. Muroppy would be putting their heads together to invent some new, wild form of magic. Rhys and his thriving second sight would be offering his invaluable insight.

I wasn't without support, and giving in to this woman would only ensure the deaths of the people I'd come to care about.

So instead, I would trust.

I had to, or we were lost.

I bared my teeth and leaned towards the barrier of my cage, sneering at the woman who was forced to stare up at me if she wanted to meet my gaze. "Go fuck yourself, Cartwright. I will not make deals with you."

A flicker of anger danced in her eyes, then went out. "That is disappointing. I'll be sure to let your sorceress know."

She turned on her heel and marched out, and although I wanted to scream and tear apart the concrete floor to hurl the slabs after her, I found myself grinning at the hard line of frustration her mouth had become.

I'd stonewalled her. At least for now. Hopefully long enough to buy us some time.

Come on, Kat. Mîn êcnes. *Find your way free.*

21

Katerina

I WOKE UP to pain.

To nails scraping along the inside of my veins. To scalded nerve endings.

My throat was raw, adding a scratchy agony with every swallow. I must have screamed myself hoarse but didn't remember doing it.

I had no idea how long it took my eyes to focus on my surroundings, but what I saw when they did made me wish I'd stayed in oblivion. Bloody tools lay on a tray beside my head, and a man wearing a blood-spattered apron leaned over me.

Notes and anatomical sketches were pinned to the walls, and I had to wonder—though I didn't really want to know—how many pertained to me. How long had I been out?

"She's waking up. Want me to dose her again?"

The voice sounded far away, as though I were drifting under water. I didn't know the speaker, but the rasping voice of the woman who replied struck me as familiar.

"Leave her. She's not going anywhere. It might be interesting to see what we get once she's able to communicate."

I tilted my head so I could put a face to this demon and found myself staring at the woman from the highway. She wore her brown hair in a harsh bob, with a pair of glasses perched on her nose. In her blue scrubs and with the gauze taped to her face from where my fire had burned her, she should have looked smaller. Diminished. But everything about her screamed *leader*.

Now that I saw her in the light, I recognized her from before tonight. She'd been on the news often enough, giving statements about magical-related events in ways that shielded mundanes from picking up on the subtext. This was the witch hunter general Tony's friend had told us about. The leader of the pack. She'd always rubbed me the wrong way. One of those political types who understood the art of the spin but proved time and again they'd lost their soul somewhere along their career path.

Nice to know I hadn't lost all my instincts about people.

I wished my aim had been a little better with my fire. Maybe then I wouldn't be in this position.

"Witch hunter general," I croaked. "I'd say it's nice to officially meet you, but fuck you."

Her thin mouth curled into a humorless smile as she approached the table where I'd been bound.

How long had it been since anyone had strapped me down like this? I marked it as eight hundred years, and even then, Emrick had done it to keep me safe. To help me heal. Not to inflict more pain.

And these people accused magicals of being a force of evil in this world. Bastards.

"Hello, Katerina. My name is Margaret Cartwright."

"That's 'sorceress' to you. Only friends get to call me by my name."

Cartwright maintained her smirk, but I caught the tightening around her mouth. I'd barely spoken two dozen words, and I'd irritated her. Point to me. "I thought it fair to treat you with the same familiarity as I've treated Emrick. But then, he doesn't have a family name, does he?"

Double points to the bitch.

Rage swept away the last of my haze, and I reached for my magic only to find it out of reach. There, but unresponsive. My anger doubled, combined with my horror that once again I was vulnerable. Helpless.

I prayed Murisa and Poppy had made it back to the house without trouble. If they could contact the main hunters, it didn't matter what happened to Emrick or me. These fuckers were going down.

But would the hunters agree to help?

Ontario's witch hunter general was not only aware of this scheme, she was *involved.* Leading the charge. The same woman who'd publicly vowed to protect the world from dark magic objectively, fairly, and without prejudice.

Either all the hunters under her command were soldiers in her rogue offshoot, or she'd hidden her treason well enough to fool the rest of the top brass. I didn't know what the odds were one way or another, or if the other members of the upper echelon would be willing to go to war with their commander.

If they didn't, I had no idea how we'd fight our way out of this. But I also wasn't about to give up. This woman had Emrick. She could have a chest covered in medals, but that wouldn't stop me from slicing her to ribbons. Once I got my hands free, of course.

First, I needed information. "Where is he?"

Her smirk deepened. "Oh, he's here. Alive and well, I assure you. Much better than you are—or, I should say, than you were. Your body has already healed from most of what Wayne put you through."

I turned my head towards the man with the bloody apron and scowled at him. The lines around his eyes tightened and his cheeks paled, but he clenched his teeth and once more set his scalpel to the inside of my arm.

A hiss escaped me as he dragged the blade from my elbow to my wrist. Blood spilled onto the metal table beneath me.

"The last healing effort took ten minutes and thirteen seconds from open wound to not even a scar," he said once he removed the blade from my skin. "The one before that took exactly the same amount of time. To the second. My observations suggest the subject's body works on a cycle, a timed schedule, if you will. I would guess that all broken bones would take the same length of time to heal. All bruises would have their time, scrapes theirs, open wounds, etcetera."

"I don't want your guesses, Wayne, I want reports. Data. Keep testing it, and don't stop until you have a complete understanding of how this healing works. Then you can move on to figuring out how to replicate it. I want blood samples, urine samples. Any fluids she produces, collect them and test them." Her lip curled back in a leer. "I don't care how you get them."

I shuddered with disgust, but it wasn't heated. I was too amused by this woman's assumptions to be turned off by her idle threats.

Despite the pain cutting through me, my shoulders shook with laughter, and soon I couldn't hold it back. Every giggle made my ribs ache, my torn flesh scream, but I couldn't stop. "You think I heal quickly because of some genetic factor in my blood or something? Because I eat a balanced diet or have some natural superiority?"

I sucked in a breath, then kept on laughing. My entertainment was heightened by the confused alarm written on Wayne's face and the increasing blandness on Cartwright's. Unlike with Barrett's unreadable stoicism, I picked out her frustration in every hard line around her mouth. How much money had she wasted digging into me to peel back my secrets?

I hoped it was millions.

I hoped these bastards bankrupted themselves only to learn they could never replicate my healing ability because the root of it lay with the man they'd captured. If anything happened to him, the only thing Wayne's butchery would achieve would be my death.

If they really wanted to discover my secrets, they should have focused on replicating Alodie's ritual. Unfortunately for them, they'd missed their chance. The only two people who knew the details were dead.

My laughter tapered off as my breath ran out, and I sagged against the table, ignoring the deep, labouring itch as the tissues in my arm stitched themselves back together.

Wayne shook his head. "Fascinating."

Obviously he wasn't discouraged by my little outburst. He would continue cutting me open and breaking my bones just to watch me heal.

Good for him. Everyone needed a hobby.

Cartwright cocked her head, and my amusement dried up

like a puddle on a hot day. I didn't like the look in her eyes, at once curious and depraved. "What about your limbs, Katerina? Do you grow those back as quickly as your bones snap into place?" I clenched my teeth as she nodded to Wayne. "Get me a finger, would you? Maybe that will be enough to encourage the reaper to work with us."

I glowered at her. "If Emrick hasn't agreed to help you yet, a finger won't convince him. If anything, you might piss him off enough to smash through whatever you're using to hold him. Believe me, you won't want to be anywhere near him if that happens."

She leaned close enough that I caught the whiff of stale coffee and peppermint on her breath. "Be grateful I want you alive, *sorceress*. One shot of that compound, and you'll lose your healing as well as your magic. Then what would happen if we cut off your fingers one by one? Either he cooperates without any further fuss, or what you've endured so far won't compare to what's coming."

I was still glaring at Cartwright, refusing to drop my gaze, when a pair of shears closed down on my left ring finger. The blades snapped shut.

Blood filled my mouth as I bit my tongue to hold back my screams.

22

Emrick

DREAD SEEPED INTO my gut when the door at the back of the room opened for the second time in one night and Cartwright walked in wearing an expression so smug it oozed onto the concrete floor.

The gauze was still taped to her face and neck, evidence of this woman's stubbornness. A dab of magical ointment and whatever injuries those bandages hid would be healing already. If I'd been in a more generous mood, I would have given her a nod for sticking to her principles. Instead, I wished her a nice case of sepsis and a long, drawn-out demise.

She didn't carry gloves this time. There was no arrogant passing of leather through her fingers in a silent showcasing of her dastardly plans. But she did have a tight grip on something small enough to hide in her fist, and when she tossed it to me, I instinctively caught it as it flew through the unseen barrier of my cage.

The object was sticky and cold, smooth to the touch except at one end where it was hard and the other end where it was wet.

I needed a few seconds to identify it as a finger. A ring finger, severed at the joint, still weeping blood where bone and flesh had been sheared from the hand.

My heart stalled in its steady rhythm before the beat picked up at a galloping pace. My breaths came quick and shallow. I knew this finger as well as I knew my own hand. I recognized the soft skin and dimpled knuckle. The tiny scar halfway up that Kat had once told me was from a brawl with her sister when she was barely more than twelve years old.

My vision swam.

It didn't matter that in a few days, she would have likely regrown most of her lost digit. What mattered was that they'd taken it from her. That first they'd stripped her of her gloves, and now they were removing pieces of her. What else had they taken? How else had they damaged the woman I loved more than the world itself?

"Continue to say no, and we won't stop at her hands." Cartwright was so damned cold I swore frost bled from her feet to cover the concrete floor. Torture didn't seem to faze her at all.

Was she hiding her discomfort to prove she wouldn't be moved, or did she honestly believe magicals were less than animals, not even worth basic humanity?

"You are walking a dangerous path, General," I growled. "Every step you take down this road will earn you fiercer retribution. You believe you're untouchable, but your bad judgement will be the end of you. I'll petition Death to have claim on your soul, and you can't begin to imagine the joy I'll have in dragging your screaming spirit to the afterlife and sticking you somewhere you'll never escape. No river to take you to your final end. No peace. An eternity of suffering."

She cracked a smile. "Watching you find a way out of this prison might be worth my future agony. After the amount of time and effort and money that has gone into building this cage, I would be beyond impressed. But you're wasting time with your empty threats. I've instructed our doctor to remove another finger for every five minutes you delay." She checked her watch. "He should be removing the next in a few seconds."

Evil.

That's what I was staring at right now.

We thought we'd seen it in Mikhail, in Shogaur, but they were nothing compared to the woman who'd manipulated this game from the beginning. We were simply pieces on her chessboard, and she was enjoying every play, knowing she would be the last queen standing.

How long had the game been running? Cartwright looked to be in her fifties, which made no sense to the timeline. Alodie had been around for at least sixty years, if not longer.

"You inherited this plan, didn't you?" I asked. With every passing second, Kat's suffering would increase, but we needed answers. Only with information did Kat stand a chance of bringing these people down. "You act like you're the mastermind behind all this, but you would have been—what? Ten years old when the first move was made?"

A faint flush crept over Cartwright's cheeks, and her jaw ticked. "I wasn't born yet." She shifted her weight on her feet and crossed her arms. "Witch Hunter General Hautman came up with the idea. He'd watched you and the sorceress for years, knowing the secret to ridding this world of its greatest blight rested somewhere with you. When he heard rumours of an immortal sorceress trapped in the infernal realms, he summoned Fegor and put everything in motion." She checked her watch again. "Do you really want to risk a third finger? Tick-tock."

I clenched my teeth and sucked in a breath. Kat would have to forgive me. "Was this Hautman guy so incompetent he didn't know what to do after he brought Alodie here? Sixty years is a long span for a whole lot of nothing."

Cartwright drew her shoulders back. "He was content to sit and wait. As was General Snope after him. But I'm able to see what they didn't. The hold of magic in this world is growing stronger, its grip tighter." She held up her hand and squeezed it so hard her knuckles bled white. "We don't have time for a long game anymore. We need to act now, or we won't have a future to protect."

She dropped her hand and stepped closer. "Now you have a decision to make, Emrick. Your precious Katerina has just lost a third finger. Once we've removed her hands, we'll start on her toes. Or maybe her eyes. Or her teeth? She might recover from every wound, but how long will it take, and how much agony will she be in while she does?"

My heart throbbed against my ribs, and my insides writhed.

Kat wouldn't want me to break down for her sake. It was her life against the rest of the world. She might suffer, but she would rather endure the torment than leave billions of others to the same fate.

I knew this as well as I knew the feel of her body beneath my hand, but I couldn't do it. Not only because my blood boiled at the thought of her screams as they peeled her flesh and sawed her bones, but because, if we wanted to win, Kat had to be free. Barrett and the others would fight valiantly, I had no doubt, but Kat was their leader. We stood no chance without her.

I clutched Kat's finger tightly in my grip. We would get through this, and when it was over, I would have my sorceress by my side. Whole and well.

And if she failed and the rest of the world burned, so be it.

Once the magic that tied the universe together dried up, she and I would go together, as we were meant to.

"Fine," I gritted out, hating myself for saying it even as I knew it was the only answer I could give. "You promise me that Katerina will not be harmed further and that you'll deliver her to me—safe and alive—and I'll do what you want."

Cartwright's smile sent a chill through my bones so deep my marrow cracked into shards, but there was no backing out. Not if it saved my sorceress more pain and gave her a fighting chance.

"Of course," she said. "We won't lay another finger on Katerina."

Something in her tone waved red flags in my head.

"Whatever your plan is for me, I want Kat brought here first. I want to see for myself that she's safe."

She'd refused me once, but I suspected this time would be different. I'd given her what she wanted—she would consider agreeing to my request my reward for good behaviour.

A furrow formed between her brows, but, sure enough, she jerked her head in a nod and raised her hand. A hunter standing near the door stepped forward. "General?"

"Bring the sorceress. Tell Wayne his games are over for the time being."

I flexed my jaw but said nothing, and the general and I glared at each other through the invisible wall as time stretched on. The seconds went by in heartbeats. In ragged breaths. I worried I'd made a mistake, but I refused to change my mind.

If I were being honest with myself, saving the rest of the world had been a secondary motivation for my decision. For fifteen hundred years I'd walked this earth and witnessed so much, but only with Katerina had I ever truly felt alive. I could never have left her to suffer at their hands, regardless of the consequences.

Finally, the doors opened, and two hunters dragged Kat between them. Red danced in my vision, and I lurched towards the edge of my cage. She was barely conscious, her eyes rolling in her head. Her clothing, her face, her hair were covered in blood. Hers, I guessed, though I couldn't see many open wounds on her except for a healing gash on her arm and two missing fingers. Not three, which I found interesting. It made me wonder if Cartwright's doctor was more squeamish than the general had so far proved to be.

"Let her go." My voice shook so badly I barely recognized it.

Cartwright chuckled. "I don't think so. She stays where she is until we're sure you won't change your mind and turn us all to dust."

I glowered at her, but she didn't blink at my reaction. On the contrary, she nodded at her people, and one of them pulled their gun and set it against the base of Kat's skull.

"Any hint that you intend to betray us, Emrick, and John

pulls the trigger. Ms. Palon has proved she can survive most injuries, but we've yet to test what a bullet through her brain stem will do. What do you think? Could she bounce back from that?"

I didn't know how my body was still in one piece, my rage having expanded so far past the invisible barrier holding me here. How had every mortal in this room not burst into flames with the intensity of it?

Kat met my gaze, and although her expression was blank, I spotted the fear lurking deep within it. I wished I could say something to reassure her, but at this point, I had no idea what would happen next. All I could hope was that after I did whatever Cartwright demanded of me, Kat and her people would find a way to reverse the damage before it went too far.

The general reached into her pocket and pulled out a benign-looking, grooved metal sphere. It fit comfortably in the palm of her hand, little more than an ugly paperweight.

She held it up between her fingers. "All we ask is that you deliver this to the afterlife."

I narrowed my eyes. "That's all?"

"That's all." She smiled. "You see? Not so bad. A few minutes of your time, and you'll be free to exist on whichever plane you wish."

"And Kat will be free as well?"

"Oh yes. We'll have no further need of her."

I didn't trust her. Not even a little bit. But I couldn't see any way out. I looked to Kat, hoping to see a spark of rebellion in her expression, some certainty that she was ready to throw her magical weight around, but she still looked dazed. Pain had left her eyes glassy, and I suspected if the men holding her let go, she wouldn't have the strength to stand on her own.

Her best bet was for me to follow through with my end of the deal, and my innards coiled into knots knowing it might prove to be no deal at all. I was no stranger to making bad agreements. Once again, I was trading an unknown future because of my love of a woman.

For the barest of breaths, I hesitated. The consequences of my actions sprawled out before me like so many grains of sand. Each one would have repercussions that affected millions of others, but it all started right here. Right now.

With a love that might destroy the world.

I held out my hand, and Cartwright stepped forward. Again, she nodded to her people, and this time the walls of my cage fell away. My connection to the afterlife slammed into me so quickly my breath caught. My chest expanded, strength surged through my limbs, and the desire to throw my power into the room nearly overwhelmed me.

The only thing holding me back was the click of the safety on the gun.

The general's eyes gleamed, as though she was aware of

every thought, and I scowled as I twitched my fingers at her, once again requesting the sphere. The sooner we got this over with, the better.

She dropped it into my palm, and the weight surprised me. Whatever this sphere contained, it was no small deal.

"Anywhere in particular you'd like me to leave it?" I asked, sarcasm dripping from every syllable.

"Not at all. All it needs is a connection to the spiritual plane. We'll take over from there." She looked to Kat. "You see, my dear, your sweet Emrick is helping us make history. Once that sphere is in the afterlife, we can begin our plan of stripping this world of every speck of magic. Within a week, every magical on the planet will be either dead or mundane like the rest of us. An even playing field for the first time since time began."

Her face shone with zealotry and insanity, and a shudder ran through me.

Awareness leached into Kat's eyes as they widened. "Emrick, no." Her terror was so intense I tasted the sourness of it on my tongue. She thrashed against the men holding her as her strength returned, but they tightened their grip until she cried out in pain. "You can't. You know what it will mean!"

I curled my fingers around the sphere. "If it keeps you alive for another few days, it's worth it. Everything for you, Kat."

She struggled again, and the man on her left jerked her arm so hard I heard a snap. She screamed. My rage flared, my power surged, and Cartwright stepped between us, defending her lackey.

"Once you do as you're told, Kat is no longer our concern. You want to save her? Deliver the sphere. Now."

I gritted my teeth.

Everything told me to turn on her, to unleash my power, wipe them out, and pray I got to the hunter with his gun aimed at Kat before he had time to pull the trigger.

But my window would be too small. One move, Cartwright had said, and I believed her. Her level of obsession couldn't be underestimated.

I met Kat's gaze and read her wild desperation. I wished I could have one moment alone with her—a single second to explain. All I could do was hope that when she had a moment to think, she'd realize why I was doing this. But I didn't let myself hide from her fear. I kept my gaze locked on hers as I summoned the mist and opened the doorway to the afterlife.

Her lips moved in a soundless *please stop*, and I swallowed against my uncertainty and doubt. We had one way forward. Unless I gave myself to Death right now—abandoned Kat and became a wraith—this was our only option.

I stepped through the doorway and readied myself to launch the sphere as far as I could into the afterlife, hoping it would break on impact and foil their plans.

The weight of the sphere shifted in my palm. A crack

appeared, spilling light through the seam.

Horror filled me. I had no idea what was happening, and I was one hundred per cent sure I didn't want to find out.

I wasn't left in suspense for long.

A spike jutted out of the sphere and stabbed through my palm, impaling my flesh until the tip pierced the back of my hand. Then the spike twisted, the top opened, and hooks drove into my skin.

The sphere had attached itself to me.

My racing heart climbed into my throat. I grabbed the sphere with my free hand and tried to rip it off, but more hooks flew out, attaching it more securely to my already trapped palm.

I'd expected betrayal, but this was far beyond what I could have imagined.

I was aware of Kat crying out, but I couldn't hear her, drowning in fear made worse by Cartwright's smile.

"Thank you, Emrick," she said. "You couldn't have performed your task better. Believe me when I say I fully intend to keep my end of the bargain. Katerina is no longer of any concern to us, and you're free to decide whether you wish to remain in the afterlife or continue here as our guest."

She pulled a remote out of her pocket, hit a button, and another flash of light surrounded me. A similar barrier to the one before appeared, but this one was visible, stronger, and infused with something that rattled my bones and raked its energy over my bare arms until I collapsed to my knees.

Something tore in my chest, and I clutched at my sternum.

What in Death was—

I looked up and met Kat's gaze once more. Watched the confusion enter her eyes, then the terror, then the despair.

She raised her hands, and her eyes dropped to the slash on her arm before she once more looked at me.

I followed her stare, and my mouth went dry.

It would have been difficult to tell around her missing fingers, but that gaping wound in her arm made her situation all too obvious. Her healing had stopped.

Whatever was in this barrier, it had blocked our bond.

Once again, my unbreakable sorceress was mortal.

23

Katerina

I FELT TOO much and nothing at the same time—at once buried too deeply inside my body and hovering too far above it. My bond with Emrick had been blocked again, the missing tether a gaping hole in my chest, the void replaced with numbness. My poor, scattered thoughts were too overwhelmed to process the full nightmare of my situation.

I'd barely been aware of the hunters dragging me off the table in that lab and carting me down an empty hallway, into an elevator, and down to the basement. I'd begun to come back to myself when they'd hauled me through an empty concrete room. A pinprick of awareness had returned when Emrick had come into view—an angel whose wings had been clipped, a bird trapped in a cage.

The sight of him had chased away my pain and filled me with so much hope I'd almost found the power to fight off the men pinning me in place. I would have given anything to go back in time and put a stop to things right there.

But then Cartwright had opened her mouth, that sphere had appeared in her hand, and she'd spoken words that even now didn't fully register.

Their goal was to wipe out all magic?

Did they not understand how disastrous that would be for the entire world?

And yet Emrick had agreed to help her. Believing it would save me?

The romantic fool.

Now here he was, my beautiful angel, trapped in an even narrower cage. I'd suffered the sucking hollowness in my chest when our bond had been blocked, the agony matched by horror at the sight of the strange sphere stuck to his hand. No blood dripped from the wound, but his expression was ravaged with an anguish that shattered my heart.

The broken shards clattered throughout my ribcage, slicing through the numbness. Sharp, stabbing pain followed in their wake, chased by an anger that burned so intensely and so hot steam rose from my skin. Surprise scurried alongside my magic that I was able to access my power at all. Whatever they'd dosed me with earlier must have worn off, and no one had thought to administer more. An oversight on their part. They must have believed my display on the highway and Wayne's subsequent care had taken too much out of me for my power to return so quickly. Or maybe they'd believed blocking my bond with Emrick would also block my magic. Their mistake. This power was all mine.

"Uh, General?" the hunter on my left called. His grip on my arm loosened, and he hissed as the heat burned his palm.

I ignored him and kept my attention on Emrick. I took in the sorrow on his face, his apology.

He'd made a deal but hadn't considered all the terms. Or he had and had deemed the consequences worth it. These people had caused Adrian's death. These people had summoned Alodie's demon and set in motion a chain of events that had torn holes in the magical community that would takes decades to repair.

Or not, if these fanatics had their way. The holes would only get larger until the makeup of the universe was devoured.

Goosebumps pebbled my skin in spite of my heat, so I summoned more fire.

"General?" the man repeated.

Cartwright turned, and whatever she saw on my face must have made her realize the precarious situation her people were in because she nodded at the men beside me. "Get rid of her."

"No!" Emrick shouted.

I didn't wait for the hunter to obey.

Cartwright wanted to deal in spheres? We would see how she liked mine.

On a deep breath, I released my flames in a wide ring. The men standing closest to me barely had time to scream before they were consumed by it.

Cartwright fled.

I turned on my heel and launched a fireball at her retreating back—fucking coward—but the fire extinguished before it reached her. The bitch must have activated an anti-magic ward.

The hunters slammed the doors shut behind her. The floor was scorched black, the rest of the room unscathed except for the charred remains of my unfortunate captors. Whoever had thought to keep Emrick encased in concrete had thought ahead.

Emrick and I stood alone in the room, but my rage didn't settle. I ran towards him and hurled myself at the prison that held him bound. My fingers went numb when they came into contact with the anti-magic barrier, the heat of my fire disappearing so quickly my teeth chattered. I threw myself against the wall again. The cage sizzled and sparked, the ward drew on my magical reserves, but I ignored the pain and pressed on, determined to break through.

The discomfort flared, and the harder I pushed, the more my magic waned.

I became aware of Emrick shouting my name. At first I

ignored him, refusing to accept defeat, but as the last of my magic seeped out of me, I dropped to my knees and forced myself to look at him.

"I'm so sorry." Tears streamed down his face. His moonlight eyes bored into me with emotions so deep, so hopeless, that the fragments of my broken heart fractured into another million pieces.

But it was fine. If he'd lost hope, I'd cling to enough for both of us. "I will get you out of there."

Doors slammed open behind me, and I whipped around. The second I broke contact with the ward, my magic surged. I channelled all the throbbing, pulsing, stabbing pain from each of my hunter-induced injuries and used it to fill my palms with fire that I hurled at the dozen hunters creeping into the room. Three of them were hit with the blast, but the rest advanced. Their weapons were drawn, and I suspected their guns were loaded with bullets that would strip me of my magic before they killed me.

I dropped my fire and tapped into the stillness in the air.

Months ago, this switch in focus would have taken time. Effort. Energy. But I was too angry to feel the effects on my broken body. Later, maybe, I would register the damage Wayne had done. I would think about the fingers I wouldn't grow back, the gash on my arm that would take weeks to fully heal, and the snapped wrist that hadn't quite repaired itself.

In this moment, I was focused only on taking my revenge.

I raised my arms and let my lightning fly. Bolts struck the walls, the floor, and the guns aimed at me.

Not satisfied with one burst, I let loose another, and another.

Then I switched back to my familiar fire and released a ball of flame so big it consumed the doors and spread out along the walls.

"Kat, stop. If you don't, you'll burn yourself with the rest of them."

Emrick's despair hit deep in my soul, but I couldn't obey. Stopping meant giving in. Meant leaving him here. And I wouldn't do that. He had agreed to work with these people to save me, and I wasn't about to turn my back on him and abandon him to whatever their next step was.

My fire spread, devouring everything it could grab. Shadows appeared in the doorway, and without hesitation, I sent another blast towards it. Anything I could do to keep these monsters away from me and Emrick.

"Kat, stop!" someone yelled from beyond the flames.

Beneath my rage and panic, recognition tweaked at that voice.

A secondary fire blazed as white-hot as mine, pushing my magical flames back. In another moment, Barrett and Gavin sprinted through the temporary gap.

Something in my chest cracked. What were they doing

here? *How* were they here? How had they found me? How had they gotten in?

Confusion, wonder, and fear for them made the hold on my magic slip, and I scrambled to grab it so I could be ready to protect them if another wave of hunters appeared.

They were calling for me to come to them, but their pleas swept over me. I wasn't about to leave. A few hours ago, I might have gone. Before Emrick had made such a foolish, short-sighted decision and gotten himself even more deeply mired in the hunters' games. But not now. Not when all I wanted was to stay by his side until whatever end came—even if that end came now.

But my friends had reached me. Were reaching for me. Urging me to follow them.

I backed up until I nearly pressed against the barrier. Despite the slight distance I kept from it, the tingle of the ward buzzed along my skin, draining my magic, my strength, and my hope that I was strong enough to take down every hunter by myself.

"Kat, come on." Barrett sounded as calm as if we were waiting for a table at a restaurant. "If they haven't figured out we're here yet, they will soon. We should make tracks while the fire's still burning."

I snarled at them. "I'm not leaving."

Barrett and Gavin exchanged a look. Probably silently debating which one of them would tackle me and drag my stubborn ass out of here, but they were in for a surprise if they tried.

"You have to go, Kat," Emrick said. His urgency was gone, replaced by cold, driven practicality. "I agreed to their games to give you the best chance of ending this, but you can't do it from in here. I'll do whatever I can to slow them down, but you need to go home and get to work. You know what they want to do. You know they can't win."

I squeezed my eyes shut. "I don't fucking care about them. What is this world to me if you're not in it? They've locked you in and bound you to that—that thing. They blocked our bond again. I won't let them do anything else to you."

"Kat, look at me. Look at me."

I didn't want to, but my body couldn't help but obey. I struggled to make out his beautiful face through the wet blur of my tears.

"I love you," he said. "If they think they can keep us apart, they're more clueless than we thought they were. We'll find a way. I promise."

"I love you." It came out as a croak.

At least I'd had a chance to tell him, which was more than I'd worried I'd have this morning. At least my final time hearing his voice hadn't been that scared half-message before they'd taken him.

He rested his empty hand against the barrier and winced as sparks flew. "Go now. While you can. I'll see you soon."

He said it as a promise, but we both knew it was an empty one. Against a group of zealots willing to go to any lengths to reach their aims, there were no guarantees.

Choking on a sob that this might be the last time I saw the man who'd filled my life with so much love and joy, who'd brought me back from the pit of despair more times than I could count, I backed away from him. Barrett wrapped his arm around me, and in another moment, he'd swept me off my feet and was running towards the door.

Gavin summoned his magic and released a blast ahead of us, once more creating a gap between the flames that allowed us to run through unscathed.

My attack had spread well beyond the room holding Emrick, and I sent a passing thought to the lab where I'd been held. I regretted we were so many floors away from it that my fire wasn't likely to spread so far.

Yet.

As Gavin kicked open a reinforced door and Barrett carried me outside, I swore I'd be back. Tonight, I'd offered an appetizer of how far I would go to protect what mattered to me.

Soon, I'd serve the entrée, and gods help Cartwright and her people if they didn't submit.

Emrick's rumours from the afterlife, the years of people terrified of the immortal sorceress bringing destruction in her wake, were about to come true.

24

Katerina

I COULDN'T STOP shaking.

Maera had wrapped me in three blankets after placing a cup of tea on the table beside me—tea I'd spilled twice already—but the tremors had taken over, and nothing would calm them.

It made Gavin's task of bandaging the stumps where my fingers had been extra challenging.

"She's in shock," Barrett said to Rhys, who sat on the edge of his seat picking at his fingernails. He set a plate of chocolate-dipped cookies next to the tea and settled on the armrest beside me.

"She's pissed off," I corrected through chattering teeth. "The hunters have lost their minds. Wiping out *all* magic? What are they thinking?"

The entire team had migrated from Manitoulin to Adrian's—my—house in Toronto to set up our base of operations. A smart move given everything we'd learned tonight.

Poppy sat in the armchair across from me with Murisa on her lap and a thick bandage around her left arm. I remembered her yelp as she'd run towards the car.

"They get you, too?" I asked.

She shrugged. "A graze. Bunch of Stormtroopers."

Gavin sat on the coffee table in front of me to give himself better access to my hand. He'd already bound the gash on my arm and my broken wrist, but my fingers were giving him trouble. Maera puttered in the kitchen behind us, slamming a few more cupboards than was absolutely necessary.

Rhys shoved his hands between his knees, rescuing his poor cuticles. "I don't get it. I'm not saying I agree with what they're trying to do—obviously—but you're all acting like it would be the literal end of the world."

Barrett's expression turned even stonier than usual. "It would be."

A surprised laugh escaped me, and I heard the touch of madness creeping around the edges. "I would have thought you'd be glad, Barrett. That you'd believe Doomsday was an acceptable consequence if it meant magic was stripped from the bones of the earth."

He gave me his standard bland look, but it carried no heat,

and I didn't push it. We'd already had our talk about his shifting opinions when he'd shocked me into speechlessness with his admission that he didn't hate magic nearly as much as he used to. But needling him had become a deeply ingrained habit. A comforting ritual. He knew it, which was why he allowed me to poke without biting back, and tears flooded my eyes at the simple, silent act of kindness.

Bastard.

"Science is just magic we understand," Murisa explained to Rhys as Gavin drew the bandages closed around my missing fingers. "Magic follows the same rules as the rest of the universe because the universe is made up of magic."

Rhys nodded slowly. "So if they get rid of magicals— witches, Seers, dragons—they'll also get rid of the magic we take for granted."

"Exactly," Barrett said.

Maera dropped onto the couch beside me and buried her head in her hands. "The short-sighted fools. This is what happens when ignorance prevails."

"The worst part is we won't get to enjoy the looks on their faces when they realize they fucked up." I allowed the depth of my bitterness to seep off my tongue as I pulled my wrapped hand away from Gavin. "The hunters of this generation will only live to see the deaths of us magicals. They'll believe they won. The rest of it, the magic that encourages crop growth, for example, might take a few decades to dry up. So their kids might have reason to regret the idiocy their parents were involved in—their grandkids definitely will—but there likely won't be any grand moment of revelation for Cartwright that she's doomed the planet."

Poppy sank deeper into her chair and tightened her arms around Murisa. "No worries there, kitty Kat. We'll give her reason enough to regret what she's done. Ideally before any of us has to worry about losing our magic."

I let out a heavy breath. "I guess this explains all of it. Those texts they were collecting, Rhys's vision. *Death coming for Death.* They did their research, found a way to capture Emrick, and will use him to end the world. We need to find out how they're caging him."

"From what you describe, it's a variation of the anti-magic ward," Murisa said. "There must be a device in the room controlling it. If we destroy that, Emrick should be free."

Free except for that sphere trapped to his hand. Free except for being stuck between this world and the next.

Poppy nudged my leg with her foot. "We'll get him out of there. I promise."

Murisa kissed the top of Poppy's head, and Poppy tilted her head back to claim her mouth. I found myself glaring at them and forced my gaze in another direction.

I was glad they had each other. Glad they had someone to

hold on to in the darkest moments. That connection would see them through the trouble to come. Same with whatever connection had developed between Barrett and Gavin over the past couple of months, even if it had begun over their shared loathing of everything I was. Rhys and Maera had each other as well, the beautiful bond between mother and child.

I had no one. And I had everyone. Just like before, when I stood in that hall in front of Emrick, I straddled all and nothing. I couldn't find my footing. The ground was crumbling beneath me, and I was falling so fast my stomach flip-flopped and my breath trailed behind me in a shimmering wave until I had no air left. My vision shrank to pinpoints, and I lost all awareness of my surroundings.

Gentle hands grabbed me. Then I wasn't sitting anymore but airborne, moving, being laid down gently. The blankets Maera had wrapped around me were draped over me, and soft fingers stroked my hair.

Low murmurs urged me to breathe, and it took a while, but finally my lungs cooperated and regular airflow swept in and out.

More time passed. My heartbeat slowed, and my vision crept back. Once it did, I found myself alone in the living room with Barrett. Both his hands were clasped around my uninjured one, and his brown eyes were fixed on me. Steady. Calm. As self-assured as Adrian had ever been.

I absorbed his quiet until my pulse settled, and then I drew in a final deep breath, and the tension in my shoulders released its hold. "I'm all right now. Thanks."

He held my gaze for a few extra beats before he nodded and let me go. But he didn't go far, leaning forward in his chair with his elbows resting on his knees. Cuddles had squeezed himself between the arm of the chair and Barrett's meaty thigh, purring contentedly as puffs of fur blew off him and found a home on Barrett's black pants.

"When you're ready, we need to talk about what you saw while you were in that headquarters and what that woman did to Emrick."

My insides twisted, and I threatened to bring up the little tea I'd consumed, but Barrett's focused presence, his expression devoid of pity, allowed me to push through this second wave of panic.

"We also need to talk about how the hell you and Gavin got in there. How did you find me? How did you make it through without anyone seeing you?"

Barrett huffed a laugh as he leaned back in his chair. Cuddles took the opportunity to climb into his lap, and Barrett's nose wrinkled. Despite his disgust, he didn't shove the cat off him. Was he abiding by the understood rule of "Never move a comfortable cat," or had the undead feline grown on him?

"You have Rhys to thank for most of that," he said as he

rested a heavy hand on Cuddles's back.

I raised my eyebrows. "Rhys? He had a vision?"

Barrett nodded. "A few. Seemed to have some control over them, too. He Saw the building. Saw you in the basement. We knew the place was somewhere in Guelph, so we set out right away, and while we drove, he scoured satellite maps to pinpoint the location."

Just as he'd done when we were trying to find Mikhail's warehouse. In so many ways, we seemed to have come full circle, though we were stronger now despite all our losses.

"We talked about bringing in Hera's witches to help, but Rhys told us not to. He was pretty sure we'd need them later. Once we found the right place, we stayed on the phone with him and went in just the two of us. It was patchy, and we had a few close calls, but he managed to direct us away from the hunters." The corner of his mouth kicked up in a rare smile. "The kid's gaining power fast. Adrian would have been impressed."

As usual, the two of us sat with our shared grief. Pride at Rhys's progress warmed me through, though I was sad he hadn't told me himself. I'd been too caught up in my own crap to ask.

Barrett nudged us out of the lull. "We'll get back to that when we're ready to make our next move. Are you ready to answer my questions now?"

I shuddered. I really wasn't. I had to—I knew that—but I gave myself another moment to eat a cookie and steel my nerves before I dove in.

"They're doing… experiments. On magicals. Cartwright ordered her scientist to pick my bones—literally—to find out what made me tick. How many others have they dissected? All those witches that have gone missing, Barrett. Hard to think about."

I forced myself to swallow the bile creeping up the back of my throat. "The lab is upstairs somewhere. Third floor, maybe? I wasn't exactly lucid when they moved me around, but there was an elevator that took us to the basement." I met Barrett's eye. "We need to get back in there. Use Rhys's white eyes to hit them hard while we still can and burn the place to the ground."

Barrett nodded, no doubt making mental notes of every detail I shared.

"As for Emrick." I took a moment to let the pain settle. "Cartwright gave him some kind of device. She ordered him to drop it in the afterlife, but as soon as he opened the mist, it attached itself to his hand."

The visual of the spike bursting from the sphere and driving itself through Emrick's palm looped through my head, and no matter what I tried, I couldn't shake it. "I have no idea what it is, but I think we can safely assume it's going to affect the world's magic."

"That's why they needed Emrick? To use his power?"

I shrugged. "It's the only reason I can think of. Emrick is

trapped in that cage, and the doorway to the afterlife is stuck open. With that sphere, the hunters have access to this world and the one beyond. That's… a lot of reach."

The significance of their plan dropped on me like a lead weight, and my head reeled. Instead of being forced to deal with one city, country, or continent at a time, the hunters could access the entire planet in one fell swoop. Once they got started, events would move quickly. Probably too quickly for us to get ahead of them.

Barrett pressed his lips together and sat back in his chair. Cuddles shifted with him and butted his head against Barrett's rocky stomach. "I wish we had a better idea of the details. Wiping out all magic is no simple mission."

"What better organization to attempt it than the people who started the process so many hundred years ago? These rogue hunters have more in common with their brethren of old than the members of today."

"It always amazes me when groups try to take us back to a more ignorant time." I eyed him through narrowed eyes, and he chuckled, a short, deep rumble. "Yes, I recognize this goes against what I've always said. Thanks for continuing to point it out."

I glared at him a moment longer, then winked and offered the best smile I could muster. I suspected it came out more as a grimace.

Although I hated to admit weakness, I said, "We can't fix this on our own."

"We already knew we'd need help."

I sighed and tugged on my hair. "I didn't realize just how much help we'd need. We have to storm that headquarters and hope it's the only base they have. We need to take down a witch hunter general and all her top soldiers before they can ready their defences. And we'll have to plan to do it without magic."

My guts churned with nerves. Thanks to Barrett, I'd brushed off some of my old knife skills, but I wasn't nearly confident enough to think I could go up against an entire army armed only with a blade or two.

"So far we only have whoever Hera's willing to spare, and maybe Ben with his healers—though he might need some arm-twisting. Orillia's refused to help, and I don't see Kelly eager to jump into the fray. Has Poppy reached out to the rest of the hunters yet? Do we have any other potentials on the list?"

I scrambled to think of any other names, but after the pain and the drugs and the exhaustion, I was coming up empty. Despair threatened to grab hold of me, and I worried that if I slipped down that hole, I wouldn't be able to drag myself out of it.

Instead of reassuring me, Barrett shoved the plate of chocolate cookies into my face.

"Stop stressing about it. Have a bite and get some rest," he said. "The others are under strict orders to leave you alone for the next three hours."

I jerked my head up, gawking. "Three—we don't have time for—"

He thrust the plate at me again. "We don't have time for you to be knocked around. We need you sharp, and that means sleep."

I blinked. "Barrett, we are facing global extinction. I don't think—"

"We need allies, but we also need you. We can't do this without you. Close your eyes and trust us to get to work. When you wake up, you'll have enough to do."

He plonked Cuddles onto the floor, then rose from his seat and bent over to kiss my forehead. I couldn't have been more shocked if he'd torn off his mask and revealed himself to be a giraffe.

"You did good today, Kat," he said as he straightened. "You survived. Keep doing that, and there's no way we can lose."

25

Emrick

I LONGED FOR my old cage.

That one had kept me contained and limited my power but otherwise hadn't affected me.

This new one seeped through my flesh and seared my insides. It pulled at my blood and mixed with my cells. It used my power to keep itself going, and the pull drained me—but not fast enough. The part of me tied to Death fought against the anti-magic wards, replenishing my strength, keeping me caught in this horrifying, unbreakable cycle.

When I tried to walk farther onto the spiritual plane, my cage yanked me back. At the same time, the anchor that bound me to the afterlife urged me to go home. I was caught in the middle of this tug of war—my soul the white cloth dangling in the middle.

All the while, the sphere did its job. I hadn't cracked what that job was yet, but with the time I'd been given, I was determined to work it out. And stop it if I could.

Aside from the base of the spikes, I couldn't see any opening. It made no noise; it cast no light. Yet it tingled against my palm with a hum of energy, and I knew it was far from a harmless lump of metal.

I shook my hand, poked at the spikes where they'd hooked into my flesh, gripped the sphere and attempted to wrest it free. Spirit as I was, I didn't bleed, but the excruciating burn brought me to my knees, and I braced my weight on my free hand, gasping for breath as sweat dripped down my brow.

Only after the pain subsided did I notice the way the ground beneath me had *changed* close to where the sphere dangled from my other hand. The shift was so subtle I might not have noticed if I had been in the physical world instead of the afterlife. But on this plane, *change* wasn't possible. Time had no meaning here. Reality, physicality, substance—they were concepts leftover from the world of the living. Yet the dry, brittle grass beneath the sphere was different from the grass outside the sphere's range.

With the doorway between realms open, the afterlife was already a different place. There was light where there shouldn't have been anything, creating shadows where, in my fifteen hundred years here, none had ever existed. But even so, the effect of the sphere was striking.

Curious, I dropped the sphere lower to the ground, and my breath lodged in my chest as grass—earth—existence—vanished. Then the void began to spread, leaching deeper into the afterlife.

It was as though the energy of the sphere had eaten right through the makeup of this plane. I soon found myself kneeling in the middle of nothing, a dark emptiness that held none of the beauty I'd come to appreciate. The nothingness emphasized how fictional a construct the afterlife truly was. It was a waiting place, a crossing point to a realm far vaster and more final than this one, designed to offer a certain comfort and familiarity as the souls of the recently dead transitioned from one state of being to another.

I would have sworn the afterlife, as an extension of Death, stood apart from the magic of the mortal plane, but this little device stuck to my hand had proved me wrong.

The hunters intended to wipe out the magic that kept the earth running, but a side effect would be destroying the comfort Death offered them. Without any regard for the needs of their fellow mortals, they were stripping away kindness and warmth and trading it for an empty void.

With every passing moment, I expected Death to intervene. This attack on its domain would have more of an effect on its precious balance than my involvement ever would—but so far there had been no sense of the power that infused this place.

Anger spiked in my blood. If Death wouldn't step in, I would have to keep trying. I rose to my feet and clenched the sphere tightly in my fist so the spikes attached to my hand pressed deeper.

Drawing in a slow inhale—taking a moment to appreciate the irony of focusing on my breath when I'd always told Katerina not to waste time on such rituals—I tapped into my power.

It tickled the back of my neck, taunting me with its weakness compared to my usual strength, but I didn't care. Some was better than none, and I would make use of every drop.

Carefully, aware of how dangerous playing with Death's power might be for me, I wrapped it around the sphere, choking whatever energy it emitted. The hum from the device grew fainter. Still there, still leaking from my hand into the world around me, but a trickle now instead of a wave. But the more power I drew from the afterlife, the more my sense of self faded, like an ebb-and-flow of energy that left less behind with each swing. I tried to rein the power in, to find a balance between sacrificing myself and hampering the sphere, but every shift in favour of my soul caused more of the afterlife to disappear.

Until I figured out how the device worked, it would continue to gnaw at the magic of the mortal world and the one beyond. I'd promised Kat I would do whatever was in my power to slow them down, and despite what it might mean for me, I would hold to that promise.

A small gesture, not nearly enough to save the world, but I would never make it easy for Cartwright.

I just had to hope Kat made the most of whatever time I gave her before this little sphere consumed her magic along with everyone else's.

26

Katerina

IN THE END, Barrett gave me more than three hours.

By the time I blinked my eyes open, at least twelve had passed, and I couldn't bring myself to complain about it.

Aside from the throbbing in my fingers, the ache in my healing wrist, and the itchiness of my stitched forearm, I felt…

Honestly, I felt like absolute garbage, but at least my shivering had stopped and I was able to stand up without toppling over. Small wins.

I rounded the side of the couch and dragged myself into the kitchen, where everyone else sat around the table. At no point had their discussion woken me, but it had obviously been intense. Sketches of the hunters' building lay scattered across the tabletop, and I was reminded of a different day. A different emergency.

Would they ever end?

Would the seven of us—*eight*, I corrected myself, because Emrick would be with us again soon—ever sit in this room and talk about something that wasn't a total world-changing disaster?

Would Maera ever bake something for a positive reason and not to keep her hands busy while the world fell apart?

I liked to think so, but the dream seemed so far away that I had no idea what it would look like.

It would probably smell the same. Maera's panic baking was as incredible as her everyday baking, even if it tasted just a smidge like fear.

I pulled an empty chair out from the head of the table and sank into it. My right knee screamed at me as I bent my left, and I wondered how much damage that "doctor" had done to me that I wasn't aware of. "Where do we stand?"

"Rhys deserves an entire chocolate cake," Murisa said, smiling at the exhausted-looking redhead sitting beside her.

He offered a wan smile and a humble shrug in response. "I haven't Seen as much as I wanted, but at least it's something."

Poppy snorted. "*Something.* Yeah, right, that's all it is. Only the general idea of the headquarters' layout with a few inklings of what we'll face when we reach each section. Give yourself more credit, my dude."

"Between Rhys's visions and the blueprints Murisa was able to track down, we'll be able to create a solid battle plan," Barrett said.

Poppy grinned at me. "In other words, we have the makings of a decent strategy, and the knowledge that, no matter what plan we make, you'll ignore it and run in with your lightning bolts primed to get Emrick out of that cage."

Her smile vanished under a jaw-cracking yawn, and the contagion spread to everyone around the table. Only Maera and Barrett appeared to have any pep left in their step.

"Have any of you slept?" I asked. "Because either you get some rest or Poppy's right—I'll have no choice but to go in on my own."

Gavin scrubbed his hand over his face. "We did. We've taken turns for a few hours at a time. We're exhausted, yeah, but more than anything, we're done with this shit."

I didn't blame them. So was I. More than a little. "One more night and it will be over. I refuse to let it go on any longer than that."

Barrett cleared his throat. "I don't know if we'll be able to move as quickly as that."

I frowned. "What do you mean?"

He met my eye, and the smallest of smiles played on his lips. "Remember when we were hunting down those witches of Mikhail's, and I accused you of rushing in without thinking?"

"Mmhmm." I remembered, all right. Both of us had said a lot of things that night. I stood by them—as I'm sure he did—but it hadn't been the finest moment of our turbulent relationship.

"This is me preventing you from making the same mistake. You said yourself we need to come up with a plan that takes this faction on as a whole, not in parts. It's the only way we'll get Emrick out and stop them without sacrificing our entire team before we reach him. Our best chance is to gather our allies, but it will take time for everyone to get here."

I gritted my teeth. He was right. For everything that had changed between us, I still hated when he was right.

"You said you would work on that while I was sleeping. Have you had any success? Now that we know the hunters' goal is to *eliminate all magic*, you'd think more than one group might be willing to stand with us." The looks the others exchanged made my stomach wibble. "You've got to be shitting me. Are we really that hard up?" Anger sizzled like acid at the back of my throat. "Believe me when I say that after we crush these *ants*, there will be a reckoning for all the people who refused to stand their ground."

Murisa rested her fingers on the table. "Not everyone is made to fight, Kat."

I understood what she was saying—that I couldn't let my position in the magical community be the bar by which I measured everyone else. And I wouldn't. No one else had sworn the oath I had to uphold the tenuous balance of this world, that was all on me. But.

"Everyone has a responsibility to take what strides they can to do what's right, in whatever small ways they can. All I'm getting is excuses. I don't intend to forget that."

Maybe it was the blood loss and grief talking more than my anger, but I was too exhausted, afraid, and frustrated to allow for leniency.

For centuries I had helped these people, and yet the second I asked for their help in return, they had somewhere else to be.

Fine. As always, I would take care of the world myself.

Barrett shook his head. "It's not great, but it's not as bad as all that. More than one group didn't believe us. They don't understand how anyone could do something as huge as get rid of all magic. If I hadn't seen Emrick for myself, I'd probably agree with them."

Murisa nodded. "Without evidence to prove it, it's a pretty wild accusation."

I gritted my teeth. "Who *did* believe us?"

Gavin pulled a sheet of paper towards him. "That witch from Rune the Day, Ben, he confirmed he'll have a few healers ready to join us. Maybe a half-dozen. When we explained what the hunters are up to, he promised to reach out to some of his more… battle-minded friends. We haven't heard word on numbers yet."

Barrett grunted. "No surprise, no word from Kelly. No answer when I called, and her voicemail's full. She probably left the city."

My shoulders sagged. "She and her coven would have been more trouble than they were worth. Probably." I looked at Poppy. "Have you called your mother?"

"I have. She's ready and waiting to approve our plan whenever we have one to share."

We exchanged an eyeroll, then I turned to Murisa. "Did you contact the main hunters?" When she nodded and looked at Barrett, I followed her gaze.

He grimaced. "I don't know how much help they'll be. I spoke with one of their captains, Ro Weaver. We've known each other a long time, so I trust them not to take our conversation back to Cartwright, but that's about as much faith as I have. Weaver claims the actual organization has no knowledge of Cartwright going rogue. That if what I told them is true, she'd be in breach of every treaty and agreement the hunters have made with the magical community in the past two hundred years. They're aware that acting against those agreements would be a declaration of war."

So far all that sounded good. "But?"

"But Cartwright is a general. The head of Ontario's hunters. She has the respect of her peers and no small amount of influence. Weaver would be hard-pressed to convince any of the other higher-ups that Cartwright would make such a move. And if they share their concerns and word gets back to her…"

"She'll use it as another blow against us and any allies we've mustered."

He nodded, and I almost shoved my hand through my hair before I remembered the thick bandage around my missing fingers.

"It's not a lost cause, though," he continued. "Weaver has a few people they can reach out to—others who've noticed something going on who might be willing to step outside the bounds of protocol if it means preventing a greater conflict. If they can get enough people working with them, they might be able to convince the local lieutenants to take a stand."

"Think they'll rally in time to help us?"

He kept his gaze locked on mine. "It would be wise not to count on it. Not for the frontal assault anyway. Clean-up will probably be another story."

I tapped my fingers on the table. "How long are we giving Ben to get back to us?"

Barrett shrugged. "It's still early. Giving allowances for people who actually use the midnight hours to sleep, I'd suggest we wait until midday before we solidify any plans. We can take those few hours to wrestle some ideas into place." His gaze flicked to Rhys. "Maybe get another vision or two to help us navigate."

Hours. He wanted us to wait *hours* while the man I loved was trapped with the enemy? While the hunters began the process of draining magic from the world?

"Emrick is in that building being forced to act as a doorstop. I'm not about to sit around here and wait for those sons of bitches to wring him dry. We need to work with what we have and leave room for anyone who feels like saving the goddamned world to join us." I rested my injured hand over the other. "Break down what we're working with."

Poppy pushed a sheet of paper towards me. "We have an arsenal of mechanicals and potions, courtesy of Murisa and me, which covers surveillance, distraction, and mayhem." She flashed me a wicked grin. "All the things you know I'm good at."

I glowered at the map of the hunters' building. It appeared to be a warehouse attached to a three-storey office building. There were too many exits across both sections of the place, and we were seven people.

"We also have weapons," Barrett said, spinning another sheet of paper to show me the list of everything we had. "Muroppy has created a range that'll cover us under most circumstances. Enchanted blades, guns, bullets."

Murisa's eyes shone. "Even a little hand crossbow."

I had no idea where we kept any of these weapons and

understood that I never wanted to step foot in the guestroom Barrett and Gavin kept at my house. Did they even have beds, or did they throw pillows and a blanket on top of trunks of knives?

Gavin summoned a fireball into his hand. "We have you and me. After all my training, I think I'll hold up well in a fight."

"I have no doubt of it," I said with a smile. Although he'd done all the work, Gavin's progress was one of my greatest achievements. "But I don't know that I want you on the front lines."

His brow furrowed, and he squeezed his hand around the flames to put them out. "What do you mean? I throw fire, Kat. Use me."

"You're also one of the only people around this table who knows how to patch us up when we go down. We'll have Ben and his healers, but they're not fighters. You know both. That makes you valuable."

Barrett rubbed the top of his head. His hair had grown in again since Adrian's death, still short, but long enough for his fingers to sink into the tight curls. "He is, but considering what we're about to walk into?" He dragged his hand down his face and scrubbed his chin. "I don't think we have the luxury of 'leave no man behind.' If we try to patch as we go, we risk losing everyone. Blunt force is our best option, and he's one of our heaviest hitters."

"Until we lose our magic," I reminded him.

As I looked around the table, I realized the process had already begun. What I'd taken as straight exhaustion was a symptom of a more terrifying underlying condition. Which explained why Maera and Barrett appeared less affected. We hadn't even started and already we were running out of time.

Gavin's jaw tightened with determination. "I'll fight until I have nothing left to throw. After that, we'll see what happens."

I didn't like it, but I'd lost the argument. At least I could be assured he'd be armed to the teeth with Muroppy's inventions. Even if the enchantments on the knives failed, they'd still be sharp.

"What about me?" Rhys asked.

I turned to him, and in the set of his jaw and the fire burning in his eyes, I accepted there would be no talking him down. But there was no way in hell I'd let him walk into that warehouse. I'd tie him to a chair and arm Maera with Murisa's hand crossbow before I let it happen.

"You'll be on the phone with us," Barrett said, cutting in before I could. Rhys's eyes narrowed, but Barrett shook his head. "No argument. Your physical eyes are only so useful to us once we go in. We need whatever your second sight can offer. We'll set you up to be in constant contact so you can help us navigate our way to Emrick. If we're able to reduce conflict until we take charge of the anti-magic wards Muroppy described, we might stand a chance in there."

Rhys's shoulders slumped, but he nodded. "All right. I'll do what I can. From what I've Seen, which isn't much yet, you'll have a few allies showing up. They'll probably be more useful in there than me."

I slid my hand across the table towards him. "By the sounds of it, the only reason I'm sitting here right now is because you walked Barrett and Gavin through that building. If you do even half that much, at least a few of us will walk free."

Rhys forced a smile, and Maera put her arm around her son's shoulders.

I scanned the papers in front of me again, taking a mental note of our resources, rushing to fit everything together. But everywhere I looked, the gaps were too big. We would be spread too thin, and our resources would run out too quickly.

Especially with all those exits.

I kept coming back to that because, as far as I was concerned, it was our greatest weakness. If we could corral everyone into a single room, Gavin and I could set them all on fire and we would be done with it. Let the hunters try to move faster than an inferno.

But with all those doors, too many could escape, and our lives, while they lasted, would devolve into nothing more than a fatal game of Whack-a-Mole.

"It's not enough," I said.

"We'll have the witches," Poppy reminded me. "Hera says she'll make sure we have at least a dozen from the Hydrangea Circle to back us up."

I snorted a laugh. "A whole twelve? My, she's generous. What happened to the rest of her coven? Sudden case of flu?"

Poppy pinched the bridge of her nose. "Given enough time, we'd probably get the whole fifty, but the timeline is moving faster than we anticipated. But she did say that, given the nature of the threat, she'd reach out to a few other coven leaders. She'll probably net us a few more covens as reinforcements."

I rolled my neck until it popped. "Okay, assuming Ben and Hera don't come through, we'll be twenty against… a hundred?"

"Weaver is worried it might be more than that," Barrett admitted. "It'll depend on how many come in from out of province."

"Get eyes on the airport," I said. "If your friend won't commit to fighting, at least they can help us control the battle-field. I need hard numbers. I need to know what defences they might have at hand. With that information, we'll be in a better position to face them."

Barrett pulled out his phone, and while he sent off a text message to his contact, I turned to Murisa. "With whatever time we have before we march, I want you enchanting things. Give me more of those bugs or birds or a toaster if you have to.

I want our agents crawling everywhere in that building until it's time to detonate them."

She nodded and started making notes, but a furrow formed between her eyebrows. "The anti-magic ward might wipe them out before they can cause much damage. We don't know how many of those warding devices they have."

"That's why we'll swarm them. Get them in the walls. The ceiling. I want any survivors of this attack to wake up screaming at the thought of bugs crawling over them for the rest of their lives."

"You got it. I also have another little surprise planned." The sly gleam that came into her eyes reinforced how perfect she and Poppy were together. Watch out world if they made it through this fight.

I turned to Rhys. "You have another job between visions. I need you on research. I want a better view of every exit we're dealing with. Every access road, every way they might escape or bring reinforcements in." I slid the blueprints towards him. "Between your visions and anything else you find, I need you to make this sketch as detailed as you can get it."

"On it."

"Gavin, I want you and Barrett practicing. I want you so comfortable with your power that whatever they throw at you, you don't flinch. Don't push yourself too hard and make sure you get some rest, but we might only have so much time before our power wanes, so we need to be prepared to go in blazing."

He nodded, and steam rose from his closed fists. I hoped he understood I meant practicing in the gym downstairs. Near a bucket of water.

"Maera, you're on food."

She chuckled. "Of course. I've already got the chicken breasts marinating."

Poppy crossed her arms and leaned back in her chair. "All right, kitty Kat, you've given everyone else their marching orders. What about me?"

I allowed the faintest of smiles to tease my lips, ready to savour her reaction. "You and I are off to the cemetery."

27

Katerina

As I PACKED up to leave, Murisa pulled me aside. She watched Poppy gather her things and waited until the necromancer was out of earshot before she heaved a breath.

"This is all a pile of flaming garbage, isn't it?" she said.

"To put it in the nicest possible way."

She tapped her hands on the armrests of her wheelchair, then clasped her fingers in her lap, then splayed them out across her thighs. I didn't want to rush her, but if we wanted to have enough time in the cemetery, we had to get moving. We didn't have the benefit of the full moon working for us tonight, so Poppy would need all the advantages she could get.

I looked over my shoulder to see the witch pacing back and forth along the side of the car. Her nerves would be a joy to deal with on the drive.

"Okay," Murisa said, having found her words. "I know Poppy doesn't want me to know what she's doing with you, and that's fine. We'll deal with that later. But I'm not an idiot. I know what her skillset is, and I know how powerful she is. You want her to raise an army, and I can help make that army more functional."

She reached into the bag slung over the back of her chair and pulled out a metal device the length of her thumb. "I can feel the drain on my magic already, and it's only going to get worse. Poppy will be in the thick of it with you, so her concentration will be split. Once the drain gets bad enough, any control she has over her undead will disappear. This will help her hang on."

I accepted it and took a closer look, but all it looked like was a rounded metal bar. It had a hole at the top that someone could slide a chain through if they wanted to wear it, but other-wise, it was unremarkable.

Murisa grinned. "The best weapons don't look like much. Alodie taught us that with her stones. Why waste effort on appearance when efficacy matters so much more? Poppy can bind her spell to this. It's like a receiver. It'll accept the spell and hold it in stasis, so as long as Pop has it on her, she won't have to focus on keeping the spell active."

My eyebrows climbed. "Murisa, this is genius."

She flushed, and her smile widened—before it faltered.

"I love her, Kat. I'll do anything to help her survive this. If you could… maybe reassure her that I won't abandon her for playing with a bunch of corpses, I'd really appreciate it."

"You don't think she'd believe you?"

"I think she'd worry I was being nice. She won't have that problem with you."

A laugh burst out of me before I could stop it, and I took Murisa's hand. "I'll do what I can."

Murisa sat up straighter and reached behind her again. "I almost forgot. I wanted to show you these before you left. Before I gave them to Gavin. In case, you know, you didn't want me to give them to him or something."

She pulled out a pair of heavy leather gloves and handed them to me. I ran them through my fingers, taking in the craftsmanship, which, I had to admit, wasn't amazing. The seams were uneven, and the finger holes were slanted, as though someone had taken a pair of scissors and hacked away without caring. But what grabbed my attention were the runes etched into the leather—the same runes that covered mine, glinting with the same silverish compound that was now causing us so much trouble.

Murisa stroked the leather. "I thought these might help him. But I didn't know how you'd feel about it considering their origin. And considering you've lost yours."

The back of my throat burned, and I blinked away my

tears. Murisa squeezed my hand. "I'm sorry, Kat. I'll destroy them. I just thought—"

"No. That's not it. They're perfect, and they'll help Gavin." I cleared my throat and sucked in a breath. "You took me by surprise, that's all. This is the first new pair of gloves to be made since… well."

In Palonia, getting your gloves had been a mark of pride. It meant you were growing up, coming into your power. For most people, it meant they were about to step into the world of magical hunts and expeditions. For me, my gloves had held a tinge of shame because they'd never served the purpose they'd been built for.

My pair was somewhere in the hunters' headquarters, stolen from me by a bunch of magic-hating assholes who were no doubt trying to destroy them. Or maybe pull out more of their secrets. It pained me not to have them. A small part of me was more than a little jealous that Gavin would enjoy their benefits while I was without them. But he'd be a stronger fighter armed with these not-quite-beauties, and he'd more than earned them.

I returned the gloves to Murisa and leaned in to kiss her cheek. "You're a miracle, Ris, you really are. Thank you for being here."

Her flush deepened, and she threw her arms around my neck. "We're going to win, Kat. I know it feels like a question mark right now, but in my gut, I know it."

"Kitty Kat, can we get a fucking move on?" Poppy shouted from outside.

Murisa laughed and pushed me away. "You better get going. I should get back to work anyway. I have a lot to do to make my… idea happen."

The way she said it, I pictured the word *idea* with a capital letter, and by the look in her eye, whatever this Idea was, it would be memorable.

I left her to it and headed outside. We had some corpses to raise.

Five years ago, I'd warned Poppy that if I ever caught her using her necromancy for dark purposes again, it would be her last act in this life.

A few months ago, I'd caught her attempting to raise an undead bodyguard along with her decomposing cat familiar. At that time, I'd been too much in need of her help and too concerned over the transition of her occult shop into an overly pink tearoom to threaten her beyond a few pointed stares.

Now, I was actively encouraging her to cross every boundary and break every rule I'd set, and she was refusing to help me.

We stood in the middle of the cemetery by the grave of a recently deceased man by the name of Graham Reed. I'd hoped by now he would be recently undeceased, but Poppy just stood there, staring at the randomly selected tombstone.

"I don't know how comfortable I am with this, kitty Kat. Don't get me wrong, I understand the need, it's just…"

She rolled her lips between her teeth and tapped her fingers with their long, bright-orange talons against her hips.

"Spit it out, Pop."

"I don't want Murisa to think bad of me, you know?" In the darkness of the cemetery, with only a few lampposts stretched at intervals down the empty stretch of lane, it was impossible to be certain, but I was pretty sure Poppy was blushing. "She's never known me as a necromancer, and I'm worried it would go against her moral code."

Her concerns were such an echo of Murisa's, I had to tamp down a smile.

"You're not killing anyone to raise them, and when we're done, you can return them to their graves and let them sleep in peace."

I couldn't believe we were having this conversation. Of all the people whose arm I imagined having to twist to use their power, Poppy would have been at the bottom of the list.

She shifted on her feet. "I know. And I know you think I'm overreacting, but I don't want to go down this path again. When I was fighting for my last coven, I thought I was in the right. I was doing what was necessary, whatever the consequences. It was a dark place, and I was not a nice person."

"If that were true, I wouldn't have spared you. Even at the height of your villainy, you were quite charming."

That earned me a chuckle, but those orange nails still flashed with every tap.

"More than that, your motives were solid. Usually. That example of horrible judgement aside. You went into necromancy because your parents pushed you down that road, but you pulled yourself out before ambition overcame sense. And considering everything, I don't think you'll let yourself go that far again."

"Are you sure there's no other way?"

I huffed and leaned against a tree. "Probably. We could threaten Orry to stand with us. We could see if any other vampire nest wants to come out of isolation and take some revenge on the vampire hunters—and hope they don't go off script. We could bribe your mother with my indentured servitude to force the most reluctant covens to join the fight. I'm reaching at all the straws we have, Poppy. The hunters have the big guns here, while we're coming in with water pistols. They can block our magic, and once the drain on our power picks up, we'll be at even more of a disadvantage."

She winced and nodded. "It's already getting bad. It's like the edge of a migraine waiting to kick in, isn't it? How long do you think it'll take?"

"If we're lucky, we'll have another few days, but I don't want to test it. That's why we need whatever we can throw at them, be it fireballs or corpses. Or corpses on fire." I set my hand on her shoulder and forced her to look at me. "I won't let you stray too far, Poppy. I promise you. I care about you too much to let you follow the dark road. This one is more of a grey. It's one I've walked most of my life, and it's as familiar to me as the scars on my hand."

She arched an eyebrow. "How are those missing fingers treating you? You familiar with them yet?"

I smirked. "Touché."

"What happens if my power drops? I'll lose control over them, and they'll be no more effective than speed bumps. Could be useful to stop anyone from running away, I guess."

I pulled Murisa's metal device out of my pocket and set it in Poppy's hand. "Your beautiful partner thought of that."

Poppy's eyes widened. "You mean—"

"She knows where we are and why, Pop. She had this ready to go. She says you can bind your spell to this with an enchantment of your own. It probably won't survive any massive anti-magic surge, but it should give you some extra time to get out of range if your magic fails."

A tear slid down her cheek. "She wasn't disgusted, was she? Horrified? Angry?"

I wanted to pull her in for a hug, but I worried if I did, we'd both lose ourselves to sobs. "She was determined to help you however she could. She loves you, Poppy. As long as you stay on the right side of the fight, even if that means chatting up a few dead people when the situation calls for it, she's not going anywhere."

Her spine firmed, and she stared out once more over the cemetery. "All right, then, kitty Kat. Let's get this party started."

28

Emrick

I HAD JUST managed to slip my fingernail through the crack of the sphere when footsteps echoed across the stone floor. The unexpectedness of the noise after so many hours' silence made me jump, and I lost the precious progress I'd made.

Disappointment and frustration ate at me, and I looked up with a snarl. My mood wasn't helped by the sight of Cartwright's calm, level stare—and was made worse by the hint of amusement dancing across her lips, as though she knew what I'd been doing and how little success I'd made.

The gauze was still on her face, but she'd swapped the surgical scrubs for another pantsuit ensemble. There was no sign of embarrassment or anger about how her last visit to this room had gone or the hunters she'd lost. At some point, a group had come in to clear away the bodies, but the scorch marks remained on the floor as a waving flag of her failure to protect her people.

Her lack of concern made me think even less of her, which I hadn't thought possible.

"How are you feeling?" she asked when she stopped a few metres away from my cage. Two of her people remained by the door, their expressions haggard but stoic.

"Fuck you."

"At least you still have your energy. Is it draining you at all, keeping the doorway open?"

I didn't answer. She didn't need to know how exhausted I was. Every passing hour added more weight to my limbs. The pulls from both the cage and the afterlife had increased, tearing me at the seams. I felt like I was a few hours away from being ripped in two. What would happen then? Would part of my soul be stuck here while the other half was caught in the afterlife? If that was my fate, I doubted my pieces would ever find their way back to each other. I would be lost to Katerina, but where would that leave me in terms of my debt with Death?

Somehow, I didn't think it would approve of having its servant ripped asunder, but would it bother to put me back together or simply make use of what was left?

I would become the wraith I'd always feared I would, but the world... the world would be safe.

The thought hit me like a punch to the gut, and I squeezed

my free hand into a tight fist.

I could do it. I could let myself go and protect the world. Lose Kat, lose myself, and crush Cartwright's plans.

She might not know such a move was possible, but if she did, she was banking on me not taking the leap. Her people had watched me and Kat long enough to believe my love for her would overshadow every other moral principle, and so far I'd proved them right.

But how long could I let this go on?

If they succeeded, billions would die. With our bond blocked, so would Kat.

If I sacrificed myself now, while she was mortal, she would be without me for decades but could embrace her death in the end.

It was the right choice. The noble choice. But I wasn't ready to make it. Not yet.

I thought of Kat as I'd last seen her. Her desire to stay with me and fight to the end—an end that would have come quickly if Barrett and Gavin hadn't dragged her away. As painful as it had been to watch, it served as an important reminder that my brave, protective warrior was a survivor.

The knowledge strengthened me, and I stared back at Cartwright. "What do you want?"

"With you? Nothing. I told you, you've served your purpose. I'm simply here to monitor the progress of our device."

She pulled something out of her pocket. The woman seemed to be riddled with technological gadgets for every occasion. Was that why she wore such ugly clothing? Because at least it came with pockets?

I wished Kat were here for me to ask. She would have laughed.

Cartwright held the gadget in front of her, and I watched the readings on the dial jump as a high-pitched ringing rattled my ears.

When the general looked over her shoulder, one of her people approached, clipboard in hand. She peered around the general to get a look at the gadget, then jotted down a few notes. By their faces, they were happy with whatever they saw, which made me grit my teeth all the harder. Anything that satisfied them was something I needed to prevent.

As soon as she was gone, I would go back to prying the damned sphere apart. It had to have a vulnerability somewhere.

"I want someone stationed in this room," Cartwright ordered. "Regular readings every hour. Report to me immediately if you see any significant changes."

"Yes, General."

"And fix these doors. I want this room closed down, no one in or out except by my order. If that bitch comes to free her lover, destroy her. I will not allow our plans to fail. Not when we're so close to getting everything we've worked for."

"Destroying the world?" I asked.

She turned her full-watt smile on me, and it was full of ice. "Oh, Emrick, you are naive. You magicals all think the world revolves around you, but you have no idea what exists when you're gone. I've heard all the arguments, but to me it stinks of propaganda. A desperation to be needed and an excuse to let you keep breathing when the world would be a kinder, calmer, better place without you. As everyone will soon come to see."

She turned without another word and strode towards the doors, one of her people trotting along behind her while the other remained where they were, watching me with such hatred I felt the urge to flip him off.

But I didn't waste my time. Instead, I turned my back on him and set to work digging my fingernail into the gap again. If destroying this sphere was the best way to help Kat, then damned if I was going to give up.

At the back of my mind, though, that nagging thought refused to go away.

With me out of the picture, the world would be safe. Kat would be pissed, but she'd be alive to be pissed.

I wouldn't make any move just yet, not while the chance remained that I could find another way to stop them—or that Kat might—but I tucked the idea away. At least we had a backup plan. The plan would cost my life, but, to save her, it was a cost I had always been ready to pay.

29

Katerina

BARRETT'S SUV CLOSED in on the hunters' headquarters.

The first time I'd come here, I'd been too out of it to appreciate how massive the building was. On our flight from it, I hadn't bothered to look back. Now that we were here and prepared to storm the fortress, I was extra glad I'd encouraged Poppy to summon her little army.

Or not so little.

Twenty corpses at various stages of decomposition were currently tucked into the rented moving van driving behind the SUV. I didn't want to think about the stench currently filling the vehicle and hoped Poppy had a spell for cleaning it before she returned it or else goodbye security deposit, hello police investigation.

Barrett pulled over, and I took a moment to breathe before I opened the door. We had our plan. It wasn't a great one, but if I'd learned anything over the past couple months, we could plan for anything and the worst would still happen. Flexibility was a better strategy, and I was prepared to pivot.

"Everyone ready?" I asked.

The only answer I received was for Barrett and Gavin to climb out of the car. Gavin assisted Murisa into her wheelchair, and we waited for Poppy to open the truck and order her army to follow us.

As she approached us, a small creature stalked by her side, and, not for the first time tonight, I couldn't stop staring at Cuddles.

Not just Poppy's undead cat, but Battle Cuddles.

Murisa's Idea had earned its capital letter. She'd kitted him out in a little enchanted metal helmet and breastplate, and gauntlets covered his front paws, complete with metallic claws. His hindquarters were bare, leaving his kinked tail to wave free, but his essentials were protected. She'd walked us through the rest of the defences built into the armour—if he got close enough to rub against someone's leg, he'd release tiny spikes coated with a sleeping potion.

Not easily killed, quick, impervious to most magics… I might be able to sling fire and lightning, but I'd argue Cuddles vastly outpowered me.

More vehicles pulled in behind us—a few sedans, but mostly vans packed with people. At the prickle of magic emanating from the vehicles, I summoned my fire, hating the faint delay when I channelled it, but held it steady until I knew what we were dealing with.

Hera stepped out of the first car, and I let my magic go. After she spotted us, she raised her hand, and the rest of her witches spilled into the night. More than the twelve she'd said would join her. I stopped counting at twenty-four and still more piled out of the vehicles that had followed them. There had to be over a hundred witches by the time they circled us, and I stared at Hera, unable to ask.

"No one comes for our magic without us standing in their way," she said, her tone as cold as it ever was. "We bring the best Ontario has to offer. Direct us, and we'll do everything within our power to crush these hunters." She grimaced. "While any power remains."

Arnold came to stand at her side, and I pretended not to notice the way she slipped her fingers between his and clutched them tightly. She was as afraid as the rest of us, even if she was working hard not to show it. Our magic was on the line. Our *power*. Hera would still be a rich and influential woman without her magic—if the drain didn't kill her—but she would be diminished. Not a future a woman such as her would be comfortable contemplating.

Before I could give any orders, more movement caught my attention from the shadows along the edge of the parking lot. I reached into my satchel for a potion vial, not wanting to reveal my fire in case the shadows were mundane. But when they stepped into the light, I recognized one of the men. Barely, considering this time he was wearing clothes, but I got there. The alpha shifter of Orillia—the city, not the vampire queen.

"Terry?"

He bowed his head in acknowledgement. "Orillia reached out. She explained why she's not able to be here herself, and although I think she would show more strength by fighting for the future of her people rather than her own throne, I did agree that someone from our city needed to help you make a stand against these fuckers. So the Orillia shifters come to offer their support."

My throat tightened, and I blinked away my shock. We had allies. We had an *army*. Within the past five minutes, we'd gone from being a rag-tag group of five, plus corpses, to a group whose numbers rivalled the hunters within.

For the first time since we'd set out from Kensington Market, I believed we stood a chance of walking out of this alive.

I cleared my throat and scanned the largest group I'd ever had to command. At the height of my power, I'd had Emrick and Adrian to fight with me. Now, when my power was on the brink of going out, Emrick was trapped in this building and Adrian was gone. But it didn't all rest on my shoulders anymore. Not for tonight, anyway. Tonight, until the last of our magic faded, we would be a colossal force.

I just wished we had a better idea of how much time we had.

Already I felt the pull in my chest, the sensation of my magic leaking out through my pores, dripping onto the concrete with every step forward. And if I was losing the power set so deeply into my flesh and blood for so many hundreds of years, I could only imagine the discomfort the witches and shifters must be in.

Still, they were here, and we would make the most of them.

With all our players on the board, the only remaining step was to roll the dice.

I looked at Barrett and found him staring into the middle distance, his fingers to his ear. The seconds ticked on before he nodded his head towards the shadows at the back of the building. "Rhys says we should move now."

"Right." I looked to Terry. "Guard the perimeter. There are at least a dozen exits around this building, and I don't want anyone escaping."

Terry nodded, and the shifters melted into the shadows, as good as gone.

I turned to the witches. "When we go inside, I want everyone splitting up. Emrick is in the basement, so that's where I'm headed, but this is a big building spread out across three storeys. We need every room cleared, every hunter… dealt with." I didn't much care how they did it.

Arnold flexed his jaw. "We'll see to it, sorceress."

To my surprise, he didn't sling the title as an insult.

This was it. We were making our stand. By the end of the night, we would know whether magic prevailed or if the end of the world was in sight.

I returned my attention to Barrett, and he nodded his head towards a door half-hidden in the corner of the attached warehouse. "Rhys says this way."

That was all the direction I needed. The sketch Rhys and Murisa had filled in together was tucked into Barrett's waistband, but while we had Rhys on the phone sharing his visions as they came, I would trust the live version.

We didn't speak as we crossed the parking lot. Tucked at the back of the building as we were, and as late at night as it was, there were few other cars to indicate how many people waited inside. Based on what Rhys had shared with us, we weren't looking at small numbers, but they seemed to be spread out through the main building. With luck, we'd find a skeleton crew guarding the doors of the warehouse and have a solid place to set up our base of operations before we pressed deeper into the headquarters.

Barrett held up a hand to stop us a few metres from the

doors, then crept forward on his own. Once he got into position on one side, Gavin followed and crouched on the other, holding a gun loaded with sleeping potion bullets. His new gloves hugged his arms to the elbow and left his fingers bare. They looked as natural on him as they ever had on any of Palonia's hunters.

Barrett pushed one door open. Dim light spilled into the shadows, but no sound greeted us. If anyone was inside, they were ready for us.

My heart raced, and I pulled a blanket of low flames over my hands. Once we entered this building, there was no leaving it. Not until we freed Emrick.

I met Barrett's eye and nodded, and he made his way inside, with Gavin close behind. The two men had insisted on taking the lead. Nothing I'd said had deterred them. And although I longed to be the one to head the charge, I appreciated the wisdom of Barrett's choice. He was trained in this sort of advance. I had more experience in going after dragons and vampires, but he was the pro at mundane warfare. So I would trust him to lead his troops, even if that included him partnering with a man who, until three months ago, had chosen a career of patching people up instead of tearing them apart.

I counted my breaths as we hunkered in the darkness. At my side, Muroppy clung to each other. Cuddles had leapt onto Murisa's lap and was gnawing on his metal claws, trying to remove them without success.

After what felt like an age, a grunt echoed from inside. I leaned forward, ready to run, but a few moments later, Gavin was backing towards the doorway, dragging a man under the armpits. He dropped him in a heap next to the door and gestured for the rest of us to follow.

One guard dealt with.

Gavin fell in beside me, and we headed in. Poppy and Murisa followed behind me. Per our plan, Poppy and Cuddles would accompany me, Barrett, and Gavin to search for Emrick, while Murisa remained here in the warehouse. No one relished the idea of leaving her behind, but the logic was sound. We needed someone able to get out and update Barrett's contact within the hunters if everything went badly. We'd also need her mechanicals to spread the word of what the hunters had done if we failed, and no one else knew how to control them.

We'd discussed the wisdom of sending out the warning in advance, but in the end we'd agreed to hold off until all hope was lost. Avoiding mass panic among the magicals was as much a priority as stopping the hunters.

As soon as we were inside, Murisa passed around tiny potion vials for everyone to sip from, then opened her satchel and released her creations. Mechanicals of all kinds scurried and skittered and flew throughout the warehouse, swooping into the rafters and disappearing into the walls. Some would be our eyes farther inside the building; others were primed to release the potions they carried at opportune moments. As soon as they were gone, Murisa pulled a little keyboard from her bag, set it in her lap, and began typing.

Her words echoed in my head as her potion settled in my blood. The sensation was bizarre.

Warehouse. Southwestern corner of the building. Empty.

As long as her mechanicals relayed their findings to her, she would be able to type out their updates and send them to us no matter where we were in the building, all while she stayed safe as houses next to the exit. As well as being a perfect invisible surveillance system, they would target the security cameras and wipe them out, effectively blocking us from view everywhere we needed to go.

Another familiar face stepped through the door, and I heaved a breath of relief. Ben had arrived, wheeling a suitcase behind him I could only imagine was filled with healing supplies. Eight other witches entered behind him.

"We're not here to fight," he reminded me in a low voice.

I nodded and pointed at Murisa. "You can stay here with her. She'll direct you where you're needed." I swallowed hard. "But if anyone comes for her, do whatever you can to protect her. Please. I'll owe you."

He narrowed his eyes, then nodded.

Poppy pressed a kiss to Murisa's mouth and brushed her

fingers along her cheek. In quiet voices that didn't carry throughout the room, they murmured their words of encouragement. As I watched them, a steely resolve formed in my heart that Poppy would make her way back here. No matter what, the two of them would get out.

As I made to walk away, Murisa caught my arm and pressed another mechanical into my hand. This one was shaped like a ladybug, and the head was a button.

She met my eye. "A nuclear option."

She released my arm with no further explanation, but those words gave me another massive boost of confidence. Whatever the hunters thought they could get away with, we had more than one surprise ready.

Cuddles hopped off Murisa's lap and wandered towards the door, but Poppy snatched him up before he could pass through it. His feline single-mindedness and refusal to follow basic instructions made me wonder how helpful he would be on this mission, but I wasn't about to suggest the witches leave him behind. He was too damned cute in his armour to abandon.

While Poppy got him settled in her arms, Barrett, Gavin, and I did a quick weapons check. Barrett was armed to the eyeballs with multiple guns holstered at his hips, ankle, and across his chest. Enchanted knives were sheathed at his hips and around each thigh, and he'd even agreed to carry a small pouch of potions—a first in as long as I'd known him. The anti-magic wards would prevent them from doing much, but we doubted every hunter would be so protected.

Gavin was similarly armed, although, on my request, he'd swapped out a few of the knives for some of Poppy's healing salves. We wouldn't have time to stop, but if the opportunity arose to get some of our people back on their feet as we went, we had to take it.

I'd settled for two knives. With Barrett and Gavin beside me, I didn't see the point of carrying guns of my own—and I hated them. But the knives would serve me well if my magic failed, and I would enjoy the up-close-and-personal nature of gutting Cartwright before the night was over.

As ready as we could be, I gestured to Barrett, and he started towards the doors that would take us into the main building. Gavin walked with him, while Poppy and I followed.

The rest of the witches stuck with us for now, but before long we would split up to spread across the headquarters. My top priority was getting to Emrick, but I wasn't so selfish as to think it was the only goal. We had to take out as many hunters on the fringes of the building as possible before they sounded the alarm. Once our presence was known, all hell would break loose.

As for the corpses, Rhys and Poppy had worked together to figure out how best to use them—which was to ditch them as quickly as possible. The headquarters was three storeys, with twelve exits excluding those in the warehouse. The lab was on the top floor, office space was on the first two floors, and Emrick was tucked away somewhere in the basement. The corpses would spread out across the main floor, clogging the exits. Their presence would give us away as soon as they were spotted, but we figured the jig would be up as soon as the cameras went out anyway. At least the corpses might deter some of the hunters from trying to flee.

It would have been nice if we could have relied on the dead to fight for us, but hopefully they would scare a few people into cardiac arrest.

Barrett and Gavin reached the doors and waited until the rest of us moved into position on either side of them.

Fire licked up my arms, and I needed more effort to hold it back than to let it loose. Anger drove me, fueled me, made me imagine how satisfying it would be to lash out and burn the building to the ground.

But I couldn't take the risk that Emrick would be caught in his cage. Or thrown into the afterlife, unable to come back, with that sphere attached to his hand for the device to continue its work long after Cartwright and her disciples were dead.

So I restrained myself, for which I deserved a medal. If we survived.

Barrett reached for the door, and I breathed in the final silence of the night.

He nudged the door open, and the peace was crushed by a hail of bullets as the hunters welcomed us to their party.

As I readied my defences, I prayed I had enough rage to carry me until the last hunter fell.

30

Katerina

BARRETT WAS READY to return fire as Gavin came in low and blasted them with a fireball so large sweat burst from my pores.

The hunters' screams filled my ears, and I closed myself to the sound. I couldn't afford to let guilt or compassion prevent me from saving the man who had been my everything for a thousand years.

Or, you know, stopping these people from sucking the life out of the world.

I hated killing them, but they'd chosen their side. The consequences had to be theirs as well.

As soon as the screams fell silent, the rest of us followed Gavin and Barrett into the smoke-filled hallway. The walls still burned, and I reversed my heat to send frost over the flames. When the fire went out, I took a moment to assess the damage. Four hunters lay dead on the floor, obstructing our way forward, while the corridor to the left was open towards the exit at the other end. While Barrett and Gavin dealt with shifting the charred masses out of the way, Hera sent half the witches to clear the other hallway and the second storey. Arnold would lead that half of our team, and I looked away as husband and wife kissed each other goodbye.

Poppy stepped forward, and my heart clenched as I watched Arnold wrap his arms around her. For all the issues that existed between parents and daughter, it was clear Arnold adored her. I hoped they'd have a chance to spend more time together once we finished here tonight.

As soon as the bodies were clear, the rest of us started forward. The blueprints and Rhys's visions had informed us we were looking at over a hundred offices on this floor alone, and I didn't want to guess what information they kept in their filing cabinets. Dossiers on magic users? Research on how to eliminate us?

Considering how long this group of rogue hunters had existed, there had to be as much information stored here as there was in the official witch hunter's headquarters. How far had Cartwright taken advantage of her position as the head of her provincial branch?

As we passed each office, I released tiny bursts of fire, aiming for the paperwork piled on the desks. I had no hope that the fire would consume everything before the sprinklers kicked in, but any damage was better than leaving these documents untouched.

The hallway stretched on, with nowhere else for the rest of the witches to split off. And, for now, we were alone. The hunters clearly knew we were here or they wouldn't have left the welcome committee. So where were they? Their absence worried me more than their presence would have. Either at this time of night they didn't have too many people overseeing the office space—which was my hope—or they'd pulled back to a more defensible area.

Despite the silence, I never let my guard down. Especially since, with every minute that passed, the drain on my magic grew stronger. By Hera's slightly laborious breath and the faint glaze in Poppy's eyes, I guessed they felt it as well.

If our power waned too quickly, the only one of us ready to fight would be Barrett. As long as I could wield a blade, I would stand by his side, but as my magic ebbed, I couldn't guarantee my strength wouldn't go with it.

It was enough that adrenaline was carrying me through the pain in my joints and the pulsing stumps of my fingers. When that crashed, I'd be as useful as a lump on the floor. But if I wrecked everyone else along the way, the exhaustion would be worth it.

Another ten witches left us as we approached the reception area, aiming to surprise any other welcome party, while the rest of us headed into the next stairwell. We had to get to the basement, but we'd boxed ourselves in. The stairs down had been barred off since Barrett and Gavin's last visit. This route only went up.

Barrett looked my way, and I hesitated. With so many witches clearing the second floor, we wouldn't be needed there, but there was the third floor to consider. We could either head upstairs to the labs and find the elevator to take us down or fight our way across the main floor to find another stairwell. I arched an eyebrow in question, and Barrett jerked his chin towards the stairs.

To the labs, then.

I gestured for him to take the lead, and as a group we trudged up to the third floor, where the scenery got interesting and far more disturbing.

The reek of bleach and blood singed my nose, eerie in its familiarity. With my memories of Wayne's generous hospitality so fresh, I didn't want to look too closely into the rooms. Hera sent off four more of her witches to clear them as we went, and by the gasps that floated behind us, I guessed they'd found more than they'd expected to.

How many other magic users had the hunters captured?

Magic users who didn't have extreme healing capabilities and who would have succumbed to the poking and prodding after how many hours of suffering.

Any regret I might have felt in destroying these people vanished as I considered how many lives they'd ruined because of their bigoted beliefs. The fact they didn't realize they were the true monsters proved how well Cartwright had spun her stories.

Or maybe they'd been assholes to begin with.

When we reached the room where I'd been held, I froze. At my side, Barrett stiffened. He narrowed his eyes as he took in the photographs of me and my various wounds on the wall—wounds Wayne had inflicted. Gavin sucked in a breath and stooped to get a closer look at the inner workings of my exposed, dislocated kneecap.

My gaze fell on the metal surgical table pressed against the wall. More specifically, on the leather gloves lying on top of it. They were covered in blood from the battle on the highway, and by the scissors lying half inside one of them, I suspected some time had been put into trying to destroy them.

Bile bubbled in my gut. Those gloves were *mine*. The magic in my veins, the bond with Emrick—they. Were. *Mine*.

I snatched up my gloves and tugged them on, squeezing my eyes shut at the pain that shot up my left arm from my gash and wrist and missing fingers. But as soon as the leather encased my flesh, I felt more like myself again. And more than a little ready to give back everything I'd gotten.

"Get out," I ordered.

Gavin looked at me, but Barrett took his arm and pulled him out of the room. As soon as they were clear, I released my fire in a burst that left me cold. The edges of the photos curled and blackened, and the sketches on the desk crumbled into ash. The bed, the rags, and the pillows smoked, and the tools Wayne had used to cut into me flared red-hot until they melted.

Once there was nothing left, I reversed my heat and covered everything under ice so thick it would take days to chop through it all. It was a needless waste of power when every drop counted, but I couldn't leave these pieces of me behind. They'd stolen them, and the invasion of my person was an insult I couldn't overlook.

Poppy stuck her head around the door frame, and her eyes widened. "Feel better?"

"Not nearly."

We moved on, but Hera's witches increased the distance between us. Half of what was left of our group would remain on the third floor to finish clearing it out, while the remaining fifteen continued with us.

The elevator came into view up ahead. It was a freight elevator, making it easy for all of us to fit inside. Gavin hit the button for the basement, and I closed my eyes as the car juddered and started down.

Second by second, we were getting closer to Emrick. To an end. A small part of my brain screamed at me to retreat. We were weakening. We were nineteen against however many waited for us ahead. We would lose.

I squeezed my eyes shut tighter, as though not being able to see would block out the voices trying to talk me out of my stubborn courage.

Halfway down, an anti-magic ward kicked in. My fire dried up, my limbs felt heavy, and my head throbbed. It felt like being caught under water a few seconds past comfortable.

I gestured to Hera, and she stepped forward. We'd discussed in advance what purpose the witches would serve if we encountered one of these wards and agreed the only way to know for sure would be to test our options if we encountered one. On the highway, Poppy's potions had fizzled to nothing, but we needed to know if the effects would be the same at close range.

Hera pulled a vial from her satchel and raised an eyebrow at me. I nodded and braced my feet as she popped the seal and dribbled the contents onto my outstretched arm. I'd accepted the role of guinea pig before walking into this, knowing the potion needed to be tested on skin. I just prayed Hera had chosen a less nasty variety.

Typically, these vials were meant to be hurled across a battle, to smash and splash, affecting anyone nearby, but Hera was no fool. Smashing glass in here would only raise attention and cause potential harm to everyone stuck in here with us. The effects didn't have to be jarring to know if they worked.

I winced as the chill of her freezing potion ate into my skin and burrowed deep into my bones. As painful as it was, I inwardly crowed our victory. Our magic might be contained, but if we got close enough to the hunters, we could still dole out damage.

Hera's lips pulled back in a grin, and I returned the smile. We weren't helpless.

As I scrubbed my arm to warm it up, the witches spread their potions around. If the hunters thought a bit of missing magic would stop us, they were in for a shock.

The elevator rumbled as it stopped, and I set my hand on the hilt of the knife at my hip. Barrett had his gun drawn, and Gavin stood close behind him with a matching gun aimed ahead. Poppy and Murisa had enchanted both weapons, and time would tell whether their magic held up against the ward. Fortunately, even an unenchanted bullet would serve our purpose.

Yet even with all our firepower, we were on the defensive the moment the doors opened.

If we'd wondered where the hunters had been hiding, we'd found them here behind the ward. Cartwright must have pulled her people back to a point where they would have every advantage.

Or so they believed.

They fired without hesitation. I pressed my back against the wall next to the elevator door and watched the padding along the back wall get torn to shreds. Barrett slammed the close button, and the doors slid shut, but not before Cuddles launched himself free of Poppy's arms and one of Hera's witches was hit by a bullet ricocheting off the demolished wall. He dropped to the ground, his hand clamped around his arm, and in the few seconds we had, Gavin knelt beside him and applied a smear of salve.

The barrage outside slowed. Someone must have shut down power to the elevator because the doors hadn't fully closed before they'd stopped, leaving an inch of space for me to peer into the hallway. Seven hunters had greeted us, four kneeling, three standing. An eighth was on the ground, face bleeding from four bone-deep gouges across his face. Cuddles was nowhere to be seen.

Barrett waited until I moved out of the way, then he and Gavin hauled the doors open and stepped into the opening to return fire. The enchanted bullets slammed into two of the kneeling hunters. The sudden and direct hits caused more than a few of them to stumble, and Hera and Poppy used their distraction to roll their potion vials across the floor. Barrett dropped his aim to fire at the glass, and the contents splashed across hunter, wall, and floor. Screams filled the hallway as their flesh bubbled with blisters.

Barrett pulled one of Murisa's mechanicals from his pocket, hit a button on the back of it, and hurled it into the remaining group. Two of the standing hunters fled, but the other crashed to the ground, his legs caught on one of the kneeling hunters who was trying to escape. The mechanical split open and sprayed the contents of its inner workings into the four hunters' faces.

Gavin fired two more shots, and the fleeing hunters fell. The other four released shrieks of terror as hallucinations of their worst fears played out before them. The effect would only last for a few minutes—if their hearts stood out that long—so I gestured for the others to follow me, and we navigated past them.

"You're going to want to slow down with those gadgets," I whispered to Barrett, and he gave me *the look,* pointing out that he had more tactical experience than I did.

I returned *the look*, reminding him I'd been around for two world wars and more than a few smaller but no less deadly ones and was therefore no stranger to managing resources.

He responded by opening the satchel at his side, offering me the collection of shape-coded devices, and I rolled my eyes. If he wanted to be such a child about it, maybe I *would* take over.

When I didn't accept the offered bag, he smirked at me and jogged ahead. I stuck my tongue out at his back and followed close behind him.

The end of the hallway opened into a large space filled with more cubicles, but unlike the office space on the ground floor, these aisles weren't empty.

I didn't bother to count how many hunters waited for us, weapons at the ready, but there had to be at least thirty, with two per aisle and more aiming at us from the tops of the cubicles.

I wished we'd waited until the witches from the other floors had caught up to us, but it was too late to retreat. Hera gave a sharp whistle, and the witches scattered, breaking off two by two down each of the aisles until I lost track of them except for the ear-bursting gunshots and the smash of breaking glass.

I grabbed a vial from my satchel and dove in, aiming for the woman looming to my left. As I hurled the potion, I longed for my fire. With all this panel fabric covering every vertical surface, I could have lit this whole place up with a few direct shots.

Instead, I was limited by my aim. Fortunately, Adrian and I had trained for years, both with my magic and without. I was more than prepared to weave my way down the main aisle, running in a zigzag pattern, never pausing, never becoming an easy target as I hurled my vials and added to the chaos of the room.

"*More up ahead,*" Murisa's mechanical voice spoke up in my head. "*Count unknown, but not a small group.*"

She'd barely fallen silent when we reached the halfway point of the room and stumbled to a halt. The cubicles from this point on had been dismantled, and another fifteen hunters stood ready, this group arranged in a long row and ready to fire.

But Barrett and Gavin had manoeuvred into position, with Barrett crouched in an aisle to my right, Gavin to my left, as though they'd known what to expect. I wondered how many times Rhys had whispered in Barrett's ear since we'd arrived.

In a joint move, they launched what looked like hand grenades across the room. Both devices burst with puffs of smoke, and through the haze, I made out the red glow as a magical net sliced through the eight hunters standing in the middle of the formation. Apparently Muroppy had learned a thing or two since they'd dissected Alodie's demon.

The hunters dropped to the floor in slain pieces, and I winced, wondering if Murisa had considered the mess when she'd created the enchantment or if she'd focused only on efficacy.

Seven hunters remained, with however many closing in on us from behind. Screams, smoke, and gunfire filled the room on both sides of me. I pulled my knife and threw myself into the fight as Barrett and Gavin tore across the open space to launch themselves at the seven. Cuddles darted in from the right, teeth bared and a low yowl ripping from his throat. He landed on a hunter I recognized from outside the Fool & Chariot. I'd known I'd see him again. Though our reunion was short-lived as Cuddles tore his claws through the man's neck before pouncing off him to find someone else to attack. A blessing as more hunters spilled into the room.

Battle frenzy grabbed hold of my muscles, swallowed my fatigue, and allowed me to weave and block and dodge as though I were at the top of my game. I relished the familiarity of the movements. They brought me back to the centuries I'd fought with Adrian by my side.

For a moment, I was no longer in a warehouse fighting humans who wanted to exterminate our kind. I was in the northern Black Forest taking on an endless nest of vampires. I was in seventeenth-century England battling a coven of dark witches. A thunder of dragons. A basilisk. A giant.

I had faced so many greater threats over the years, and because of my team back then, I'd always believed we would be victorious.

Today was no different.

With Barrett, Gavin, and Poppy by my side, with Rhys at home relaying everything his second sight deigned to show him, with Murisa looping us into all the information her enchanted mechanicals gained, we stood as good a chance as we would have if I'd had my full power.

The certainty strengthened me. Gave me the energy I needed to tear through my enemies until my blade was slick with blood, my potion supply was low, and my lungs heaved with exertion.

Until all the hunters we'd faced in this room were nothing

more than corpses, and the four of us were still standing. I prayed Hera's witches had been equally successful with the others we'd passed.

"Some kind of maintenance hallway next. You could try to go around it, but it looks like the other corridor is blocked. They're corralling you this way," Murisa said. *"After that, more office space. A maze of hallways. Things could get dicey."*

Barrett frowned and stepped closer to my side. "Rhys tells me whatever's through that door is going to knock us out. It's dark, he can't See what it is, but he says there's going to be gasping. Vomiting."

"Always a new adventure."

I wiped the blood from my face with my arm and waited for the witches to join us. I didn't care what was through those doors—all that mattered was we would be another step closer to Emrick.

My confidence slipped when the witches arrived and I found myself staring at seven of the fifteen we'd started with. Hera looked haggard, though her gaze remained steely, and more than one of the survivors appeared to be barely hanging on. The magic drain had worsened over the past few minutes, and I suspected it wasn't about to slow down.

I gritted my teeth and turned to the door.

We'd made it this far, and we would keep going. We'd finish this quickly and leave Cartwright no chance to crow her victory.

31

Katerina

"M Y MECHANICALS FOUND *what look like traps up ahead,*" Murisa warned in my ear. "*They're working to disarm them, but while they're pretty amazing, there's no guarantee they won't miss a few.*"

"Should we wait for her mechanicals to finish?" Gavin asked, eying the door warily.

"It would be the wise decision." I pulled my shoulders back to fight the urge to let them sag. "But we don't have that kind of time. Not if we want to make it to the other end of the hallway with half our number still standing. Our strength is draining too quickly."

I looked to the other witches to get their opinion and found most of them wavering on their feet, proving my point.

Since it was my choice to push forward, I took point and heaved the reinforced door open. Immediately, the echo of working pumps and the hum of electricity bombarded me, preventing me from hearing anything that might be coming for us once we passed into the next area.

Probably for the best. One problem at a time and whatnot.

Cuddles slipped past me into the dark space. I squeezed the grip of my knife and kept it ready, though there were few places for anyone to hide. The hallway was barely twenty metres long, with a few metal doors lining the sides but no indication they were anything other than maintenance rooms. The lights were dimmer here, and the shadows created monsters out of nothing, but I got the strong impression we were alone.

An impression that was confirmed when the doors slammed shut behind us, cutting off half our witches and leaving the rest of us trapped in the darkness. Of course we were alone—why would the hunters want to trap their own in a kill room?

The hiss of gas started as soon as the doors were sealed, and my stomach lurched with dread over what was about to happen.

"Hold your breath and get down," I ordered, and my voice carried without my having to raise it.

As I dropped to the ground, I felt a draft coming from under one of the maintenance doors. The temptation was strong to take advantage of the air source to fill my lungs while

I could, but I didn't trust that this draft wasn't also laced with something set to kill me.

"The mechanicals have almost got it, guys. I've got you. But whatever you do, do not breathe. They're picking up readings from that hallway, and it's not pretty. Definitely some kind of neurotoxin."

The silence around me was thick as everyone took Murisa's advice. It might gain us only a few seconds, but I'd take any extra time I could get.

Instead of counting the moments or thinking of the burn in my lungs, I switched my thoughts to Emrick, hoping he knew we were coming and praying he was holding on.

He was my guiding light in this darkness, so he better fucking be.

The pressure in my chest built, so I focused on what I would do to Cartwright when I finally got my hands on her. The satisfaction I would feel when I watched the life drain from her eyes. Or maybe I would throw her in this room, lock the door, and let her little traps destroy her. Not quite as direct, but there would be a sort of poetic justice in it.

Cuddles padded around in front of me, unaffected by the gas, and I cursed his undead lungs.

My thoughts grew hazy, and I turned my attention to the people around me. Barrett didn't appear to be struggling at all, the bastard, and I wondered if he was one of those people who submerged himself in the bathtub to build up his lung capacity for situations like this. I wouldn't put it past him.

Gavin's face was red, his eyes watering, but he seemed to be doing all right.

Poppy looked like her eyes were about to burst out of her head with her effort not to inhale. Her nose dripped, and her cheeks were covered in tears.

By the look of it, most of the witches sat between Poppy and Gavin in terms of discomfort, with only one older woman having reached Barrett-levels of stoicism.

But as I watched, one young woman choked on an exhale. Her eyes widened in horror as she realized what she'd done, and instinctively she rushed to refill her lungs.

I couldn't even shout a warning to stop her. Her eyes rolled back in her head, and her body fell into convulsions. Blood dripped from her ears and nose, and bruises appeared on her pale skin.

It took less than a minute for her to go still.

My heart ached for her, but there was nothing we could do but avenge her. And I was determined to survive long enough to do it.

"Got it. Doors unlocking. More hunters on the other side. Be ready."

As soon as she fell silent, vents clanked overhead and sucked the gas out, and cool air rushed in. I exhaled slowly, measuring it in seconds, as I pulled my way along the floor. Only when I was closer to the entrance than the middle of the hallway did I risk taking a breath. The doors we'd entered through slid open, giving access to the witches who'd been lucky enough to get locked outside.

When my body remained unaffected, I took a deeper breath and readied another potion vial. The hunters waiting at the other end of the hallway would expect corpses when the door opened. I'd give them a fight.

Heaviness weighed in my gut as I looked at the others in the hallway with me. The witches were shaken by the brutal loss of their covenmate, and Poppy and Gavin looked ready to collapse.

I was glad Murisa hadn't joined us. At least she'd been spared from seeing these horrors. Whatever her mechanicals relayed to her was another story, but she wasn't likely to be woken by nightmares in the decades to come. Or hours. Or however long we lasted.

Barrett waited until everyone was ready, then he stalked down the hallway, threw open the door at the end, and stepped out firing.

As I'd hoped, the dozen hunters weren't prepared for us. They were slow to raise their weapons, and by the time they returned fire, three of them were down.

Gavin reached into his pocket and pulled out a mechanical. When he hurled it into the centre of the horde, they didn't think to scatter, too stunned to react. Five of them went down in convulsions as the mechanicals released their electrical spell circles—a nice variation on Alodie's enchanted stones.

After what had nearly happened to us in the maintenance corridor, I was in no mood to play nice with the other four. I threw one of my potions and followed up immediately with my knife, moving quickly enough to take them off guard. The glass smashed at their feet. While the potions didn't do much other than burn holes through the hems of their cargo pants, it was distraction enough for me to slice my blade through one guy's hamstring.

Barrett, of course, beat me to the next one, stealing my outlet for my pent-up rage. When I shot him a dark look, he winked at me.

The last two hunters rallied and squeezed off a half-dozen rounds before the witches closed in; another two coven members went down. More smashed glass, screams, the reek of fire as enchanted green flames spread across one of the hunters' shirts.

She shrieked and tore it off, revealing red, blotchy skin, but her self-preservation cost her everything as Barrett raised his weapon and shot her in the head. She dropped, and the last hunter soon followed.

My conscience twinged again at the bodies piling up, but I crushed it. I didn't usually see magicals and mundanes as an us versus them. We all lived here, and we had to accommodate for the other side existing, even if only one side widely knew about the other.

That was why my purpose over my long, long life had never wavered. Whenever a magical threatened to tip the balance, I was the counterweight. Whenever mundanes threatened to do the same, I could step in and attempt to turn the tide.

But this group, they were rare—mundanes who not only knew magicals existed but understood how we worked. With their experience within the hunter organizations, they would have learned our strengths and weaknesses and had the money and resources at their disposal to account for them.

Or block them and drain them, as the case may be.

They had declared war. It was the first time in all my years I'd experienced a move like that on such a wide scale.

Never before had I felt so vulnerable.

So afraid.

So uncertain of victory.

"*Good job, guys, but this is as far as I can take you,*" Murisa said. "*Either they found my pets, or they've got something stronger than me inside. It's a huge black hole.*"

"Rhys is on it," Barrett said. "He's only getting fragments—none of them good—but enough to guide us through." He paused, and the line of his jaw tightened. "He says we're about to be hit hard. He sounds scared."

I gritted my teeth and strode forward. I refused to let them make me feel small or helpless. They believed they were prepared for us, but I was ready to show them how badly they'd underestimated our strength. We would make them pay for every shot fired. With luck, I'd do it before this war spread beyond these walls and infected the mundane world at large.

If we failed, people would be so busy fighting each other, they might not notice the planet was crumbling beneath them.

Murisa's voice spoke up in my ear again. "*Poppy's corpses are down, but the other witches are coming your way. At least twenty by my count. A bunch of them are injured and moving slow. Not sure how long it'll take them to reach you.*"

My throat tightened as the full extent of what was at stake settled on my shoulders. Before I had time to dwell, we reached the familiar doors that would take me to Emrick.

The doors had been replaced since my last outburst, these ones heavily reinforced metal that wouldn't burn under the heat of my fire. The walls, however, retained their scorch marks, and I couldn't help but smile at the extent of the damage I'd caused.

I drew in a deep breath and let it out slowly, struck by a bittersweet memory. Emrick had always told me not to waste time breathing.

The enemy won't give you time to breathe.

It was fitting that at the last I should prove him wrong.

The original plan had been for the rest of the witches to

hold here and prevent anyone else from coming in, leaving this final battle to me and my team, but one look at their faces told me Hera was in no place to lead what was left of her coven. With whatever steam remained to them, they'd help us clear the room within, and I was glad of it. Only four still stood, including her, and based on the numbers we'd seen so far and what we might expect to find, they'd be far more useful splitting the enemy inside than fending them off out here.

I thought of the other witches making their way towards the basement. If we waited for them, we'd stand a better chance of success. But we would also be giving the hunters more time to prepare. Not to mention the tiny issue of our magic circling the drain.

I met Hera's eye, and she dropped her chin in a nod, her expression no less determined for being mixed with overwhelming grief.

Who knew—the woman had a heart. I'd never thought so highly of her as I did in that moment.

Poppy wobbled on her feet, and Gavin grabbed her arm to hold her steady. She exhaled sharply and gave herself a shake, then turned to me. The terror disappeared from her eyes, replaced by a deep, raging fury.

I understood and agreed.

The closer we got to this area of the building, the worse the drain had become. Either it was because of the passing time or because of our proximity, but we would have to find our strength in spite of it. There could be no waiting for reinforcements.

Gavin and Barrett reloaded their weapons, and I pulled Murisa's ladybug mechanical out of my pocket. *Nuclear Option.* If ever there was a time for a nuclear option, this was it.

I closed my fingers around it, and Barrett rested his hand on the door.

With one last prayer to anyone who would listen, I readied myself to go in.

He opened the door, and the sight that greeted me made my mouth go dry and my fingers go numb. Enough so that I nearly dropped the mechanical. I returned it to my pocket to keep it safe and breathed through my racing heartbeat.

Over fifty hunters awaited us within, all with weapons drawn. In the middle of them stood Cartwright.

She looked so calm, so self-assured. Irritatingly arrogant.

Red swam in my vision, and I tightened my grip on the hilt of my knife. I couldn't wait to watch her confidence crumble.

My chest tightened when I spotted Emrick beyond her.

He met my eye, and his expression was tortured. He hadn't wanted me to come back, but he had to know I wouldn't leave him here. No matter what the cost to me. Without him, I was lost either way.

I noticed all these things in a heartbeat, as though time

had stilled, but it picked up again as the first shots were fired. The bursts of gunfire were matched by breaking glass and the spray of well-aimed potions. The anti-magic wards were strong enough in here that the effects of the potions were nearly erased, but enough splashes made it beyond the wards to eat through skin and leave a few hunters heaving.

Cuddles darted into the room, back arched, teeth bared. Before I could worry the anti-magic wards would strip him of the magic keeping him alive and in stasis, he charged straight for two hunters on the far side of the room. One of them shrieked and bolted to avoid him when he pounced, but the other went down in a spray of blood before Cuddles dropped onto his haunches and set to work cleaning his butt. He showed no negative effects of the ward, somehow having dodged beneath it or—I considered his armour—repelled it?

The witches didn't hold back. There was no reservation, no saving up resources—they went in with everything they had. While I had the space, I added my vials to theirs.

Only so many months ago, I'd turned my nose up at these artificial concoctions. Magic in a bottle. Second-hand power. What a fool I'd been.

I could recognize my closed-mindedness now that their tools offered me my best chance at victory.

While I did my best to clear the path in front of me with potions that ran the gamut from bottled fire to emotional torture, I caught Barrett flinging what had to be one of his last mechanicals.

My thoughts stuttered as the device landed and the floor disappeared, taking more than a dozen hunters through the concrete to… some in-between realm? I didn't want to think about it too closely.

The floor dipped and wavered as more of the area was eaten up, and a few more hunters tumbled towards the chasm.

Then the enchantment gave out, the hole sealed itself, and three of the hunters howled in agony when they discovered themselves trapped halfway through the floor.

I didn't give myself time to feel sorry for them, and neither did Barrett as he drew his gun and finished them all. More blood on his hands, but more merciful than letting them remain as they were.

More shots rang out, and my blood ran cold when Poppy fell. Her face was pinched with pain, and blood oozed down her leg. She'd been hit in the knee, but now she was down. Vulnerable.

I couldn't go to her. I couldn't waste our one opportunity to free Emrick.

But even as I fought my way towards him, never seeming to close the distance, the nightmares kept coming. I watched in horror, unable to stop it, as one of the hunters fired at Barrett. The bullet pierced his neck, and as he dropped to his knees, he caught my eye. The hardness in his stare ordered me to keep going, begged me not to give up.

I steeled myself, swallowed my cries, and threw more vials at the hunters in my path.

The tug on my magic continued, growing stronger, and with each step, forward my legs grew heavier.

Finally, the last hunters were out of my way, bringing me face to face with Cartwright. She stood in front of Emrick's cage, a gun in her hand, that smug smile still on her face despite the hits her team had taken.

"Is your night not going to plan, Ms. Palon?"

I forced a grin. "On the contrary, General, it's going exactly how we expected it to."

Uncertainty flickered in her eyes, and my smile grew stronger.

I hadn't lied. We'd known going in we might not get out. Frankly, we'd made it farther than I'd feared we would. Almost as far as I'd hoped. We were so close. Once Cartwright was gone, I could focus on Emrick.

He stared at me over Cartwright's shoulder, his silver eyes gleaming with fear. Regret. Not a little bit of anger.

It took all my effort to return my attention to Cartwright. I wasn't finished with her yet.

Beads of sweat formed on her brow and trickled along her hairline—the only evidence that she was anything less than the cool cucumber she appeared to be. "I'm sorry you've wasted all this energy only to fail now."

"It was hardly a waste. We've decimated your soldiers, and the rest of the hunters know what you're doing. Even if you survive tonight, your minions will be few and far."

She laughed. "Once our work here is done, it won't matter how many of us survive. We've already won."

"Isn't there a saying about not counting your chickens?"

I looked around the room. At Gavin standing between Barrett and the hunters closing in on them. At Poppy on the ground, Hera standing over her with her final potions ready to throw. At Cuddles, who'd been backed into a corner. Another corpse lay beside him, but there was no way he'd be able to take down five at once.

It was time to go nuclear. Whatever that entailed.

I reached into my pocket, pulled out the mechanical, and pressed the ladybug's head. Magic flooded through me. So much weaker than it should have been thanks to this ongoing, tedious drain, but a sweet relief to the numbness of before. Murisa's solution to the anti-magic ward was an even smaller ward. Probably the same idea that protected Cuddles. I wouldn't be able to throw fireballs, but that was fine. I'd spent the first hundred years of my life mastering power I couldn't project.

Cartwright's eyes filled with horror as fire spread over my hands, and I leapt at her, closing my fingers around her throat.

Emrick shouted my name, but I ignored him. Once this evil bitch was dead, we could undo everything her group had begun so many decades ago.

The general slammed the butt of her gun against my temple. Stars burst in my vision, but I held on. Her hair smoked, her clothes blackened, but she bashed me over the head again. Again.

My hands slipped. I tightened my grip, but Murisa's enchantment was already waning, the ward not strong enough to avoid the press of the anti-magic fields. I exerted more strength, but Cartwright grabbed my injured hand and squeezed so hard that pain lanced up my arm. I screamed, flinched, and she used the opportunity to drive her knee between us and shove me away.

I'd lost my hold, my window of opportunity. Barrett wouldn't have missed it. He would have moved faster than I had. But he was down—possibly dead.

My back hit the concrete floor, and Cartwright wobbled to her feet. Her neck and jaw were covered in weeping blisters, but she had the gun and stood too far away for me to use what was left of my magic.

"I was going to let you live, sorceress. Make you suffer in a world where I held all the power and you held none, but I think I'll do you a favour and end you now."

As her thumb flicked off the safety, I looked to Emrick for the last time.

His beautiful eyes, like moonlight across a raging sea, stared back at me in horror. He was shouting but I couldn't hear him. That stupid sphere was still attached to his hand.

I carried so many regrets from my nine hundred years, but this one was the heaviest. After all the times he'd saved me, I couldn't do the same for him.

It also broke my heart that, after I fell—after I failed—he wouldn't be the one to escort me to the afterlife.

32

Emrick

MY VOICE GREW hoarse with my screams.

I'd watched the hunters fall through the floor, get mowed down by bullets and Murisa's gadgets, and be mauled by an armoured zombie cat.

I'd watched Poppy get hit and Barrett fall.

I'd watched Gavin collapse, clawing at his chest as though he couldn't get enough air.

I'd suffered through all of it, desperate to help and unable to pass through this invisible cage.

But as Cartwright aimed her weapon at Kat's head. As resignation filled the depths of Kat's ocean eyes, something within me snapped.

In less than a heartbeat, an infinitesimal fraction of a millisecond, my future flashed before me. Katerina no longer in the world and me straddling realms until Death released me. Me unable to join my other half. Separated from the only person on this planet who loved me for everything I was.

Panic gripped me, throwing my thoughts into a frenzy. Options tumbled through me with the speed of a dozen freight trains, each one barrelling into my brain until I couldn't see straight.

Especially not when Kat's death would mean the end of all hope. Who else would stand against Cartwright in time?

If I did nothing, Kat would be dead and everything she'd fought for would come to nothing. I couldn't let that happen. I wouldn't. Which meant there was only one way forward.

She would never forgive me, but I prayed she'd understand.

"I love you." There was so much more I wanted to say. I wanted to tell her how grateful I was that she'd filled my life with love and joy and beauty for more centuries than I deserved. I wanted to apologize for leaving her. I wanted to wrap her in my adoration so she would never forget, never doubt. But none of it would be enough.

So I settled for those three little words, filled with every emotion my ravaged soul contained. Although no sound came out, I knew Kat heard them. I knew the moment she understood what I intended to do.

My name was on her lips once again, a plea for me to stop.

I ignored her but refused to close my eyes. If I was about to lose my mind, heart, and soul, then I wanted my last knowing sight to be Kat's beautiful face.

I prayed on some level I would take the memory of her with me, even if I had no clue who she was or why the thought of her glowed within me like some eternal flame.

With a last soul-deep cry, I reached for Death's power and pulled it over myself like a shroud. It clung to me, sank deep into blood and bone—the cold, empty void that had embraced me the day I'd signed over my life to save a woman who hadn't deserved it.

The day Katerina had grabbed hold of my arm and changed everything I'd believed about what my future looked like, I'd forgiven Gaby her betrayal. How could I feel anything but gratitude towards the person who'd pushed me down the path to meeting the woman I would have happily spent eternity with?

I channelled more power from the afterlife, more than I'd ever needed or tried to hold before. More than when I'd dived into the still river in my search for Kat's soul. More than when I'd sunk so deeply into this plane Mikhail had turned corporeal under my hands. It burned my veins with its icy touch, made my skin prickle and stretch as though it were trying to burst through my pores.

It begged to consume me—and I would let it. But only once I was certain I'd drawn enough.

Kat's screams clawed at my ears, floating around me like the sweetest music of grief and regret. Of heartbreak. For me. Because I had been so lucky as to earn my sorceress's love.

Cartwright's brow furrowed and her grip on her weapon wavered as she watched Kat panic. Her aim slipped, and I grabbed my opportunity.

My enduring, eternal love for Kat wound through my deathly power, bolstering it, fueling it, until its coldness morphed into a heat that boiled my very soul.

Only then did I send out my conscious thought to every hunter in the room—beyond it, into the rest of the building. I sensed their life forces pulsing, so eager to endure. Unfortunate for them that they'd chosen the wrong side.

With one last look at Kat, I pulled.

In a breath, the souls of almost a hundred hunters were sucked from their bodies. They slammed into me, passed through me, and surged into the afterlife as nothing more than disembodied glimmers of light untethered to the earth, doomed to wander until they were lucky enough to find someone to guide them beyond this plane.

I felt the moment Death looked my way. Felt it like a dark cloud on a sunny afternoon.

I'd shifted the balance too far. Involved myself too deeply in the affairs of mortals. I knew it. I accepted it.

I refused to tear my gaze from Kat as bit by bit my soul

flaked away and drifted like ash into the afterlife. The sphere fell from my hand and hit the ground, no longer bound to the mortal world.

My love for my sorceress was the last part of me to fade, wrapped in regret that I'd broken my promise to her for the final time.

Katerina

I HADN'T KNOWN how agonizing heartbreak could be.

I'd thought I'd known pain when I'd nearly burned alive under Shogaur's malicious stare. I'd been drained by vampires and pulverized by giants and dragons. I'd taken hits from witches' spells, been stabbed and shot and impaled. I'd had my fingers sheared off by a sadistic doctor.

These torments were nothing compared to the soul-destroying, nerve-scraping, sanity-snapping pain that exploded in my chest as Emrick's pale skin slipped even further away from the spectrum of human colour, passing into a murky grey until he was barely visible, more shadow than spirit. No longer bound to this world but an extension of the afterlife. Gone was the solid mass of muscle and flesh that had wrapped around me for so many centuries, warming me, comforting me, worshiping me. In its place was a transparent figure, all colour and life as drained from him as my magic had been.

As my magic no longer was… because the sphere had fallen from his hand.

His eyes were the only familiar feature left—still beautiful and silver but cold. Empty.

I'd begged him to stop. Screeched until everyone else in the room had turned and stared at me.

Even Cartwright had stepped back, curious about what I knew that she didn't.

One second she'd stood there, gun aimed at my head. The next, her body had crumpled at my feet. It had happened so quickly, I doubted she'd seen it coming.

Every hunter in the room was dead, though their bodies appeared untouched. Any postmortem would show the cause of death as unknown, but I knew. Emrick had ripped out their souls.

He'd sacrificed himself to save me. To save the entire world.

And now he existed, but that was all. My Emrick was gone, as stripped from me as any possibility of vengeance towards Cartwright was.

I stumbled towards him—towards the vision of him.

"Kat?" someone called from across the room. I had no idea who it was, and I didn't care.

All my attention was on this floating figure in front of me.

His silver eyes followed me, and despite what I knew to be true, a traitorous hope refused to disperse. "Emrick?"

He didn't react. There wasn't the tiniest recognition in his eyes. No *interest*.

"Emrick, please."

Tears slipped down my cheeks.

More horrifying than the emptiness in his stare was the burn in the centre of my chest. The sensation of something frayed and broken being restored. Of our bond returning. The refuge of my mortality slipping away.

My eyes widened, and I searched the room, trying to figure out what had changed. My gaze fell on a dozen mechanicals gnawing through a metal box in the corner, destroying Emrick's cage and the anti-magic ward.

"No!" I dashed towards them and kicked the enchanted creatures away from their task, crushing them beneath my boot.

"Kat, stop!" Gavin wrapped his arms around me and hauled me backwards.

"*The wards are down*," Murisa said in my ear, and she sounded *relieved*. How could she sound happy when she'd sealed my doom?

I thrashed against Gavin's hold, but he tightened his grip. "Katerina, quit it. It's over. They're dead."

He didn't understand. It wasn't over. And now it never would be over. Gavin would get to die. Barrett, Poppy, Murisa—they would all enjoy the sweet release from their sorrows and pain, while I would be trapped here to suffer alone. For years, centuries, millennia. I would watch cities rise and crumble. I would get caught in endless wars and stand witness as the planet's beauties withered under humanity's greed and carelessness.

And I would have no one to hold my hand. No one to share my days or the long, empty nights. No one would be around long enough to get to know me or what I'd been through.

Adrian was gone, and Emrick—

A wail broke from my chest. I tore myself out of Gavin's hold and stumbled away from him. I retched as the past few hours of fear and pain and a future of despair swept over me.

"Ben and the healers are on their way, and the other hunters have arrived," Murisa said. *"They say more help is en route."*

I sagged against the wall and wrapped my arms around my knees. Vaguely I was aware of Poppy dragging herself across the floor towards me, her bleeding leg stretched out behind her. I was aware of Barrett lying on the ground. Gavin knelt beside him, helping one of the surviving witches press a wadded-up cloth against the wound. No, not a cloth. Gavin's T-shirt. At some point he'd taken it off, revealing the gashes, gouges, and bruises that covered his torso from tonight's battle.

Hera and one other witch were making the rounds, pulling healing potions out of their satchels. I had no eye for them.

They'd helped us make it this far, and they would live with their magic intact. I didn't care. Helping them had been a nice win, but my primary goal had been to rescue Emrick.

Because without him, I was lost.

I bowed my head against my knees, unwilling and unable to watch as the wraith passed throughout the room, appearing and disappearing as he escorted the witches' souls across the barrier into the afterlife. My Emrick would have turned the bodies to dust as he went, helping us clean up before the mundane police walked in on the disaster. The wraith left them, going about his duty within the limits of his obligation.

Another deluge of tears streamed down my face, and my lungs and throat burned with each breath. I was falling to pieces, and there was no one left to hold me together. Oh, Poppy and the others might try. Maera might offer to fill me with baked goods until her last breath. But when would that be? Another forty years? Fifty?

My friends would die. My next friends would die. And so it would go until there were no souls left for the wraith to gather. When it was just him and me and his fellow wraiths on this earth, and Death finally paid him a mercy, then—maybe—I would find peace.

Ben stepped into the room. He gave me a nod before heading to Barrett's side. The rest of the healers spilled in behind him, searching for people to help.

Too bad my wounds were untouchable.

Arnold and a dozen of the witches who'd fought with him came in after them. Rumpled, bruised, and bloody, he rushed to Hera's side, and Hera threw herself into his arms, for the first time since I'd met her appearing human. Apparently even the woman with no soul had found someone deserving of her love.

I squeezed my eyes shut, but even unable to see, I *sensed* the wraith moving around me, the bond between us so strong there was no way for me to ignore him. I sensed the power emanating from him as he freed the souls from their bodies, travelling from the ones who had died in this room to the few remaining in the hall. The poor young woman in the maintenance corridor, and the others who'd split off from the main group.

Along with him went Death. It filled the room with its layers of silence, the hair-raising foreshadowing of what awaited us all in the end. What awaited my friends who suffered alongside me.

They begged me to look at them, to give them my attention. I couldn't. Selfishness consumed me, leaving me no choice but to drown in my inner chaos.

As I studied the discomfort of Death's closeness and latched on to it as a reprieve from my tortured thoughts, an idea began to form. Memories long forgotten swept around me, giving the idea shape. Solidity.

Emrick had explained many times over the years how he'd

made his deal with Death. He'd exchanged his eternal rest to save his cheating shit of a wife. If Death had been open to negotiation once, maybe there was an opportunity to do it again.

It was too early for hope—I was too mired in desperation—but as soon as the idea settled, it became a decision.

"Kat?" Poppy's voice was close, and when I raised my head and opened my eyes, I found her almost beside me. She held Cuddles against her throat. His yellow eyes gleamed at me with their dead stare, but a deep purr rumbled from his chest. Tears streaked through the blood on Poppy's cheeks, and her throat bobbed with hard swallows as her gaze shifted between me and our fallen. She needed me to get up and help, to drag myself out of my brokenness and lead them. But I wouldn't.

She would have to forgive me.

I pushed myself to my feet and searched the scattered remains for a knife, my own having been lost somewhere in the fight.

"Kat, what are you—wait—"

I brushed past Poppy as though she weren't there, and the witch tending to her knee stopped her from coming after me. I didn't have time for her or her feelings. If I was going to act, it had to be now. Before the wraith drifted away. Before Death released its hold on this cursed place.

It took me a minute of kicking through corpses, but with every passing second, I felt my strength returning—not only my magic, but the hum of my immortality. All my partially healed injuries resumed their rapid repair. My fingers screamed at me as bone and flesh and tissue reformed. They would take a few days to grow back, and it would be an unpleasant experience, but the rest of me would be as good as new within the next few hours.

Unless I failed again.

Finally, I found a blade that would serve me.

"Kat, stop," Poppy called.

I didn't look her way. I couldn't afford to hesitate.

I closed my eyes and thought of Emrick. Through him, I thought of Death—that all-encompassing stillness. Once I was sure I had the connection, I set the point of the blade to my chest.

"Gavin—stop her!"

Emrick had told me how, after Gabrielle had recovered and run off with her lover, he'd fallen ill with the same sickness that had nearly taken her, but no one had come to barter for his soul.

That changed now.

For all the times he'd told me his story, he'd never explained how he'd summoned Death in the first place. I'd never pushed, never believing I would be in a position to make the same choice he had. Now that I stood here, I realized there could only be one way. I tightened my grip on the hilt. How better to draw Death than to invite him?

With one last breath, I plunged the blade into my heart.

34

Katerina

I EXISTED IN a void.

It wasn't the afterlife—which, now that I was in this place, I remembered as vividly as if I owned property there—and it wasn't the mortal realm.

Yet it was familiar.

Death had dragged me to this same fragment of existence after Alodie's spell circle had struck me down in that Toronto hotel. All around me were shapes and shadows in shades of grey, none of them clear enough to make out. There was no sense of danger. I felt no worry or concern.

The neutrality of everything struck me as strange. Surreal. Considering why I was here, surely I should have felt some trepidation.

Had I messed up so badly that I'd ruined my chance of success before I'd even begun? Had I met my final death, and Death had come for me directly, allowing me to hop over the afterlife altogether? "Pass Go, Collect Your Final Release."

If so, I accepted it.

At least it would be an end.

Yet even as the thought occurred to me, even as a blanket of peace settled deep in my chest and the allure of rest tempted me to relax into the nothingness, a question prodded my thoughts. What did I want?

There were no words to the question, no voice in my head, simply an awareness. As though the question had already existed in my mind.

I forced myself to remember why I was here.

"I've come to make a deal," I said into the void. "A deal for Emrick's soul. I want it returned to him."

For a while, nothing happened beyond a shift in the shadows as they circled me. Considered me? If so, I didn't want to know why.

Again that deep sense of peace filled me, dragging down my muscles until all I wanted was to close my eyes and lie down.

If I had a chance to bring Emrick back, would that be my choice? Or would I prefer to lay down my mantle and sleep?

I didn't know if that question was mine or another query posed by the shadows, but I allowed myself time to consider it.

If I failed and Emrick remained as he was, there was nothing for me in the mortal world. All the chaos of the past few months was over, the source of our problems dealt with.

There would always be magicals who stepped out of line, but they could be someone else's problem. I'd finally reached my closure when I'd ended Alodie's life. I was comfortable now with passing the torch to someone else if my time was up.

But it would mean Emrick was stuck here on his own. Not *him*, maybe, but what was left of him. Could I turn away from his memory without making the attempt to bring him back?

The answer was a firm negative, and I rebelled against the lethargy weighing me down. "Will you negotiate?"

Another span of time passed with no way of knowing how long. Then another question occurred to me. How much was I willing to trade? Because it had to be a trade. The balance had to be maintained.

I'd known what was coming when I'd struck down this path. Life and Death were always in check. The world would swerve off its axis if they weren't. It was the same scale between magical and mundane that I'd spent my immortality protecting.

I had given years of my life for that balance. How much more was I willing to give to save Emrick?

Everything.

The answer came to me as swiftly as my understanding of what it would mean. I didn't care. My body might continue on, but my heart and soul didn't exist if his weren't in this world.

"I offer myself. I'll make the same deal Emrick did and become your servant for as long as you need me. I will serve alongside him, collecting the souls of magicals wherever I'm needed."

It would mean saying goodbye to my friends and to contact with the mortal world. It would mean the bond between Emrick and I would be broken, but we could reforge it in a new way—one based on equality from the start instead of a tether between shattered sorceress and aged spirit-herder.

Thoughts that came from outside my mind swirled around me of the mortal world. Of werewolves, vampires, and witches rising in power and having no one to press them back. Of wyverns, basilisks, banshees and—goddammit—harpies surging in number.

Amid all these hordes, I saw myself. Not the sad, pitiful self that had stumbled out of Palonia or the depressed, apathetic self that had reluctantly pursued Mikhail, but the Katerina who'd fought alongside Adrian at the height of our power. Lightning bolts burst from my fingertips and great fiery wings spread out behind me as frost coated the ground beneath my feet.

I *was* balance.

I let out a classy snort. While it was nice to know Death recognized the role I served in this world, I found it more than a little hypocritical that I should be shown such visions now.

"If what I do is so important, why punish Emrick for helping me? Why not allow him to step in when it was called for?"

More visions filled my mind of Emrick involving himself when he shouldn't have. A video montage of the hundreds of times he'd crossed the line for me. Him finishing the ritual to banish Shogaur to the infernal realms. Him diving into a still black river calling my name. Him reaching out with his power and stripping all those hunters of their souls. As I watched those moments, Death's answer was clearer than it ever had been.

Emrick had always thought the consequences of his involvement were because Death wanted to prevent the balance from tipping between magical and mundane in the mortal world. But all this time, it had been about maintaining the balance between the mortal world and the afterlife. Today was an example of how far the scales could tip if Emrick went too far, drew too much power, and lost control.

That clarity would have been great to have a few centuries ago. Adrian, Emrick, and I could have worked with that. We could have avoided the arguments and the separation. The longing and heartbreak.

Frustration choked me. In the face of Death's explanation, my reaction made me feel like a child being talked down to by a parent, but so be it. Emrick and I had lost so much time because of a technicality.

I silently raged at Death, pouring my vitriol into the ether.

When I ran out of energy, the sense of waiting stretched on, and I struggled to latch on to hope. Death hadn't yet denied me, but I got the impression I would have to strike a hard bargain to get what I wanted. Death was not one to entertain careless deals.

"Very well," I said. "How's this for a proposal? You return Emrick's soul to what it was—every last memory and hair pigment, our bond intact—and I'll go back to my job of keeping the world at peace. When my time is up—when my purpose has been fulfilled—when I'm no longer needed—then I will serve you alongside Emrick for as long as you deem it necessary to reset the balance."

I was swearing the rest of my existence, both in life and death, to whatever came after, but I suffered no pang of doubt. I was ready to offer more if Death considered my terms unsatisfactory.

The shadows shifted again, closing in around me, sucking out the air until I was ready to collapse—which was a strange sensation considering I wasn't here in any physical sense—and then they retreated, spreading out, letting in more life, more definition in the faceless shapes.

I held my breath, and apprehension squeezed my chest.

I wouldn't die here today. Death had already presented me with that choice, and I'd refused. With my role as magical counterweight a non-negotiable term of our deal, I knew I could open my eyes at any moment and be right back in that concrete, corpse-filled basement.

The question was whether I would wake up there alone.

The light grew brighter. Brighter. So bright I had to close my eyes and look away to avoid the discomfort. The wind picked up around me, pelting me in the face like bits of forest debris, teasing my hair, clutching at the sleeves of my T-shirt.

When the wind died down and the light faded, I carefully opened my eyes.

I didn't know what I'd hoped to see. A pair of silver eyes, probably. Emrick standing whole and hale in front of me, ready to curse me out for taking extreme risks on his behalf—the hypocrite.

Instead, I was back in the hunters' headquarters, exactly where I'd been before my little meeting. Well, not exactly. I found myself on my back. Ben, who'd been tending to my self-inflicted wound, jumped away with a yelp when he found me staring at him. The knife that had taken me to Death lay on the ground beside me, and the stab wound had mostly healed.

With a groan, I rolled onto my side and took in the rest of the room. Gavin was on his knees, gaping at me with tears dripping off his chin. Barrett lay beside him, his neck bandaged and his eyes open as he watched me. Poppy and Cuddles sat nearby. Poppy's knee had been bandaged, and Cuddles's armour was gone, his grey fur matted to his wasted body. I noted the black blood oozing from a wound on his back leg. Hera, Arnold, and the other witches sat with some of the newly arrived hunters.

But no Emrick.

A sob escaped me, and I squeezed my eyes shut as I swallowed the pain.

Poppy didn't leave me to suffer alone for long. As soon as she got over her shock, she threw herself at me, squeezing her arms around my neck so Cuddles was pressed between us.

"What the fuck were you thinking, you foolish, ignorant, rash—" She continued for so long I was amazed she'd found so many adjectives to express herself.

By Gavin's expression, he agreed with every word, while Barrett stared at me with curiosity, as though he suspected what I'd done, where I'd gone, and what I'd tried to offer.

The reactions of my team made me smile for the first time in days.

I was back, and we had won.

I had no idea what my world would look like going forward, but we'd triumphed. And although Emrick was still gone, I refused to give up hope that Death would honour our deal.

35

Katerina

OVER THE NEXT hour, more and more people arrived, until the building teemed with witch, vampire, and guild hunters. The tension in the ranks of all three groups was palpable, and I suspected there would be a major overhaul in how the organizations were run.

I also suspected the League for Magical Freedom would enjoy an influx of new blood. The odds of the group remaining uncorrupted were slim, but if the visions Death had dropped into my head were correct, they would have me to look forward to if they took the world too far the other way.

No one questioned the hunters' authority here. Their people had gone rogue, so this was their mess to clean up. By the expressions on the witches' faces, they weren't thrilled about it, but no one spoke against them.

Hera had stayed close to Poppy and me as the dead hunters and witches were arranged and wheeled away. Although she and Poppy didn't exchange many words, it was impossible to miss the way mother and daughter leaned on each other. Some bonds were impossible to break, no matter how hard we might try to snap them. Did I think this battle would be a turning point for their relationship? Not likely. But in the moment, I was glad they had support.

Barrett had accepted Ben's immediate magical treatment without fuss, but when he'd refused anything further to speed up the healing, Gavin had been the one to glower him into submission. Two magic-haters embracing change. I'd never been prouder. I also wondered how much it would cost to keep Ben on retainer.

With every person that came and went, every wound that was patched up, every second that passed, I watched the corners of the room for any sign of white mist. Any hint that Emrick might be coming back to me.

And with every disappointment, exhaustion gnawed another chunk out of my energy. It was closing in on four o'clock in the morning. My magic was gradually returning to its usual levels, my broken wrist had healed, the stitches in my arm had fallen out, and my hand with the missing fingers was itching like mad. I wanted a bath, my bed, and to hide under my covers until the thoughts in my head went quiet.

Until the hunters cleared us, however, we were stuck here, and I was pretty sure I wasn't the only person who wanted to tackle their lieutenants to the floor and force them to show mercy.

Finally, we were given leave to go.

Drained, limping, holding each other up, we returned to the warehouse.

The moment Murisa saw Poppy hobbling in on her crutches, she let out a shriek that nearly scared one of Hera's surviving witches to death. Poppy tossed her crutches to Gavin and leapt into her girlfriend's lap, spattering her face with kisses, which Murisa promptly returned.

My heart warmed at the sight of them, but the ache was just as intense. I left them to their reunion and continued to the car.

Barrett and Gavin stayed with me. More accurately, Gavin stayed with me, and since Barrett was leaning most of his weight on the other man, he had no choice but to keep up. The soldier didn't make a single sound of complaint despite the pain he had to be in, and I made a note to have Maera make him pancakes for a week once he finally dragged himself out of bed.

Gavin, the only one among us not currently recovering from severe physical injury, stowed Barrett in the passenger seat of the SUV and climbed into the driver's seat. In another few hours, I would be safe enough to take the wheel, but the last thing I wanted to do was wait here until that happened.

The hunters had added to my fires, spreading the flames to ensure all evidence of the rogue headquarters would be shielded from any prying, mundane eyes. At another time, such destruction would have been a joy to watch, but I'd seen more than enough of this place. Later, when the ashes had cooled, I'd return to ensure nothing remained that another group might use to their advantage. But that was a later problem.

Eventually, Murisa and Poppy realized they could delay their reunion until after they got home, and they piled into the back seat with me. The hunters had taken possession of the moving van, and their in-house necromancer had promised to see that Poppy's soldiers were returned to their rightful beds. I took that to mean our security deposit for the van had been lost after all, but if that was the cost of someone taking over our mess, I considered it a sound investment.

From Murisa's description of the corpses' journey, they'd all made it to their assigned points before Poppy's magic had drained. A few rogue hunters had been discovered hiding in a closet, having believed their actions had triggered a zombie apocalypse. One of my greatest regrets in life would be that I hadn't been there to hear their screams.

The last thing I saw as I stared out the window was Hera standing in the parking lot watching us drive off—before she turned to Arnold and put us behind her.

Rhys and Maera were waiting for us when we returned to the Kensington Market house a little after six in the morning.

Maera had obviously spent the entire night baking because the place smelled of chocolate and sugar and butter. She must have read my mind about Barrett's reward.

The table was covered in food, from sweet to savoury and everything in between. My stomach grumbled at the sight, but I didn't know which section of the table to start at. In the end, I bypassed the food and headed straight for the shower.

Fatigue and pain kept my thoughts blissfully still as I scrubbed the blood from my hair. More than once, I had to rest against the tiled wall to catch my breath. Each time I looked at my various scrapes and bruises, I was both surprised and relieved to find them fading.

My bond with Emrick hadn't been blocked for too long this time, but even so, without knowing he was all right, it felt strange for it to be intact.

At the same time, it was nice to know my body was working for me again. If my fate was to continue on as I had for the past eight hundred and fifty years, I was happy to have the healing perk in my arsenal.

Once I was clean, dry, and comfortable in a pair of dove-grey leggings and a low-back sapphire shirt, I plodded downstairs to the kitchen.

Maera filled up my plate, her eyes hooded with sympathy and her lips pressed into a thin line. Someone must have told her what Emrick had done. I didn't want to talk about it, so I focused on stuffing as much food as possible into my mouth.

Barrett went to bed after taking a few bites, and Poppy and Murisa escaped to their room as well. Maera, Rhys, and Gavin stayed around the table with me. Gavin filled the others in on everything that had happened from the moment we'd entered the warehouse, and Rhys responded with all the gasps and wide eyes I would have expected of him.

"I knew it was intense, but that's…" He shook his head. "I don't want to say I'm glad I didn't go with you, but—"

"*I'm* glad you didn't go with them," Maera said. "It was bad enough watching you See it happen."

Rhys paled with the memories, and I hated that he'd be stuck with them the rest of his life.

"That was the most in-depth I've ever gone," he said. "I was only getting flashes, but in those flashes, I was *right there.* Standing in front of those guns. Getting caught under the spray of those potions."

Maera stared at him. "He shared everything he Saw as soon as it came to him. Lucid as if he were out of the vision. I've never seen anything like it."

The shadows that had crossed over Rhys's green eyes cleared, and his gaze fell on me. "I'm sorry about Emrick."

I stared longingly at the chocolate chip cookies piled on the plate in the middle of the table, but eating my problems away wouldn't prevent the others from expressing their sympathy. Better to address it and get the details they didn't know over with.

I cleared my throat and shifted in my seat, prepared for the response that awaited me. "It might not be a thing."

Rhys stared at me in confusion, but Maera—sharp as a tack, that one—narrowed her eyes. "What did you do?"

Gavin scowled. "She stabbed herself in the heart and died, that's what she did."

His dark eyes blazed, and fire encircled his rune-gloved fist. I raised my eyebrow at his show of protective anger, surprised it should come from him. His cheeks flushed, and he shook out his hand and reached for a cookie. My heart swelled at his retroactive concern for me, and I winked at him as he slumped back in his chair.

"I made a deal. Nothing that will affect any of you, so no need to worry." I glanced around the empty room. "Though I'm still waiting to see if Death will deliver."

If Emrick was back, where was he? Why hadn't he come to see me? What if Death had sent me back to keep managing the world without actually agreeing to reunite us?

I wished I'd had a little more control over my exit from that plane, but against Death no one had the upper hand.

"What about the rest of Cartwright's plan?" Rhys asked in a much-appreciated subject change. "Will the official hunter organizations pick up where these guys left off?

Anger simmered in my blood at what the rogue hunters had come so close to accomplishing. The magical hunters who'd arrived to help process the scene hadn't appeared too pleased at the reason for the destruction. From what I'd overheard among their ranks, they'd suffered the same drain on their magic as we had and didn't intend to let the near catastrophe go overlooked by their superiors.

I caved and reached for a cookie. "I think there will be much tighter oversight into what the individuals within the organizations are doing. Cartwright had copies of all the files about known magicals. And what they found predated her role as general. They'd planned this for years, and no one noticed. I don't see anyone getting away with it a second time." Not as long as I was around, anyway.

Rhys blew out a sharp breath. "Thank goodness. That was not fun. The headaches got so bad, we had to sit in here with the lights off. I probably wouldn't have felt it as much if I weren't trying to trigger so many visions, but I wasn't about to leave you to handle this without me."

"I'm grateful. Without you, we wouldn't have stood a chance. I always said you were our secret weapon."

Maera put her arm around her son's shoulders and kissed his hair. Although the maternal concern was present, it lacked the bone-deep worry she'd shown since Rhys's first vision at fourteen. She'd come so far from the woman who'd claimed she would rather Rhys struggle with his blocked visions than master them if it meant keeping him out of danger.

She caught me staring and said, "I'm not too proud to say when I'm wrong. You're every bit the woman my grandmother said you were. Yes, you walk into danger constantly, but you never leave anyone behind. Your promise stands, though. For however long my son walks with you, you'll never stop protecting him."

My throat tightened at the level of trust she'd placed in me. "You have my word, Maera. Of course."

She nodded. "Only you could stab yourself in the heart to have a word with Death and come back from such an exchange unscathed. Poppy was shot in the knee, Barrett in the neck, and yet both of them have come home and will recover to head back out sooner than is good for them. You're touched by the gods, Katerina. I suspect Rhys could be in worse places than your company."

I started to smile at her and say something about how she never had to worry about me going anywhere if she kept putting so much delicious food in front of me, but the words dried on my tongue as goosebumps bubbled on my skin and my hair stood on end.

The temperature in the room had dropped.

I pressed my lips together to stop them from wobbling, and my insides churned with an agonizing sense of anticipation. My hopes rose, and I squashed them down, refusing to give in to them even as I searched the room, begging Death that I would see the mist that had always followed the chill.

It started in the corner next to the fridge and stretched across the room towards the stove. The mist thickened and swirled despite the lack of draft, and in the next moment, I found myself staring into Emrick's deep silver gaze.

36

Emrick

A SOB CAUGHT in Katerina's throat, the emotion no less thick in mine.

There she was. Alive. Recovering. More beautiful than I'd ever seen her—especially considering such a short while ago I'd believed I would never see her again.

She rose from her chair on shaking legs and crossed the kitchen towards me. I faded into the mist and appeared again on the other side of the room.

Kat stopped, turned, frowned at me, and the hurt in her eyes was matched by her irritation. I offered an apologetic smile, but I couldn't risk it.

Although the evidence was right there in the fingers that, cell by cell, were regrowing, in the fading bruises on her face, and in the tug of our bond in my chest, I couldn't bring myself to tempt fate so soon after the last time.

Not when I didn't understand how I was standing here.

I'd come back to myself bit by bit, as though parts of my soul had been dragged across the river of the afterlife and reassembled by an unseen hand.

It shouldn't have been possible. I'd known the consequences of my actions. That I was back meant something else had to have been taken to maintain the balance.

My thoughts stumbled over that simple idea, and I narrowed my eyes at Kat. "What did you do?"

Maera, Rhys, and Gavin needed no other hint that this conversation was not for their ears. They started to rise from the table to make their escape, but Kat waved them down.

"You stay," she said. "We'll take this chat elsewhere."

She glanced at me and headed up the stairs to her bedroom. I followed, keeping my distance.

Watching her as closely as I was, I noted the faint limp in her usually smooth gait and the way her hand trembled as she reached for the door. Her missing fingers—the stumps healed and the bone pressing through the sealed flesh—made me see red.

I wished I could seek out Cartwright in the afterlife and tear her apart a second time, but she was nothing but motes of energy drifting through the emptiness of the world that came next. I had no idea what sort of existence a soul trapped in that condition experienced, but I hoped for her it was torture.

I followed Kat into her room, closed the door, and leaned against it as she walked to the end of her bed, creating space between us.

Seconds passed, and we stood in silence, staring at each other. My heart thrummed against my ribs, a sensation I'd believed behind me. Sweet exhilaration. Blessed apprehension. I had never been so grateful to feel so uncomfortable.

For her part, Kat watched me as though she'd never seen me before. Her blue gaze trailed over me, and I felt it as tangibly as if her fingers were taking the tour.

At the thought of her hands on me, my mouth went dry and my body hardened. Longing to take her into my arms and run my lips over hers nearly overcame me.

But not yet. Not until I was sure.

And not until she explained what she'd done to bring me back. Because I knew she'd had something to do with it. Somehow she had bargained for my life.

Although I didn't want to crush the glow in her eyes—that glimmer of hope and joy—I popped the silence with a sharp, "So?"

She blinked, her expression cleared, and my soul cried out at the detachment that fell between us. It was as painful now as it had been for those seventy-five years we were apart.

"It's nothing," she said. "Nothing has changed."

I tried to swallow my frustration that she would lie to me, but it burned through my soul. Because what else could it be but a lie? Death wasn't altruistic. It wasn't compassionate or merciful. It just was.

Since I couldn't bring myself to accuse her outright, I continued to stare. After a while, she threw up her hands and paced the width of her room.

"Fine. I tried to trade myself for you, all right? I'll admit it. I offered myself to Death so we could be together. It turned me down. Something about me being a requirement to the running of the universe or something. Like I didn't already know the world would fall apart without me."

My lips quirked in a smile at her contempt. If Death itself had confirmed her importance, there would be no living with her now.

Still, I stayed quiet. I needed to know everything. Guilt had settled deep in my bones, and I needed to know what I was supposed to feel guilty about. What had my choices pushed Kat into?

"Death isn't much of a talker—as I'm sure you know," she continued, "so I don't really know much more than that. Except…" She trailed off with a shrug, and my heart kicked against my ribs.

"Kat."

"When my time is finally up, I become what you are. That's it. In exchange, you got *you* back. All your memories. Your colour. Your feelings—whatever they might be now." Her deep ocean eyes flicked towards me and away, and my heart cracked and swelled at once that she should doubt for a moment that I loved her.

Her throat bobbed with a swallow. "I asked him to put you back the way you were when we met. But I don't know what that means. You clearly have all your memories of our time together or else you wouldn't be looking at me like I'm some wayward child who's made some horrible life decisions, but there might be… changes? I don't know."

Her lower lip wobbled, and she caught it between her teeth as she took another lap across her room. "I don't regret it. Whatever you're thinking right now, whatever mistake you think I've made, you can shove it. You left me. You *left* me. You gave yourself up for the sake of destroying those people, and I would have been alone in this world with no one except a shadow of the man I love. Not even a shadow. You don't know—" Her voice caught, and her tears broke through her long lashes. "There was nothing of you left, Emrick. Nothing at all. I looked at you, and you walked right by me. I called to you, and you didn't turn your head. It was your face, your eyes, but there was *nothing* of you left. What other choice did I have? If I'd failed…"

She hooked her hand around the bedpost at the end of the

bed and met my eye. I stared back at her, my hands trembling. Every muscle yearned to go to her, but fear held me steady.

"I'm sorry." My throat was so tight my voice came out gruff, but I pushed through. "I didn't mean to leave you behind, Kat. If there had been any other way… But she was about to kill you, and if you'd died…"

And there we were, right where we'd been before she'd sent me away seventy-five years ago. Both of us terrified of losing the other—me terrified of her dying, her terrified of me losing myself and becoming a wraith.

All those years apart only to have our nightmares realized last night.

Only to come back from them.

It was nothing short of a miracle, but why should I be surprised when everything about this woman was miraculous?

Of all the villages in all the world, I'd been called to Palonia on the night when Kat needed me. Of all the women in all the universe, my sights had landed on her, and my heart had burst open with a desire so deep and so pure, it had never closed again. Of all the odds in all of probability, this woman loved me so much she'd bargained with Death for my soul.

How could I ignore the pull of fate? How could I not trust that everything about this moment was meant to be?

And if that were true, how could I stay away?

My breath caught in my chest, and my feet stepped towards

her before I knew I was moving. I stopped at the bedpost opposite her, only a few feet between us.

"I'm sorry," I repeated.

"I'm not." She raised her chin. "Though I might be a little put out if I sold my soul and don't even get a kiss in gratitude."

That earned her a full smile, though I didn't feel overly joyous. Uncertainty held me back. Death had agreed to Kat's terms, but what if there was a loophole somewhere? What if our bond no longer protected her? What if—

"Hey." Her soft voice drew me out of my mental spiral, and I found her standing closer. Less than a foot away. It would be so easy to slide my arm around her waist and pull her against me. The work of a moment to lay her on the bed and fit myself on top of her.

Whatever she saw in my expression turned her eyes dark with desire, and my own swelled.

"Nothing. Has. Changed." Her chest brushed against mine. She rose on tiptoe but kept her mouth infuriatingly, tantalizingly away from mine.

I was a statue. I refused to lift a finger—refused to breathe—in case the tiniest movement closed the gap between us and she melted to ash in my arms.

"Do you know what Death showed me when we were… negotiating?" She paused before the final word, as though appreciating for the first time how surreal it was that she'd experienced it. I understood all too well. I didn't believe it myself sometimes. "All this time, all these years, all the pieces of your soul you lost when you stepped in front of danger for me? The greatest risk was that you would lose control and go supernova with your power. Which, in the end, you did anyway. We've already faced the worst-case scenario, Emrick. You can breathe now."

No. I really couldn't. Not when she left me breathless.

I found it interesting, though, that the balance Death had set in place wasn't about my helping Kat but helping her *too much*.

We could use that knowledge going forward. Thanks to Kat's bravery—or madness, time would tell—we had a second chance.

Was I really going to waste it?

"Besides," she whispered, edging ever closer to me, "what happens if you're right and at the first kiss I die? I come back. You and me. Nothing can keep us apart now."

On a moan of surrender, I clutched her to me and caught her luscious mouth with mine. Energy surged between us, tingles of electricity buzzing under my skin, bringing me to life—our first contact since the hunters had blocked our bond. Since that morning when my obligations had pulled me from this exact position. I'd promised her we'd pick up where we'd left off. It was time to fulfill that promise.

Kat smiled against my lips, but I growled against hers. She wanted to be smug? We'd see who held the power by the time I was through with her.

I tugged off my gloves, then twisted my fingers through her hair as I deepened our kiss. Her body melted against mine. With my hold tight around her waist, I turned us until she sat on the edge of her bed and trailed kisses down her neck.

She clawed at my shirt, but I took hold of her wrists and pinned them above her head, meeting her eye as I did. Her parted lips called to me, but for now, with a self-restraint that deserved a million accolades, I ignored them and returned my attention to her neck. I nuzzled the spot between her throat and her collarbone and slid my free hand under her shirt.

Her gasp sent shivers of pleasure under my skin, urging me to tear away the barriers between us and take her. But I refused to hurry. For weeks, life had kept us apart. How strange for it to be Death that had brought us back together.

I wasn't about to rush this.

For as long as possible, I would take my time and savour every moan, every gasp, every arch of her back.

I released her wrists to pull her shirt over her head. My control slipped just enough that I couldn't deny her beautiful mouth on my way back down. I trapped her lips and explored her tongue as she wound her fingers through my hair to hold me in place.

My hands travelled lower, hooked into the waistband of her leggings, and with a few wiggles and more than one panting moan, threw them to the floor to lie with her shirt.

I'd sacrificed myself for her.

On the one hand, I would do it again tomorrow if it meant keeping her exactly as she was. On the other, I had no idea how I'd worked up the courage to lose sight of her. To forget her.

Honestly, I was amazed that I *had* forgotten her. Seeing her now, I couldn't believe that the vision of her naked perfection hadn't seared itself so deeply into my being that even without knowing who she was, I hadn't loved her.

But was that true?

My time as a full wraith was hazy. Cold. An empty space in my mind. But through all that nothing, there had been… a spark. The faintest glow that made me appreciate how incredible this world could be. Despite the carnage and the brutality, there was beauty. And for me, that beauty was all here.

I slipped down Kat's body, leaving a trail of kisses as I went. She squirmed beneath me, but I tightened my grip to keep her still. My tongue swept across each nipple, teasing her, and I chuckled at the pleading whimper that escaped her throat.

I kept going, travelling across the smooth planes of her stomach, down to the softness of her thighs.

She tasted of nectar and ambrosia. The gods would never dine on sweeter. Though as her body shook beneath me, as her back dipped and a scream slipped between her lips, I felt like a god myself.

I lingered where I was, decorating her thighs with more kisses, but when her hands found my shoulders and her fingernails scored my back, earning her a sharp hiss of pleasure, I kissed my way back up. As I went, I stripped off my clothes, enjoying every press of my bare skin against hers. Her warmth. The shape of her that fit so perfectly against me—how could I believe we'd been created for anyone else?

She captured my mouth and, in a move I wasn't expecting, hooked her leg beneath mine and flipped me onto my back.

I grinned up at her as her black hair draped like a curtain around us, obscuring the rest of the room—the rest of the world. No one else existed but us.

I groaned as she took me in. Her pupils dilated until the only blue remaining was a darkened ring around the edges. My beautiful sorceress. For a moment, we stayed exactly like that. Still. Breathing. Together.

Then she rocked her hips, and my hands curled around her waist, holding her firmly against me as she found her rhythm. I met her thrust for thrust but allowed her to lead. I needed her to get what she wanted. Trusted her to take me with her on her way.

Equals. As we had been for so many centuries.

"I love you," she said against my mouth.

"*Mîn êcnes*," I replied. My eternity.

Her pace quickened along with her breath, and I wrapped my hand in her hair and devoured her mouth, swallowing her moans as her climax peaked and she tumbled over the edge.

I followed her seconds later, blood rushing in my ears, skin flushed, heart racing.

All for her. Everything I was, everything I had to offer, was for her.

And so it would be for eternity. *Mîn êcnes*. My Katerina.

Epilogue

Katerina

Ireland — Four years later

ALL RIGHT, BARRETT, break it down for me," I said as I entered the kitchen.

Half the table was covered in blueprints, sketches, mechanical devices, and potions. The other half was covered in plates of munchies, courtesy of Maera's stress.

Barrett searched the table for something, and at his frustrated huff, Gavin plucked out a map and handed it to him with a wink.

Barrett's cheeks flushed faintly. "The harpy nest is here along the coast of Galway Bay." He flattened the map on the table and pointed to an area marked with the remains of Poppy's tracking spell. "Murisa's spies say there are at least a dozen in the roost."

A mechanical bird on the table chirped and hopped around, and I patted it on the head in recognition of a job well done. A moment later, a low *mrow* sounded from the end of the table, and I caught a streak of grey as undead cat snatched mechanical bird, and they tumbled to the floor.

I looked over the edge to find the bird's head in Cuddles's mouth as his back legs kicked at its gut. A claw popped out of his back paw, and I hoped Poppy was ready to patch him together.

Leaving him to his metallic feast, I heaved a sigh and returned my attention to the map.

Goddamn harpies.

"All right then, what's the plan?"

Gavin came around the table and flipped a device in his palm. "Muroppy came up with something to mess with their echolocation. They'll clear the perimeter and do what they can to keep the creatures contained."

I grinned. "And leave the fun for us?"

A snort sounded behind me, and I turned as Poppy and Murisa came into the room. Poppy's shorts exposed the twisted scars around her left knee. The healers who had come to the house after the battle with the rogue hunters had offered to heal her in a way that would leave no trace, but Poppy had refused. She wasn't afraid of scars. "No one will fuck with me with these babies," had been her response.

So far, when the weather was nice enough to show them off, she was right.

But maybe that was because she was Poppy, half of the best technomancer duo the world had ever seen.

"We're not leaving anything for you," she said. "If you don't think those bitches will try to run, you haven't learned anything about harpies."

I scowled. Obviously Rhys had opened his big mouth about my last run-in with the flock's sister so many years ago.

"Barrett and I will take the western side of the nest." Gavin nodded to me. "You can take the east."

I frowned. "Sure, leave me next to the water."

He grinned. "You can handle getting wet."

I flicked a fireball at him, but he absorbed it with one of his own.

Murisa wheeled her way to the table and scattered a bunch of tiny metal beetles across the map. One second, they were motionless; the next, they skittered across the table towards the food. Gavin rushed to grab a chicken wrap before the mechanical touched it.

Murisa watched her babies run. "I want to test these new portable wards. With a word, they'll stop and throw up a barrier, linking to the next one."

"Creating this cool magical net," Poppy finished, her eyes

shining with pride as she leaned over to kiss her wife. "My genius witch."

Murisa beamed, then cleared her throat and looked at me. "You'll recognize the magic at work, so don't be surprised when you see it."

My skin crawled as I thought of the anti-magic ward that had caged Emrick in the hunters' headquarters. Four years, and those few days still haunted me. How long before I was able to put them behind me? Ten years? A hundred? Memories that ran so deep weren't shaken easily.

The temperature dropped and white mist swept around me. In another breath, Emrick's arms tightened around my waist, and he pressed a kiss on top of my head. "It's a great idea, Poppy," he said. "I can't wait to see it in action."

I turned in his arms and stared into his silver eyes. "I didn't invite you to this party."

His smile warmed me straight through. "You didn't. I'll try not to feel left out."

"Harpies are off-limits to you."

"They are."

"So you're not coming."

"I am."

I opened my mouth to argue, but he stopped me with a kiss that curled my toes. Once he was sure he'd left me speechless, he pulled away and left another tiny kiss on the tip of my nose.

"Someone has to escort those poor creatures into the afterlife once you're through with them."

Poppy gagged. "Gross, you guys, come on."

Maera bustled her way to the table with another plate covered in food—mini cheesecakes this time. Bless the woman. "I thought that year away would be enough for you two to get it out of your system. After the harpies are gone, we're sending you off again."

I smiled at Emrick, and his moonlight eyes gleamed with dark promises. "I think that's a brilliant idea."

The stairs creaked as Rhys joined us. His green eyes were white, but he walked without stumbling into the kitchen.

"Feathers falling like leaves. Screeches echoing across the water. Blood. Bone. Empty nests, and blacked-out skies."

Barrett scowled. "Sounds like they're planning on packing up."

"Any idea of time?" I asked.

Rhys canted his head. "Soon. Not immediate."

Maera and I exchanged a look, and my housekeeper nodded. "No point delaying. I'll pack up the food, and you can take it with you. You'll want to make sure you're energized before dealing with these ladies."

Muroppy set to work packing away the mechanicals in the satchel Murisa carried on the back of her chair—Poppy doing her best to pry the bird out of Cuddles's stubborn jaws. Barrett and Gavin gathered the maps and sketches that would help us plan our strategy.

I watched them mobilize, and for a moment I couldn't breathe. My heart was too full.

Once upon a time, I'd watched my father and his team prepare for similar missions. Heard them poke fun at each other and practice their skills so they could be ready for whatever came. I'd listened to my husband regale me with stories of how those missions had gone while I dandled Rowan on my lap. I'd been surrounded by people I loved but had always felt left out.

Even after a thousand years, the loss of my family remained a dull ache—and I hoped it always would—but I was no longer incomplete.

"Anything else, Rhys?" Emrick asked. He tightened his arms around me as though he knew where my thoughts had gone. Knowing him, he probably did.

Rhys looked my way and smiled, his eyes clearing to their usual bright green. "Anger. A lot of anger."

Everyone in the room turned to me, and I grinned back at him. "Good. They must know I'm about to ruin their day."

Thank You for Reading

Thank you so much for taking a chance on an independent author. We're living in a wonderful age where it's easy to upload a book to the internet, but that doesn't reflect the blood, sweat, and tears that go into making a book the best version it can be. It takes time, patience, perseverance, and to have the final result end up in a new reader's hands is the best reward. You are the reason we keep writing, so thank you.

If you enjoyed the read, please help support the author by leaving a review at the retailer where you purchased the book. Reviews make a world of difference for an author, helping us reach new audiences and bringing more people into the worlds you've spent time in.

For exclusive character content, announcements, promotions, and special offers, sign up for Krista's mailing list at https://www.kristawalshauthor.com/pages/about-the-author

Acknowledgements

We made it to the finale! My sixth series wrapped up, as well as my 25th book.

Because holy smokes. You have helped me produce 25 individual titles. Books that would not exist if you hadn't shown so much support and encouragement.

Special thanks and appreciation to:

Kate Sparkes, my FAKAs, and the Blood & Pulp gang, for helping me shape this series, title it, cover it, and for holding my hand through all the ups and downs.

Christopher Barnes for all those fine editing touches.

My Street and ARC teams—you are so amazing! I love how the further into this series we get, the more your reviews become fireworks in my heart. You've become as invested in Kat's struggles as I have, and your reactions make me dance like a wild one.

My Patrons, for your feedback, your engagement, and the community you're helping me create over on Patreon. You make it so much fun to create content to share with you.

Chris Reddie. Your constant reminders to celebrate my wins make every accomplishment that much sweeter. You never let me get so bogged down in the work that I forget to look back to see how far I've come, and I'm so grateful for that. And little girl, my sweet daughter, I feel like every book I release is a reminder of how quickly you're growing up. Maybe that's why my release schedule for the next series will be a bit slower.

My readers. Thank you for being with me, for sharing Kat & Emrick's story. Fourteen years in the making, and now it's over. Thanks so much for giving me the opportunity to tell it.

About the Author

Known for witty, vivid characters, Krista Walsh never has more fun than getting them into trouble and taking her time getting them out.

When not writing, she can be found reading, gaming, or watching a film – anything to get lost in a good story.

She currently lives in Ottawa, Ontario with her husband, toddler, and epileptic blue heeler.

You can find her at www.kristawalshauthor.com or at the local Second Cup coffee shop… but only if you come bearing a Vanilla Bean Latte, half-sweet.

Other Works by Krista Walsh

Epic Fantasy

The Meratis Trilogy

The Cadis Trilogy

The Nayis Trilogy

Urban Fantasy

The Dark Descendants

The Ghostmaker Trilogy

The Immortal Sorceress Series